Hoarding Gold

Kiera A. Reynolds

Contents

CHAPTER ONE
THE JOB

Money is the root of all evil. I've heard that so many times; from media, social media, strangers, my mother. Greed takes humans to dark places, hurting anyone it comes in contact with. These big companies step on the backs of others to make billions without a thought for who is hurt along the way. No one cares, but someone has to.

That's where I come in.

My black leggings bunch in the back, so I work to fix them and make sure there's no gap between my pants and black turtleneck. Leather gloves and knitted hat find their way into my pockets, again all black. I am the night when I do jobs. I'm nothing but a moving shadow.

After making sure all my needed equipment is in my bag, I slip out of the room. Lex sits at his desk in the living room, all three monitors giving his face a ghostly cast. His brown bangs fall over his eyes as he leans to look closer. When his glasses slip down his nose, he pushes them back up.

Lex's dark eyes, glowing an eerie shade of blue from the monitors, find me. My best friend and roommate looks at his watch. "Two hours?"

"Yeah. I want to get there and do some last-minute reconnaissance. Don't forget."

"I don't forget things, Eddie."

"Counting on that perfect memory."

He waves me away, returning his fingers to the keyboard. I stop by our ratty couch and give Clancy, our orange and white tabby, a scratch. The only sign that he feels my attention is the purr that rumbles. Clancy is so lazy he can't even bother to open his eyes. I shake my head and walk away.

At the door, I try to remove the chain. It decides to stick, as it often does, and I jiggle it until it moves. The deadbolt comes next, then I'm yanking on the door. It's stuck. No matter how often we call the building manager, he never sends someone to fix the door. It could be worse. At least this helps keep people out. When I finally yank the door open, I jump and cover my heart with my hand. Jared laughs on the other side, finding my startled state funny.

He looks me over and shakes his head. "You'd be prettier if you'd wear lighter colors more often."

"Good thing I don't care about being pretty."

I glance back at Lex, who shrugs. "He'll help keep me awake."

"Just don't get caught up in whatever game you two are playing and lose track of time."

Jared is Lex's close friend. He's almost always here, and I've come to tolerate him. The blond is the typical jock type, which makes their friendship feel a little cliché, but it's none of my business. Why Lex enjoys his company, I'll never know. I don't have the right to judge who he chooses to hang out with.

I slip past the man at the door and walk down the hall. Paint chips from the dirty walls. The carpet in the hall is full of holes. Mrs. Barlow stands on her welcome mat, purple slippers on her feet. Her faded pink bathrobe swings open, revealing a stained jogging suit. As usual, curlers make her gray hair colorful.

And, as usual, she's arguing with Mr. Elsher from across the hall. His poodle barks so hard that it hops. These two fight like cats and dogs, which I guess is a little ironic since they're always fighting *about* their cats and dogs. There's not a day that goes by that they're not bickering in the hallway. The problem right now is that he's blocking my path out of here.

"Your mutt went after my precious Marshmallow," Mrs. Barlow says. "It's a menace to society and should be put down."

"Keep your cats in your apartment. They're not supposed to be roaming the halls."

"Neither is your dog, but I don't see that stopping you."

"She's on a leash."

"And still almost ate my cat."

Examining the poodle, I find it hard to believe it could eat the fat white cat in her arms. They're about the same size, but the cat probably weighs three times what the dog does. I try to walk around, and the hopping bark turns my way. I'm not really afraid of something so small, but I don't see a way to get around her without being bitten. She bites everyone, except her owner. The last thing I need tonight is an open wound that'll leave DNA.

"Excuse me," I say, feeling the immense heat of their anger turn on me. "I really need to get through."

"Go around," Mr. Elsher says.

"Your dog is in the way."

"She doesn't bite."

Tell that to the five complaints to the manager this month that say the opposite.

I bite my tongue. It's hard to remain inconspicuous while getting in a fight with a loud neighbor, so I wait it out and keep my mouth shut. Thanks to my interruption, their argument has lost momentum, so Mr. Elsher huffs and walks to the elevator.

Mrs. Barlow turns to me. "Eddie, my toilet isn't working again."

Sighing, I silently curse the fact maintenance is useless and the little old lady doesn't have anyone else. "I'd love to help, but I have an appointment. Can you make do until tomorrow?"

"Sure, I'll just let everything sit in the bowl until you get here."

She slams the door hard enough to make me wince. Great. Why am I always the one to get roped into helping her with the nastiest of her problems? I grimace and make my way toward the elevator. The trip down is accompanied by a few jerks of the descending box of death getting stuck and releasing again. Maybe I should start taking the stairs.

Outside, I walk down the sidewalk in the opposite direction of the bouncing poodle. I get a few jeers and catcalls, but I don't stop. Thanks to Lex's obsession with all the different martial arts that I can't name, I know enough to keep myself safe. He said that living in this neighborhood means I need to know the basic moves at least. This always leads to a conversation about moving elsewhere. It's not that we can't afford it, but that would mean we can help fewer people. No matter how much we hate the living situation, we're both dedicated to the cause of being modern Robin Hoods. We only keep what we need to survive and a little saved for emergencies. The rest goes to those in need.

A block away, the little parking garage holds our car for a small yearly fee. I make my way there and park it in the business district, a block away from tonight's target. I have a half hour left by the time I reach my destination and hide in the shadows of the alley across the street. Watching, I memorize the schedule of the front guard. Every fifteen minutes, he gets up to make rounds. That's my time to make a move, but I need Lex to loop the camera feed he's been recording for the last few nights.

As the time nears one in the morning, I slip my bluetooth into my ear and dial my roommate's number. There's no answer. He better not be gaming with Jared and ignoring that it's go time. I try again. Nothing. I let out a low growl as our time slot passes by. There's no way I can make a move when the cameras are still recording. When the guard returns to his post, I sigh and resign myself to another fifteen minutes.

Five minutes before the next patrol, my phone rings in the speaker attached to my ear. I press the button to answer. "Dammit, Lex."

"I'm sorry. I was playing with Jared and lost track of time. How bad is the damage?"

"I have five minutes until my next window. Are you ready?"

"Give me a minute to hijack the feed. Are you sure you'll find something worthy here?"

I scoff. "Three of the largest financial institutions merged into one building. One of them handles corporate banking. I'll find plenty."

The guard stands and walks toward the back rooms. From there, he'll enter the alley behind the building and circle. I have a limited time to reach the elevators. As soon as Lex gives me the go ahead, I dash across the street and past the bushes of the white stone building. Lex uses his skills to unlock the electronic lock, and I slip in. Dashing to the elevators, I press the up button and try not to hop around with impatience. Stairs would be better, but they're in an area where I'm sure to be seen.

I glance at my watch, urgently swearing at the elevator to hurry. As soon as the doors open, I press the button for the third floor. I'm thankful when it closes before the guard returns. "You're sure the third floor is clear?"

"Of course. Do I question your skills at every turn? No one is there, and the safety deposit room is actually quite easy to get to. The firewall was a bit rough, but the building is an open book once through. Stop worrying and do your job."

"It would be easier to do my job if my coworker was on time."

"You don't let things go, do you?"

I smile. "You should know me better than that."

The doors open to darkness lit only by running lights. I blink to adjust to the dimness as I step out. Walking down the hall, I bypass security rooms and offices until I reach my destination. Glass sliding doors separate me from my target. The keypad glows blue around the numbers. I wait for Lex's instructions.

"I can deactivate the alarms, but when I do, you'll only have five minutes," he says into my ear.

"Five minutes isn't very long."

"It'll have to do. I tested it earlier. There's some kind of failsafe that even I can't bypass. If power to the alarm remains off for more than five minutes, the backup will trigger."

"You tested it?" I ask. "Without getting caught?"

"I'm not an amateur, Eddie. I know what I'm doing. Since we have such limited time, I dug deep. Get ready to memorize box numbers because I was able to find the richest pricks available that need to have their pockets lightened. Tell me when you're ready to memorize."

I roll my eyes. "I don't need time. Just tell me."

"98, 102, 120, 176, and 214."

Repeating them back to him is easy, and he gives me the signal that it's safe. I run over to the first box while pulling out my lock picks. The first lock clicks to reveal travel documents and deeds. Bust. The next gives me birth certificates and social security cards. I grunt with frustration. Next, I find a wad of cash. Lex gives me the two-minute warning, so I just skip to the last box because it's closest. Jackpot.

I reach behind me and pull the black bag from my back pocket. Jewelry and watches make their way in with the wad of cash I found earlier. Then I shove it all in the pack on my shoulders that also holds rope and a change of clothes.

"Forty-five seconds," Lex says in my ear.

I relock the boxes, careful to leave no evidence. When the owners return for their things, it'll be too late. Nothing will trace back to us. I hurry through the door and shut it. Lex releases his control, and I hear the locks click. Listening for any sign of trouble, I breathe and will my heart to calm.

"No alarms?" I ask.

"Not even the silent one. I suggest moving to the elevator now. The guard will be doing rounds in two minutes."

I rush back and push the lobby button. The ding of the elevator makes me wince. Lex assures me the guard is now out back. They can't see me, but my hacker best friend can. He suggests I go the back way because the guard is walking toward the front. Following his instructions, I find the back door already unlocked and waiting.

As soon as I'm out of view of the cameras, he stops looping the feed. "What did you find?"

"I only got through four boxes. The first two were nothing but paperwork. I found a stack of money that probably equals close to ten thousand and a bunch of expensive looking jewelry."

"Good. I need a new router. I feel like this one is giving me issues."

I'm about to offer agreement because we need to make sure our operation is in the best shape. I'm stopped by a hand that snakes around my stomach. Another covers my mouth.

"Thinking to sabotage us again, mangy mutt?" whispers into my ear.

"Eddie, what's going on? Can you hear me? Answer me!" Lex's panic tells me he hears the voice.

I try one of the moves my friend taught me, but my captor only chuckles. "Smart, but it will do no good on one such as me."

The pressure holding me releases. My feet immediately decide running is the best option. I don't make it far. Something hard hits the back of my head, and I fall with a grunt. Blackness works its way into my vision. The world goes dark while Lex screams at me to say something.

CHAPTER TWO
A NEW OFFER

"For someone as clever as you are, you're a bit of an idiot."

The voice with a tone of calm authority breaks through the fog of forced sleep. My head feels as if it's splitting open, and I want to tell the voice to keep it down. Somehow, I think that wouldn't go well. I remember enough to know I was caught during my escape. I'm not sure how because Lex assured me I didn't trip any alarms. Unwilling to open my burning eyes, I lay wherever I am and listen to the conversation around us.

"Excuse me?" This one has a gravelly tone with a pinch of attitude.

"You shouldn't call him an idiot. It was a simple mistake." And this one is soft and gentle, little more than a hum.

Now that I've categorized my captors by how they sound, I need to formulate a plan. My headache is easing a little, but they sound like they're right in front of me. Opening my eyes will alert the men to the fact I'm awake. Best to wait until I can get more information.

A sigh follows the last comment. It sounds tired. "You're right, Warrin. I'm sorry for insulting your intelligence, Draven. I just can't wrap my head around why you knocked her out. We could've turned her description in to the police and let them handle it. You know how humans tend to get snippy when you show them their authority isn't needed. You've put us in a bind."

Strange way to address cops. We're all humans, aren't we? Draven and Warrin. Why do those names sound so familiar? I hate how foggy my brain feels right now. I'm going to assume my throbbing head and lack of thinking capacity is due to Draven. My silent curses involve his name. How do I know these names? Figuring that out is important if I want to get out of this alive. The fact he knocked me out instead of turning me in is concerning.

"I thought she was one of them," the gravelly sounding Draven growls out. "I acted in the heat of the moment. Don't tell me you never do the same."

This would be so much easier if I could see their expressions. I hate flying blind, but my supposed unconsciousness is the only advantage I have right now.

"How could you think she was one of them?" Mr. Authority with an unknown name asks. "She doesn't even smell like a wolf."

Now that is a strange thing to say. I'm both flattered and confused by that last statement. At least he doesn't think I stink.

"What if someone comes looking for her?" the gentle Warrin cuts in.

"Relax," Draven drawls. "I found her car and moved it to our private garage."

Lex is going to be so angry when he's done worrying about me. It took forever to find a car that works but looks like an inconspicuous clunker. I'll worry about that when I get out of here.

"You're sure it's hers?" Mr. Unknown says.

"It smelled just like her. There was another scent, but I'm not that worried. Anyone who knows what she was up to won't want to involve authorities. We can do away with her as needed, and I'll send her vehicle to a chop shop. Regardless of your earlier statement, I'm not stupid, Anders."

Maybe I do stink if he can tell my car by just his sense of smell. Either that or he has super smell. Wait...

Warrin.

Draven.

Anders.

The third name kick starts my pained brain. Anders Hayes, Draven Pierce, Warrin Carter. HPC Financial Incorporated. The shock is too much. Gasping, I sit up and wonder why the CEOs of the company are holding me hostage. I would think they'd want the proper authorities to take care of this situation to save their reputation. After all, reputation is everything to these huge corporations that horde wealth while the poor suffer. Unless they have the resources and clout to cover their dirty laundry up; like a chop shop to dismantle the car of a thief caught red-handed.

Shit... This isn't good at all. I'm dead.

The conversation stopped the minute I displayed wakefulness. Now, silence reigns supreme. Opening my eyes hurts, but I force them to comply. Sharp pain shoots from my eyeballs to the back of my head. The world spins as it blurs and unblurs. I really shouldn't have sat up that fast. I feel sick.

"Sleeping beauty is awake," Draven's voice says through the swirling colors in my disturbed vision.

"Technically, sleeping beauty was pricked by a needle that put her to sleep. You clocked me on the head like a barbarian. It isn't really the same," I say through the agony that comes with my words. "Besides, I believe your initial pet name for me was 'Mutt.'"

He chuckles. "Technicalities don't interest me; ask my friends here. Mutt seems good enough to me. I'll make sure to use it as much as possible before we end this nuisance."

"Draven," Anders says, "no need to threaten the young lady. There will be no ending. I'm sure we can come to an understanding. After all, sweeping this under the rug is the best course for all parties. I'm sure Edith here doesn't want the authorities involved either. Who knows what other thefts they'll connect her with?"

I'm not sure if that's a threat or a plea. Maybe just a statement of reason. Either way, I'm willing to come to a compromise. I'd rather leave these bars for freedom, not different captives. And yes, my vision is clear enough to make out that I am actually in some sort of prison.

Leaning on my bars, I recognize Draven Pierce. His long black hair lies halfway down his back. His dark green polo shirt hugs a lithe figure. Thin doesn't mean weak. No, Draven carries muscles on his thin frame and stands as if he's ready to pounce like a graceful but dangerous panther.

Anders Hayes leans against the white-painted brick wall, arms crossed over his broad chest. Under his white dress shirt, strong muscles bulge for anyone to see. Where Draven's dark eyes watch me with hostility, Anders's browns watch me with patience. His brown hair is short and impeccably styled.

Warrin is more of a shock. He's huge, towering over the other two with his hands in his pockets. Under his shirt, I don't see muscle. While he's not muscular, he isn't doughy either. The large man stands somewhere between the two, soft if you will. Blond hair covers his head in an organized mess. Despite his huge size, there's a gentleness in his light blue eyes.

Their looks don't surprise me—give a professional a little credit for her internet research—but I do find that the pictures on the company website don't do them justice. I thought they were handsome eye candy to begin with. In person, they're downright drool-worthy. Not that now is the moment to be drooling. I need to get out of this situation.

"Where am I?" I ask, not expecting them to give me that advantage.

Anders surprises me. "The bowels of the building you decided to rob last night. We have returned what you stole, and

I'm quite impressed you were able to get as far as you did. That takes some skill."

Draven scoffs. "She learned the layout and used a few lock picks. She probably had some basement hacker helping her. That's not that impressive. She got caught, didn't she?"

Warrin's ice-blue eyes leave me to look at his attitude-filled companion. "That basement hacker broke through the cyber security you assured us was the best, so I'd say you should be impressed."

"Whoever was behind the keyboard is probably just lucky."

If I was anywhere but my current location, this conversation would be amusing. It's unfortunate that's not the case. I am behind these bars, at the mercy of men with lots of resources and connections. I'm not in the position to be amused. Poor Draven would be upset to learn that his hacker never went to school. Lex learned all his skills from his big brother—in his parents' basement. That thought almost makes me laugh.

"You keep a prison in your office building?" I say, refusing to rise to the bait and give up my best friend.

"Let's just say we have enemies, which is why I'm going to make you an offer," Anders says.

I purse my lips, but Draven growls. "Why does she deserve this offer? She'll only stab us in the back the first chance she gets."

"I highly doubt that. I don't peg her as a petty thief. Why did you steal from us, Edith?"

Hearing my birth name for the second time today makes me wince. The ill-tempered man that stole my car must have gotten my identification from inside it. I will no longer bring it along on jobs. Who would have guessed one of the men in charge of the company could smell me?

"Because you can afford it. You greedy corporations horde wealth while the helpless suffer. You're sitting on a massive amount of money, and normal people are one medical emergency or lay-off away from living in the streets. Homelessness is rampant. None of that bothers people like you."

Okay. Maybe I didn't need to go on that rant, but I can't help myself. As Anders said, I'm not some petty thief. I don't steal for myself; I steal for the people who need the money these people keep in bank accounts and investments. The money they use to live in excess. They don't deserve it just because of who they are.

"Steal from the rich, give to the poor?" Draven laughs. "That's rich. You expect us to believe that?"

"She seems sincere," Warrin cuts in, casting furtive glances my way.

"I highly doubt it. This criminal calls us greedy, but she's the one stealing from others."

I open my mouth to argue, but Anders cuts me off. "Ignore them. Tell me what you do with the money you earn from your thefts?"

"I keep enough to keep the operation running, then I allocate the heavy profits to those in need."

"You make it sound like a one-person operation."

"It is." *You're welcome, Lex.*

He grins. "We aren't stupid enough to believe that, but we don't care who helps you, only that they help us with this compromise. You see, we aren't the greedy people you seem to think we are. Like you, we keep enough to run our business and to support a rainy-day fund, but the rest we try to give back to the community."

I look over their name-brand clothes with disgust. "Oh, really?"

Anders chuckles. "We have to look the part, and I will admit that we enjoy the pay given to us, but I assure you that we do give back as much as possible."

"Please. You say you aren't stupid. Neither am I."

"Fair enough. We understand your skepticism. If you'd like, we'll give you access to our financial statements and charity reports. How you think of us doesn't affect our situation, which is why I want to make you an offer. The other option is to let Draven do what he seems to desire. I'd rather not do that because I believe everything can be solved through negotiation."

I swallow hard and look around more. White brick walls show me no windows and only one door out. The odds of me escaping on my own are slim to none. "Fine. What is this offer?"

"Work for us. No, let me finish. It's obvious we have some major holes in our security. We, including the scowling Draven, would like you to help us fill in those holes. You and your hacker friend can test and rework whatever needs to be done."

Laughter bursts from me. "You want to employ a hacker and a thief to improve your security?"

Draven grunts. "I told you this was pointless, Anders. Let me get rid of the nuisance quietly."

"Now hold on," I say. "I didn't say I wouldn't do it. I simply don't understand the reasoning. Also, besides life, what else do I get out of it?"

Anders waves his less diplomatic companion's concerns away. "Let's say this. You'll be free, without police involvement. I will give you access to what I said to prove we are who I say we are. We will also pay you a ridiculous sum to do whatever you want. You can keep it. You can give it away. It means nothing to us."

"What's to keep me from doing a half-ass job and making a run for it?"

"For every year we don't have a successful break in, we'll give you a bonus."

I bite my lip. The number of people I can help with all the money is unimaginable. They really thought this through. I help them, then I help others in need. This is a no-brainer. "Very well. Set me free, and we can discuss terms."

"Warrin will drive you home. I'm sure your hacker is probably worried. We will return your car and phone this evening, along with contract terms."

My eyes narrow. "Why can't I drive myself?"

"Let's call it insurance. We expect to see where you work and that you gave us a proper address. It will be returned unharmed."

"Fine," I say with a sigh of defeat. It's not like I was planning on weaseling out of it when I have plans for their money, but that doesn't mean I like being at their mercy. At this point, I just want to be home.

I hope I didn't make a deal with the devil to get that.

CHAPTER THREE
SARDINES

"Just so you know, I think what you're doing is very noble."

Glancing out of the side of my eye, I watch Warrin warily. How can someone think it's good that I tried to rob him? I mean, of course, I feel his words are true. But I don't steal from myself. The gentle giant's admiration feels strange in my ears.

"Uhhh, thank you," I say, unsure what else can be said.

"I'm serious."

"I can see that." To be truthful, I can't. It's hard to take a guy seriously when he's scrunched over the steering wheel and still rubbing his head on the ceiling. Maybe that's why his blond hair seems so messy. The ceiling is too close.

I let the silence stretch a little longer before the irony of his words gets the best of me. "You do realize I tried to rob you?"

Warrin chuckles. "I'm not slow. As much as I don't like being the target, I still feel you're doing a great thing. I like helping other people too."

Of course you do, Mr. Billionaire.

"So, mmmm, have you been rich long?" What kind of question is that? Maybe I'm still fuzzy from the knock on my head. I'm pretty sure there's a decent lump on the back of my head, but I'm afraid to touch it to make sure.

"Nope. My dad didn't come home one night, so Mom had to raise me on her own on a waitress salary."

"Oh," I say, for once at a loss for words. Words of comfort tumble around in my head, but I come up with nothing. "Then how did you become the head of a corporate bank?"

Warrin smiles. "Anders found me begging for money to get my mom a present. He offered to help get me on my feet. Mom now doesn't have to get yelled at for forgetting the extra ranch any longer. I bought her a nice place."

"Oh," I say again, letting the silence stretch between us.

My attention turns away from the big man who looks like he is stuck in a sardine can. It's not guilt that keeps me from meeting his gaze again. How could I know he had such a rough life? Okay, maybe I feel a little bad. That doesn't mean guilty.

The rich deserve any judgment given. He may use his money to help his mom, but he's still a billionaire, sitting in his corporate office while others toil around him. No one gets to the top without stepping on others.

As far as Anders is concerned, he doesn't gain a green light for helping Warrin into a better situation. I'm sure he had a selfish reason for doing so. They all do. How selfish? Well, I'll reserve that judgment for later.

None of this changes my opinion of Draven at all. He's still a complete arrogant ass. One capable of murder and who knows what else. As much as I don't want to give Anders the benefit of a doubt, he at least kept me from ending up as minced meat.

As we enter my neighborhood, I glance at the big man again. His almost invisible eyebrows are drawn together. "Why do you live in a place like this? Are you a terrible thief?"

I purse my lips and look out the windshield. Homeless drift around aimlessly. Thugs sell drugs on the corners. Most of the buildings are in various states of disrepair. It may look like nothing special, but it's home.

"I told you. The only money I keep is enough to keep the operation running. Everything else goes to the needy," I explain.

"Right. You're not afraid of living here?"

The thought makes me laugh. "Can't be worse than the world I grew up in."

Warrin licks his lips, and I go back to staring out the window until my building shows up outside of it. With amusement, I watch my chauffeur try to reach the handle of the door and wonder why they don't buy him a big pickup or SUV. Anything where the hulking man can get in and out of without a crowbar.

I hold up my hands. "No need to get out. I can get home from here."

"I'm supposed to find out where you live."

"This is it. Apartment 215. Listen, I promise I'm not going to make a run for it. While helping people in your position goes against my ethics, in doing so, I have the ability to help a lot more people who actually need it. I'm not going anywhere."

When I open my door and throw one leg out, he reaches over to grab my wrist. I look back at him to see him looking at the people loitering with suspicion. "I don't like the looks of it here, Edith."

With a shake of my head, I pull my wrist free. As expected, he doesn't force the issue. "First of all, call me Eddie. I'm convinced my mom named me Edith because she hates me. Second, I've lived here for years. People know me. I'll be fine. You, on the other hand, will be prime pickings. Careful when you come back."

I slip from the car before he can argue. When I look back, I see him reaching for the handle of his door. Sure, I can reach inside before he can ooze out of the open door, I rush into the lobby of the apartment. Looking out tells me Warrin is debating on whether he should trust I'm safe or run into the seedy undergrowth of this building to try to catch up with me. My breath whooshes out when he decides it's best to pull away.

I move toward the elevator and take it to my floor. Mrs. Barlow sticks her head out of the door. "Oh! You're back. My apartment stinks."

It takes me a few seconds to realize why that's my problem. A grimace threatens when I understand what she's saying. "I'll be back in a few minutes to fix your toilet. Let me run to my apartment and get changed real quick."

"Okay."

Her head slips back into her apartment, curlers and all. At my door, I'm ambushed and knocked back by my best friend. Lex's hug jars me enough to remind me of my misery. I gasp.

Pushing him away, I say, "Easy, Lex. I got a nasty bump on the head."

"Bump from what? I was worried. I wasn't sure if I had to call the cops, the fire department, or go into hiding."

"Sorry about that." I usher him far enough into our apartment to close the door, then head for the medicine cabinet for aspirin. "There were difficulties."

Lex hands me a bottle of water because we don't trust the liquid that comes from these pipes. I swallow the medicine I hope will stop the small throb still affecting the back of my skull.

"What kind of difficulties?" he asks. "I kept checking. You made it out clean."

"Draven Pierce caught me outside when I was ready to head back to the car."

"*The* Draven Pierce?"

"Do we know any others?"

"No, but he's got connections, Eddie. He could toast you."

"You have no idea," I say with a sour taste in my mouth.

"What's that supposed to mean?"

I recount everything that happened, or everything I can remember. By the time I'm done, Lex is pacing the apartment. My story ends, and I wait in silence for what I know is coming.

"We are doomed." Yep, there it is. "Do you have any idea what this means?"

"Since I was there, I'm pretty certain I do. They're not going to turn us in, Lex."

My best friend plops down on the couch with a huff. "And if they change their mind after you give them what they want? And why did you have to pull me into it?"

"I didn't mean to make your existence known. They kind of figured it out that I couldn't have done it on my own. If you don't want to help, you can go ahead and make a run for it. I'll tell them you weren't here when I got home."

"What kind of friend do you think I am?!"

Blinking, I stare at him for a moment. What does he want from me? I'm yelled at for bringing him into the middle of this. I'm yelled at for giving him an escape. I sigh, letting my temper cool. This is the typical Lex. When the shit hits the fan, so does he.

He needs time to cool down, but I'm not sure we have that time. "I—"

A knock interrupts my next words. Lex jumps, startled enough to almost fall off the couch. With a growl, I walk over to the door. Mrs. Barlow is trying to look through the peephole.

I sigh. "I have to fix Mrs. Barlow's toilet again. Think about it. You don't have to help but think of what we can do with the money they're giving us. It's one gig, and then we move on while still collecting cash to donate. At the least, you can hear them out for yourself and make a decision then. I'll find a way to make sure you can back out if needed."

The knock sounds again, louder this time. Not for the first time, I curse the family that leaves the abrasive little old lady helpless. I open the door without waiting for an answer. He'll either still be here when I get back, or he won't. Losing my best friend will be a blow, but I won't force him to suffer for my mistake.

Mrs. Barlow looks annoyed at the delay, so I apologize and follow her to her apartment. As usual, the smells of dirty cat litter and cat vomit assault my senses. I wiggle my nose in an attempt to ease the nostril abuse, but it doesn't help. Every time I enter this apartment, I find myself glad I only have one. The only reason I was allowed to have Clancy is because Betsy, her old calico, kept trying to kill him.

Betsy is a mean one. Most of these animals either don't care or rub up against my ankles, like the three weaving through my feet now. Betsy, well, let's just say she's not very friendly. I still have scars on my shins to prove how sharp her decaying teeth are.

Under the smell of cat waste, I catch a whiff of the reason I'm here. As soon as I open the door, my eyes water. I rush over to the toilet, lift the top, then pull the chain like I've shown my neighbor multiple times. She still can't seem to do this on her own. I think I'll use my newfound money to buy her new toilet insides.

Reaching for her bathroom spray, I press the nozzle to fill the room with the scent of soiled linen as the can sputters to empty. That doesn't help much. When I go to throw it away, I drop it. Leaning down affords a cat the chance to jump on my back.

Please don't be Betsy. Please don't be Betsy. For the love of God, don't be Betsy.

"Chancelor, what are you doing, you silly boy?"

Air rushes out of me in relief as she lifts the cat off my back. Not Betsy. No new scars tonight. I stand and rush from the bathroom into air that doesn't smell much better.

"I'm going to pick up some parts for your toilet and fix it for good," I say.

"Why would you do that? It still mostly works."

I purse my lips. "But then it won't get so bad if I can't get to it right away."

"Whatever you think is best. Just as long as you don't expect payment. My checks are barely enough for me to live."

I trip over one of the reasons my neighbor runs out of money so quickly and make my way to the door. "On the house, Mrs. Barlow."

Pepper makes a dash out the door when I open it, and I hear the poodle barking before she takes chase. Sighing, I close the door behind the little old lady, leaving her to deal with her arch nemesis on her own. I'm too tired to break up a cat fight.

Upon entering my apartment, I find Lex staring across the living room with wide eyes. I follow his gaze to find a surprise.

"What are you doing back so soon?" I ask.

Warrin turns with a small briefcase in his hands. "They worked on the contract while I drove you home. Anders is parking your car in the garage Lex directed him to. I'm permitted to start discussions, and Anders will be along to help answer questions or negotiate."

Warrin opens the briefcase and starts pulling out folders. I give Lex a quick look, silently telling him now is the time to run if he wants to. My friend shakes his head and leans forward with a sigh. I close the door and walk over to join them, really just wanting to go lay down in my dark room to relieve my headache better than the aspirin is. No help for it now. Time to negotiate with businessmen.

ANDERS

"I can't believe you're stuck on this idiot idea," Draven says with a scowl.

My anger rises, but I squash it back down. Anger never leads to good decisions, so I do my best not to partake in the emotion often. Draven has a habit of bringing it out of me though. Business partners and bonded brothers doesn't mean peace, especially with his tendency toward negativity and attitude.

"It's in the best interest of our business and keeps you from killing a harmless human woman," I reply.

"Harmless? She broke into our office and almost made it out with client property. Warrin would have been on the hook for losing it. How is that harmless?"

"She thought she was doing good."

"And you believe that?"

"I do."

"Are you sure you're not just turned by a pretty face like Warrin seems to be?"

I feel my eyes harden at the thought. Edith is human. Yes, she's pretty. Yes, I admire her spirit. No, I'm not looking for more. My jaw ticks with the force of my clenched teeth.

Draven doesn't read the cue. "Looking to replace your mate?"

My roar halts his words. "Don't you dare bring my mate into this. No one can replace her, and I'm insulted that you think I'm so fickle as to be swayed by a pretty face. I may never take another mate, but if I do, it will be with someone I know is worthy. Don't you dare ever say anything like that again."

His eyes darken with an unknown emotion for a moment. "Then think clearly here. This woman is a thief that I caught red-handed. She has no loyalty to us and has already proven not to be a trustworthy person."

Draven's stubbornness makes me shake my head. How can he not see this opportunity? Nothing in her breathing or heart rate indicated deceit. His views on her are colored by his past, which none of us can blame him for. He's not wrong about Warrin. Our third is already smitten with the thief. Draven feels it's because his mother is human, but I think it's deeper than that. Despite his hard upbringing, he's a big softy who isn't tainted by the same kind of traumas we are.

I know there's no point arguing. "So, you're not coming."

"That didn't sound like a question."

"Should it have been?"

"No. You know my answer."

"Exactly."

He grumbles behind me, but I walk away from him. As much as he hates this, we have decided that decisions only need a majority. There is no doubt Warrin is in on this plan. He's probably already waiting excitedly by the car. I'll need to talk to him about taking it easy. The last thing I want is for him to be hurt over a human who doesn't even know who we are. He always lets his heart lead him. A pretty face with noble intentions is enough.

And there Warrin is. Twirling the keys in his hand while pacing by the driver's door. This should give us enough of a chance to talk about how he needs to be careful. We don't need him falling for a human who doesn't reciprocate the feelings. That would be devastating for him... and us.

CHAPTER FOUR
THE CONTRACT

"Where were you?" Anders asks when he enters.

So far, what Warrin shows me looks tempting. The pay will help many people, and Lex says their financial statements are impressive. The list of charities they are involved in is extensive. It's starting to feel less like a punishment. That still doesn't mean I like the thought of helping them.

"What does it matter?" I answer while not taking my eyes off the contract in front of me.

"I thought maybe you made a run for it."

Insulted, I look up at the buff man wearing the professional suit and tie. "When I say I'll do something, I do it. I may be a thief, but I still have my honor."

Anders holds up his hands in a bid for peace. With a huff, I turn back to the papers. Stupid rich people don't understand the need to keep your word. They're all tricky like that. How can I trust them to keep their end of this bargain? I chew my lip in thought, wondering if it's too late to back out. My dilemma must be plain on my face.

"As we can trust you, you can trust us. No police involvement if you help us, which the contract states, with the stipulation that you don't tell them of our little prison in the basement," Anders said.

The man in charge walks over and drops a stack of hundreds on the stained coffee table. "Is this a bribe or an advance?"

"Call it a leap of faith."

I grimace. He's giving me trust that I won't just run off with his money. Not that this stack will be missed with the net worth of these men, but it's something. Lex stares at it with stars in his eyes. I sigh and decide it won't hurt to give a little in return. "I was fixing the toilet of the crazy cat lady down the hall."

Anders purses his lips. "Isn't that what maintenance is for?"

My laughter only makes him look more confused. Men like this are always out of touch. "It's what they're supposed to be for. They're more of a decoration to keep the city from fining the building. Before you start spouting about legality, don't bother. Welcome to how the rest of the world lives."

Warrin blinks, and I wince. It's hard to remember he came from a very low-income childhood. I shouldn't care if I hurt these men's feelings, but the gentle giant seems almost innocent. For some reason, I find myself not wanting to hurt him.

I change the subject. "No Draven?"

As Warrin sits back, he's surprised by Clancy jumping into his lap. I watch the orange and white tabby circle a few times before settling in for a nice nap. The owner of the lap he's occupying relaxes and scratches his head. Purrs vibrate the still air in the apartment.

"Draven does not approve of our deal and plans to stay out of it as much as possible," Anders confesses.

"Will that be a problem?" Lex asks.

"Not at all. Before we continue, what apartment does the cat lady live in?" Warrin cuts in.

"Why? Are you guys going to send her to a chop shop for taking me away from you for a few minutes?"

He laughs. "That's Draven's specialty, and no. I want to hire a plumber for her."

"Why?"

Blue eyes widen in surprise and confusion. "To help someone who is falling through the cracks."

I sigh. "211."

Warrin writes down the apartment number, and I smile at the thought of a plumber dealing with Betsy. Something tells me Warrin might just be able to tame the wild ball of angry fur, but the plumbers will be eaten alive. I wish I could be there. Although, I'd risk the chance of becoming collateral damage.

Taking the initiative to bring the meeting back into focus, I point at the terms and ask the questions I have. Lex chimes in with questions of his own. We go back and forth, negotiating terms that will suit everyone involved. As much as the thought of working for a large corporation that I should be robbing makes me feel icky, I'm happy with the offer and what we can do with the proceeds.

"One more thing," I say. "I want an extra clause about this yearly bonus. If something should happen to me, I want the money owed to go to charities of my choosing for as long as the company still operates."

Anders sits back, freezing when our couch creaks under his heavy weight. I smother a smile, hoping that the leg will finally give out and leave me the memory of the great CEO lying in a mess of broken furniture. Even Lex falling with him isn't enough to take the hope away. He'll survive.

"That's doable," Anders says when he decides he won't be thrown to the floor. "Sign the contract as is—we will write a note that this is only preliminary until the revised contract can be drawn up—and we will leave the two of you be. Can you both come into the office to sign the finalized contract and take a front-side look at our security?"

We do as he asks and agree to the meeting. When they exit, Lex grabs the majority of the stack of money while muttering about needing new equipment for the job. I won't begrudge him the proper tools to do what we need to do. There's plenty more to come. In fact, I order celebratory pizza.

Lex grabs his wallet and prepares to leave the apartment. I stop him. "You could've run."

His hand drops from the doorknob. Brown eyes meet mine. "To be truthful, I thought of it. While I'm not happy with the risk you took, I do know this can help a lot of people. Besides, I'm impressed by their own investments in charities. Even if they're doing it for the tax breaks, they're doing good. That much I can get behind. That's not the biggest reason."

"What is?"

My best friend holds my gaze without blinking. "We've known each other since elementary school. You may be an idiot, but you're my idiot. I'm not leaving you to deal with this on your own."

Before I can respond, Lex slips out the door with his wad of cash hidden in an inner pocket to protect it from being lifted. Tears threaten, but I push them away. He'd only tell me I'm being overly sentimental. As gruff as my best friend is, he has a heart of gold. That's a given, seeing the work we do, but that doesn't stop me from loving him like a brother because of it.

The pizza arrives, and I slip a hundred out of the stack, telling the delivery guy to keep the change. Judging by his excited thanks, I feel like I just became a favorite customer. Food seems to help my headache a little, but it's still too prominent. Exhaustion weighs heavily on me. A forced nap isn't a restful one. Even though it's early, I turn off our TV, put the leftover pizza in the fridge for Lex, and fall onto my bed. Clancy curls up behind my knees as I drift off to sleep.

Shouting wakes me in the morning. Reaching for my phone, I notice I slept about thirteen hours. My headache is finally gone, and I feel like a thousand bucks. I stand with a yawn, stretching tired muscles until joints pop. With some clothes in my hands, I step out of my room and make my way to the bathroom.

Jared and Lex shout at the cars they race against on the TV. Both are oblivious to my presence, but I find myself wondering what the jock is doing here so early. He usually sleeps until noon, so his presence here is interesting. Not enough to deserve more than a passing consideration. After my shower, I enter the living room to find them eating leftover pizza for brunch.

Without a word, Lex holds out a card to me. I take it without thought. All three cell phone numbers are on this company business card. "Where did you get this?"

"Warrin gave it to me when he first got here. I forgot to pass it along. He said to put their numbers in your phone in case they need to get a hold of you."

"Warrin, huh?" Jared interjects cluelessly into the conversation. "Finally have a hot date?"

I shake my head. "Business associate."

"Suuuure."

Throwing Lex a glance and a thanks, I ignore Jared trying to get a rise out of me. I'd have to care what he thinks to be bothered by the immature teasing. Good thing I don't. Lex treasures Jared's friendship, so I deal with his presence by ignoring him when he becomes obnoxious, which happens to be pretty often. As strange as it sounds, I've gotten used to the annoyance enough to block it out.

Once in my room, I enter the numbers into my contacts, but I use the original nicknames I came up with; Mr. Authority, Mr. Attitude, and Mr. Gentle Giant. I know Warrin's nickname is new, but Anders didn't give me a chance to give him another before identifying him while I pretended to sleep. A text comes through before I can put my phone down.

Mr. Gentle Giant: I hope all is well. I apologize for our rough meeting yesterday. Is your head feeling better?

I bite my lip, trying to figure Warrin out. Draven wants nothing to do with me. Anders is all business. Warrin is sweet and curious, considering me noble for trying to rob him the other night.

Me: I'm fine. I got some good sleep. See you Monday.

Trying to make sense of the smiling emoji he sends back is pointless because I'm not sure what to make of this man. Instead of dwelling on it, I slip my phone into my pocket and decide on a walk. Today is Saturday, so two days until I become a cog in the machine. I remind myself it's for a good cause and decide a walk is a great idea.

The boys are back on their game when I walk through. I'm glad to avoid Mrs. Barlow on my way down the hall. My guilt plagues me over the fact I'm working for the enemy, so I do the only thing that will make me feel better; I turn my feet to take me to the soup kitchen. It's not my day, but they're always happy for extra hands.

Entering, they prove me right by handing me a pitcher of water. I walk between the tables, refilling glasses without being asked. As usual, many of the elderly stop to tell me of the family they lost or miss. I smile and nod, happy to give them an ear to talk to. This is something I've done since childhood. It helped keep me out of the house where I wasn't wanted, the mistake that ruined my mother's life. Making others smile always took the pain away.

This is probably how I came across my current line of work. I started by stealing expensive sunglasses, watches, and spare bills from the children more well off than I was. Even then, I didn't spend the money I got on candy and CDs. Instead, I walked the street and dropped my stolen wealth on the homeless after fulfilling my needs. Them getting a solid meal was better than all the chocolate in the world.

By the time I leave, I'm smiling and feeling lighter again. I stop at the mailboxes before I make my way to the elevator. An unmarked envelope is wedged between the bills and circulars. Curious, I slip it into the back pocket of my jeans and walk toward my apartment. I hear the boys laughing in Lex's room after a loud thump penetrates his closed door. I shake my head and sit on the couch, pushing the empty pizza box to the side.

The bills go onto the table without a glance spared. I know what they want, and it won't be hard to pay them. We always make sure to have enough, plus we have the leftover cash I hide in the safe behind our table by the door. My finger slips under the flap to break the seal. Opening the paper, I stare in confusion at the note made of letters cut from a magazine.

We know what you're doing.

CHAPTER FIVE
DELVING DEEP

The steering wheel is cool beneath my touch. It's hard being in this vehicle after Anders drove it. A faint musky smell of expensive cologne saturates the still air. When I turn on the vents to circulate it, the smell only gets worse. With a grimace, I turn it off. It's not that he smells bad. I just don't like the thought of a stranger in the only means of transportation we have.

"What about bugs?" I ask.

Lex turns away from the view passing by outside his window. He looks at me, pursing his lips in thought. "If you don't trust these men, why did you make a deal with them?"

Leave it to my hacker to get to the heart of the issue. No, I don't trust them. Warrin may be wiggling his way in, but the other two... not so much. So, why did I make the deal? To avoid time behind bars? Yes. To have unlimited funds available for our mission? Definitely. The only issue is deciding if it's smart to think that they won't renege on their deal once they get what they want. Contract or not, once I complete this job, I'm expendable.

As usual, Lex reads my silence. "Sometimes, I wonder if your heart or your brain is bigger."

"Well, I've never known a big heart to be a bad thing."

"It can be in certain situations. Your job needs a good deal of brain usage."

I laugh. "Without my heart, I wouldn't be here in the first place. Besides, I like being guided by my instincts. They haven't steered me wrong yet."

"But you're doubting them now?"

Clenching my teeth, my knuckles turn white on the steering wheel. Damn my friend for always making sense when I don't want him to. The ever-distrustful Lex Adler, questioning me on my lack of belief in complete strangers; hot strangers, but still strangers. It's like our roles have reversed.

"I don't know," I say. "This is completely new to me. I have never done anything this reckless."

It's Lex's turn to laugh. "Eddie, you break into high security corporations for a living. You don't even keep what you steal. How is this more reckless?"

He needs to stop having good points. "We steal from people like them. Now we're working for them after I got caught."

"Fine. I'll sweep the car when we get back. Will that make you feel better?"

I grumble. "Would have felt better if you did it before we left the apartment."

"Maybe I didn't because I trust your instincts," Lex says with a grunt that effectively shuts my mouth.

My roommate may be gruff and unwilling to trust, but we've always been like two peas in a pod. Mom hated that I had a friend as close as him and always tried to wiggle toxic waste between us. Kids at school always sang the song about Edith and Lex sitting in a tree. We graduated together. We went to prom together; platonically, of course. We moved out and into this place as soon as we turned eighteen. Inseparable friends forever, taking on the coldness of the world without fear.

And I'm throwing us into the lion's den.

Maybe his unconditional trust in me is misplaced. For once, my instincts have led me into danger. Was I following instincts or the basic need for survival? My possible mistake has the potential to ruin my best friend's life. Maybe that's why I'm second guessing my intuition on this.

My heart races as I turn the wheel and pull into the massive parking lot behind the headquarters of my current employers. They offered to allow me to park in their private garage beneath this monstrosity of a building, but I couldn't accept. Hiding our only means of escape away in an area they control is not something I'm willing to risk. It's important for anyone living on the wrong side of the law to have an escape route planned.

Even through his bravado, I see Lex tense beside me. This is one of the reasons I didn't tell him about the letter. It's most likely a prank or an empty threat, but the timing would break through the false calm my friend does his best to keep. I'll help him save face by keeping a harmless joke from destroying his confidence. It's safe in the drawer under my panties.

Once I turn the engine off, we sit and stare at the building before us. White stone and shiny steel reach for the bright blue sky. Windows glint in the sun. In the lower levels, we can see people walking by the glass, making copies, staring at their phones, and filling their bottles from the fountain in the break room.

I take a deep breath. "Are you ready?"

"Are you?"

Grimacing, I release a heavy sigh as my answer. I pull the keys from the ignition, open my door, and climb out. Lex only waits a moment before joining me. The air is cool but not so much that we freeze. We are edging into winter, where the weather can change back and forth from hour to hour. November warmth is always fleeting.

The weather report as told by Eddie Hart is now over. There is no more stalling what is to come. As if as one, we take our first steps toward the building. Entering the lobby during the day feels wrong. There is no darkness to hide my movements. Too many people walk through the vast open space. Is there an opposite to claustrophobic? If so, I think I'm feeling it right now.

I'm meant to prowl this environment with stealth, not walk right into the shark's feeding grounds when the kings are at home. This is stupid. It isn't until Lex squeezes my shoulder that I realize I've stopped walking. I take a few deep breaths to calm myself.

"Eddie!" Warrin's great big presence is on us before we realize what's happening. "Welcome. And to you too, Lex. Anders sent me to greet the two of you. I'm supposed to take you to the conference room where we can finish the contract process, then we can show you our systems after. Although, I believe you both know most of it already."

There's no hint of sarcasm or resentment in his words. If anything, he sounds excited and impressed. This is the last man I'd expect to be a coldhearted CEO. Yet, here we are. Maybe his upbringing makes him different. No, I've seen even the most destitute consumed with greed when the chance presented itself. It's almost like this large man isn't corruptible.

That thought is like a bucket of cold water to the face. No one is that innocent, but I don't sense any duality to him. What we see is what Warrin is. There are no hidden alarms blaring from the depths of my natural instinct. This man is the gentle giant I assume. This is strange, not something I'm used to dealing with. I'm not even sure how to handle it.

Warrin's chattering about anything and everything as he leads us to the row of elevators. None of it infiltrates my mind while I watch the numbers climb higher and higher. The weather, his favorite food and movie, and even the bedtime routine Warrin follows batters at my ears. It's all white noise at this point, and I feel guilty for not listening.

Anders—and Draven, to my surprise—are waiting at the oblong table sitting in the center of the room. I barely notice the cliché plants and pictures hanging on the white walls. A large screen hangs on the wall at one end of the room. Tall buildings make an impressive view. All this registers to my subconscious, but my eyes are locked on the two men waiting for us.

Warrin takes a seat, his hair the usual mess. His blue eyes twinkle and shimmer. He leans on the table with his elbows, as if excited for this meeting.

Draven sits in his seat, arms crossed over his chest and legs up on the table. His dark eyes regard us with a coldness that leaves goosebumps all over me. Long black hair is pulled into a bun at the nape of his neck. Cat-like grace lends a certain beauty to the angry man that I can't deny, even as I throw him a scowl.

Anders smiles warmly, his brown eyes at ease. He sits straight, with a confidence I wish to possess. As with the last two times I saw him, his brown hair is gelled into place, not a hair standing on end. Broad shoulders strain the fabric of his suit jacket.

Lex and I take seats next to Warrin. We look over the new contract to make sure that the proper changes were made. Our final signatures fill all the proper lines by the end. Warrin is practically jumping up and down. Anders looks pleased. Draven grimaces, as if he ate something rotten. In the end, I feel like I just sold my soul. I can only hope that some good comes from it.

My friend is sitting at a computer terminal in the security room, going over every entrance into the system that he may have missed during his recon. While he does this, I look for every blind spot I may find helpful in my nighttime pursuits. It's amazing how many weak spots we are finding. It seems the three men employing us were ripped off by their security company.

"Look at this," Lex says beside me.

I roll over to inspect what he shows me. Too bad I have no idea what I'm looking at. "What is it?"

"Not part of the system, but it seems connected to it. I have never seen something like this. I'm not sure if I need to remove it or leave it."

I yell for the head of security. Jeff walks over to us, his belly straining the uniform. He wipes his balding head with a green handkerchief. "Yes?"

"What's this file?" Lex asks.

"Oh, that's something that the cyber team added to the system. It blocks intruders from critical systems."

"Mind if I take a look at it?"

Jeff shrugs. The three men enter and offer to take us to lunch. Lex waves them off, in his element, even if it's being done in front of others instead of hiding away behind his personal setup. He has something to nibble on, and he won't put it down until he figures out where it came from, where it goes to, and what function it performs. I consider doing the same, but the look of hope on Warrin's face is too much. I can't help feeling like I can't let him down.

Anders drives, giving me the passenger seat, much to Draven's annoyance. I can feel his dark eyes drilling into the back of my head. I ignore it as best I can, listening to Anders tell me the history of their companies and the merging. "And that's the story. We merged out of the greatest of needs."

"Because someone was threatening a takeover? I think you have a strange way of looking at needs," I say as we pull into a restaurant that looks way too expensive for my taste.

"If our companies go under, thousands of people will be out of work."

I let it drop because I don't want people to lose their jobs and become destitute. That doesn't mean I concede to his point; it's simply not worth arguing over. With extreme reluctance, I follow them into the restaurant that looks like it only caters to those way above my station. At the table, I sit and take a menu.

The prices are steep. I grimace. "Maybe I'll just have water. Even the bread is way too much. Is it made of gold?"

Anders chuckles. "Get what you like. It's on us."

Draven glares at Anders while Warrin rattles off his favorites. Since I'm new to food like this, I take one of his suggestions, feeling uncomfortable with eating something that can pay a week's salary to someone who needs it more than me.

"What have you found so far?" Anders asks.

"Lots of holes. It will take a few more days just to scour everything, then I'll work with Lex on a plan of action."

Before we can talk further, the food arrives. While eating, they listen to the issues I have found so far. Draven rolls his eyes but remains silent. Anders asks questions, and Warrin simply smiles. Despite my reservations, I find myself looking upon this agreement with confidence. The men discuss lighter topics, so I zone out.

A tingling washes over me, making the hairs on my arms stand on end. Curious, I glance around the restaurant. Nothing is out of place. Everyone is eating or laughing, minding their own business. So why does it feel like I'm being watched?

DRAVEN

It's hard not to outright snarl at the human woman. Lots of holes? I handpicked the security team that we used. The only holes in our systems are the ones she probably put there. I'm not sure why Anders is so keen on letting a human in to destroy everything we've built. It's not like we don't have enough trouble as it is. What is he thinking?

My eyes roam over the interloper to our lunch. She listens to our conversation, but she's pretending not to. Typical. As if I wouldn't notice the duplicity. Her blonde hair lies down her back, the dark roots showing a little at the top. Nothing about this woman is real and truthful.

Keeping up with the conversation, I continue to observe our new *consultant*. Warrin is already head over heels for this woman, idolizing the very thing that put us at risk the other night. Anders is too friendly for my comfort, too trusting and professional. Am I the only one that can see how untrustworthy she truly is?

Sure, she's pretty. Her dark eyes hold kindness that I don't believe. While her falsehood has sucked in my companions, I won't be so easily tricked. The woman sips at her water without a care for the world. There's something haunting in her gaze, but it's just one more secret I don't know.

When her eyes start to look around in search of something, my senses pick up. I can smell the scent of canine in the air. It's not strong enough to be close, but I can still smell it. There's no way she can. Although she seems to know they're there. Why is that? Did they tell her? I can't let my guard down. My newfound brothers may have let her deceive them, but I won't.

I'll remain forever vigilant. That's the thing about lies; they come out eventually. I'll have to watch for them and hope they come out before she brings our ruin. No outstanding citizen sneaks into a business to steal from its clients. There's much more to this woman, and I will watch her until I know for sure what it is. I won't let her pull a fast one on me.

Not for the first time, I find myself wishing that Anders would have let me take care of the nuisance while I still could. My associates would have made it look like she never existed. This Eddie would simply disappear. Even her friend would never find her.

Those two never listen to my knowledge. I know humans. They shoot first and ask questions later. They take down anything they don't understand. There's always an ulterior motive. It's only a matter of figuring it out. Well, I won't let anyone pull a fast one on me, and I certainly won't let a human female hurt Anders or Warrin. I'll figure her out.

And I'll do it without falling into her trap.

Unlike my two business partners, I understand the duplicity of her species. I will get to the bottom of it. Maybe then the other two will take me more seriously. Humans are dangerous and to be avoided unless necessary. She can look beautiful all she wants. I won't fall for it.

CHAPTER SIX
EMPTY SHADOWS

The drive home is too quiet. Since I drove in the morning, Lex insisted he drove home. Instead of having traffic to distract me, I'm staring out the window, lost in my thoughts.

The rest of lunch went well. As much as I hated them paying, they insisted I order dessert. Well, Anders and Warrin insisted. Draven spent the entire time I ate my cheesecake glaring with heated eyes. It made eating a little uncomfortable, but I refused to let his attitude ruin the creamy goodness that melted on my tongue.

Even then, the feeling of being watched persisted. I must have just been paranoid because I didn't see anyone around me who was staring, besides Draven. Even his annoyance didn't match the malevolent feeling that sent chills up and down my spine. It didn't stop until we returned to the car.

None of the men seemed to feel it, but I couldn't shake the paranoia. Anders and Warrin were oblivious to any strange happenings. Draven was too caught up in trying to make me feel his wrath to care about what was going on around us. It had to be all in my head.

"Everything alright?" Lex asks, dragging my attention from my miserable thoughts.

"Yeah," I sigh, watching the window mist with my warm puff of breath. "Just feeling a little off. Did you figure out the file?"

"Yeah. It was just what they said it was. Very interesting system."

Silence engulfs the vehicle again. I have nothing else to say about our current job. Lex becomes lost when he's working on the computer, and I have my own part to play. I have a nice list of areas in need of improvements from the security footage and speaking to employees. Tomorrow, I'll test locks. Although, I already know the safety deposit boxes are easy to break into.

We pull into the garage, and Lex hops out. He pauses when I don't follow. "Earth to Eddie."

Blinking, I look around and get out. "Sorry."

"Is everything alright?"

"Hmmm?"

"Eddie?"

I jump. "Sorry, Lex. My mind is just circling a bunch of unimportant stuff."

"Are you sure? If those men did anything to you at lunch..."

I laugh. "You'll do what? You're not a fighter. A good friend, but the only violence you have in you is video games."

"True, but I'm a mean keyboard warrior. I can ruin their reputation until they're begging on a street corner. And don't even think I'll let you help them."

"I'm sure you would. No, it's not the corporate brutes. Not even Draven. I'm just tired."

"Draven," he mutters. "What's up his ass?"

"Metaphorically? The thief that broke in and tried to rob him is now working on his weak security. Physically? I don't want to know."

"Good point."

Now that my mood is better, Lex falls into silence. The only people that get to see this devoted and protective side of him are me and Jared. Everyone else is met with silence or gruffness. It's flattering to think I'm worthy of this side of the great, antisocial hacker.

Upon entering the apartment building, I offer to be the one to grab the mail. Lex is back to his usual self, so he only shrugs and walks toward the elevator. I hesitate with the key in the lock. After a deep breath, I turn it. It's not that I'm afraid of the idiot sending prank letters. My friend's easy paranoia is something I need to protect him from.

Paranoia. That's funny coming from someone who thinks she's being watched when no one is looking at her. Shaking my head, I open the little door and pull out the newspaper. No envelopes follow, bills and creepiness absent.

I rush to catch up as the doors to the elevator slide shut. Instead of helping, Lex grins and waves like a madman. The doors clamp shut less than a second before I reach them. I growl and threaten to give Lex a good lecture when I get to the apartment.

Standing there, alone in the lobby of our rundown apartment building, an eerie feeling washes over me. Goosebumps prickle my skin as the light on the ceiling flickers. I hit the button with the up arrow a few times in illogical hopes it'll speed up my steel carriage. It's taking much longer than I think it should.

Glancing around shows me no one is here to give me this sense of foreboding. Shadows stretch outside the smeared glass of the door leading into the fresh air. My gaze travels to all the dark alleys and areas the light can't touch. The streetlights make more darkness when their beams are interfered with. I swallow, sure anything could be watching me from the shadows.

The sense of doom grows, and I reach over to hit the button again. Once. Twice. Five times. An inner alarm tells me it's best if I hurry, but I can't until the damn elevator returns. By the time the dinging echoes, the stairs are beginning to look like a good idea.

As soon as the doors part, I rush to get in, plowing over those pushing to get out. Glares and curses don't stop my mad dash for safety. I hit the button for the second floor over and over. Relief is almost unbearable once the doors close. Even the lurch of the elevator moving up isn't enough to dull my sense of relief.

In the hall, I pass the plumbers as they exit Mrs. Barlow's apartment. One has a nasty scratch running from his eye to lip and a very unhappy expression on his face. I wince at the jagged red line slicing over his cheekbone. That's got to hurt.

Opening the door, I shout, "Damn you, Lex. Why did you leave me there alone?"

His eyebrows scrunch together over his bowl of cereal. "I figured you're an adult and could make it up on your own. Didn't think you'd get bent out of shape over a joke. Guess I was wrong."

Sighing, I realize sentimental Lex is replaced by his normal grumpy self. "Did you not think of the trouble I could get into in this neighborhood?"

"Not really since we have lived here for years and you wander alone all the time. You're a thief. You can't handle standing in a lobby? What's wrong with you today?"

I clench my teeth and stomp to my room. He may have a soft spot for me, but that doesn't mean he's a different person altogether. He's also very right. That doesn't stop me from being angry at him. Just because I'm twenty-two doesn't make me impervious to the nightmares of this world, of which there are many.

Slamming my door puts more emphasis on my unhappiness with my best friend. It's not until I'm sitting on my bed that I realize I'm hungry. Oh well. I'm not going to go back out there and deal with him because my stomach wants to betray me. I went from being grateful for my best friend to being angry with him. Well, I'm not the only one. He shows me his soft spot, then he covers it up and abandons me.

This isn't fair to either of us. I've been on edge all day, and my emotions aren't anywhere close to stable. I think I just need to call it a day. A shower should come first, but a headache is sneaking up on me again, so I slip off my socks and slide under my covers. I'll shower in the morning. Maybe my mood will be better by then.

My alarm going off reminds me that headaches don't always go away with sleep. Swearing under my breath, I reach over and pick up my phone to shut it up. I fall back onto my pillow with my hands spread out over my twin-sized mattress. Blinking the sleep from my eyes is hard when my head hurts, but I somehow manage to drag myself up and to the bathroom. The shower helps a little. The aspirin I open will help more.

Lex is waking up when I walk across the living room and into the tiny kitchen. I set the coffeepot to make a cup of coffee and dig through the cupboards for a bagel. My stomach grumbles to tell me it won't be enough after skipping supper last night. I push the annoyance away.

My roommate meets me on the couch with another bowl of cereal, this one of the fruity variety. Lex can live on bowls of crunchy sugar in milk. I need a little more. The bagel is gone too quickly, so I take a few cautious sips of my coffee.

"I'm sorry about my attitude last night," I mumble.

He shrugs. "Tensions are high."

"They are, but I shouldn't take it out on you. We've been thick as thieves since childhood."

Lex grunts. "It's easy to be thick as thieves when we're actually thieving for a living."

"True."

"Listen, Eddie, you are like a sister to me, and I'll defend you to the death. Just don't ask me to not abandon you for amusement."

Those words may mean little to many, but it's a semi-apology from Lex. "Ready for another day of work? I never thought I'd say that."

"As ready as I can be. Once I get all the information I need, I think I can work some of it at home. I hate leaving the apartment."

Isn't that the truth? Lex's wish to turn into a crusty hermit is the reason I have to deal with Jared as much as I do. No help for it. Like he says, I can enjoy his love and occasional affection, but I can't change who he is. Not that I want to. Lex is Lex, and I wouldn't change him for the world. I only wish I didn't bring him into this.

After our meager breakfasts, we make our way to the parking garage. The air is cool, making me wish I would've worn more than my light jacket. As the year continues on, it will only get worse. The bite will get stronger. Light clothing will no longer be enough. It almost isn't now.

Lex offers to drive, and I let him without argument. My head still hurts, so I don't really want to be the one responsible for our lives on the way to the building. I wonder when the aspirin is going to kick in because I don't feel like dealing with this all day. Maybe I need more food. A bagel isn't much on a starving stomach.

My mind wanders from topic to topic as I watch the people walking on the sidewalks pass by. Once in the office building, I make my way straight for the break room and take a provided water. Lex is already clicking through different folders when I join him. I take a look at the list of locks I need to examine today. My hand marks a red check beside the deposit boxes because I know for a fact they aren't adequate to keep the likes of me out of them. Not many locks are, but we'll do our best to add at least a little challenge to any future breaking and entering attempt.

As I finish the list, Warrin walks in. "Eddie! Lex. I brought donuts."

My stomach grumbles, and it takes all I have not to lunge for the box. A bear claw makes its way into my hand. Warrin smiles at my choice with a small glint of amusement in his eyes. I'm not sure why my pastry tastes amuse him, but I won't let him keep me from enjoying it. The throbbing bouncing around in my skull calms slightly when I take a second.

"Thank you," I mumble, not caring how rude I am for talking with my mouth full. "Just you this morning?"

That big smile lights up his face, and the twinkle in his light blue eyes makes me forget to breathe for a second. "They have clients to attend to. We know you're going to be examining locks and weak points. I'm to act as your escort."

Well, if any of them are escort material, it's Warrin. Anders is a bit over professional at times, but he's still kind. Draven is laughable. I'm not sure there is a hospitable bone in his body. I'll take the gentle giant over the other two. The day shouldn't be too boring or uptight.

CHAPTER SEVEN
FLEEING MICE

"And most people don't understand that this can be a bit of a weak spot," I say, turning the knob to a utility closet. "See? Unlocked."

Warrin's eyes narrow in confusion. "It's a closet. There isn't anything worth stealing in here."

"You have to look at the bigger picture."

I walk into the tiny room with the giant man in tow. Once inside, I find myself wondering if this was really a good idea. The closet is tiny. The man is massive. I feel squished.

"How can a room this small hold a big picture?" Warrin says.

"If I was slithering through the halls and was risking discovery, I could slip into this closet and wait for patrols or whatever threat is past."

"I can't see you slithering. That sounds gross; not at all like you."

Blinking, I turn my head to catch Warrin staring at my ass. He realizes he has my attention and looks up quickly. His big adorable cheeks redden. Well, despite being groped with his eyes, I don't feel violated. Nothing Warrin does feels like assault. That's an interesting thought, one to examine further later when I'm not so squished with the subject at hand.

"Regardless of whether I slither or not, this would be the place to do it. Also, there are many objects to use as a weapon," I say.

"Like the broom or mop."

I point at one of the metal shelves along the wall. "And chemicals to burn or use to start fires. Then where would you be?"

"In a lot of trouble."

A squeak grabs our attention. Curious, I tap the bucket it came from with my toe. A gray mouse runs from beneath. Warrin hisses and jumps back, a giant man afraid of a tiny mouse. His broad back slams into the shelf with the chemicals on it. As it tips, a bottle of bleach teeters on the top. Warrin throws himself on top of me like a warm shield, and the bottle thunks on his head.

Breathing, I find myself squished against the hard wall. The gentle giant's body feels oddly good against my front. As I thought when I first saw him, he's neither hard nor soft, some perfect place in the middle. Strong enough to leave no doubt to the muscles underneath, but enough non-muscular give to make him feel like someone that would be good to cuddle with.

His massive hands pin me in, one pressed against the wall on both sides of me. I find myself wondering if the hands are as gentle as the owner, or if they're rough and demanding. Blinking, I push the thought from my head and follow the tendons in his throat up to his face. When my gaze reaches his lips, they part with what I imagine to be an invitation I consider accepting. To stem further temptation, I look up to find an intensity in the ice-blue eyes that makes my mouth go dry.

They're not cold like the frozen liquid they resemble. No, just the opposite. There's a fire in them that would melt the largest iceberg within seconds. I lick my lips, locking my gaze on his. He smiles, bringing warmth to my core. This is dangerous territory, but oh, how I'd like to explore it.

Clearing my throat, I break the magnetic field drawing our eyes together. "I think the mouse is gone now."

Warrin bites his lip and moves away. "I'm sorry. That was rude of me."

"No. You saved me from a massive bump on the head. Speaking of, how's yours? Do we need to get you some ice?"

He shakes his head, his blond hair swaying like a field of fresh wheat in a windstorm. "I'm fine."

I might not be. When he turns to walk out of the storage closet, my gaze falls on his backside, and I find myself wishing for the ice he rejects. The heat in me grows with each step, leaving me feeling as if I've been traveling the desert for a week with no water. Parched is too weak a word. Dehydrated a little closer. A dried husk just right. My tongue sticks to the roof of my mouth.

With a deep breath, I follow Warrin out, make a show of locking the door, and close it with a louder bang than I was expecting. We spend the next couple of hours going from floor to floor and door to door. At the safety deposit room, I stop.

"These were particularly easy to break into," I say.

Warrin sighs. "Yes. It is my responsibility to keep my client's personal belongings safe, but I failed to do it properly."

"Well, to be fair, I'm a pretty good thief."

"A very impressive one, but I still failed. I'll look into better locks and alarms. I've already started."

While the first words fill me with pride, the tone of the rest sends an emotion I'm not used to feeling when it comes to the job. Guilt. I steal from the rich to help those that need it more. I don't regret my actions, but I hate knowing I made Warrin doubt himself. These thoughts sit uncomfortably in my stomach, like the time Lex swore to me that the funky tasting apples weren't bad. I'll never get over that betrayal, or the sickness I dealt with for a day. I hoped never to feel it again, but I do now.

"Lex is an awesome hacker. Your security was almost air-tight. I'll help you make sure it is," I say, trying to cheer him up. "I can help you find the right locks if you want me to. Just give me a budget."

"Unlimited."

"What?"

The big man turns to me, a look of determination rekindling the fire in his eyes. "It is my duty to keep these boxes safe. I will do so by whatever means necessary. Cost isn't an issue."

And that reminds me who I'm dealing with. I bite my bottom lip and turn away. Warrin may seem sweet and gentle, but he's also one of the high society men I despise. To make sure I don't make any foolish decisions, I need to remember it. He's not some giant, cuddly bear. He's a man with the means to make my life and the lives of those around me miserable. I can't forget again.

The elevator dings on the bottom floor, and Warrin lets me exit first. The other two are waiting; Anders with a brochure-worthy smile, and Draven with a smirk mixed with a grimace.

"Lunch?" Anders asks.

Thinking of the overly expensive meal that may have cost the same as a normal car payment makes me wince. I need to remember who I am, where I come from. "Not today, but thanks for the offer. I'm sure Lex would be happy to have me as company."

"Nonsense," Anders says. "He can come too."

I'm desperate for another excuse. Work. Yes, I have a lot of work. Before I can utter the words, Lex thumps me on the shoulder. They must have already told them. My scowl makes my friend look confused. What does he even want with rich people food anyway? He eats cereal out of the same bowl all the time, sometimes without washing it first. As if reading my mind, he shrugs.

"This one doesn't speak much," Draven says with a dark chuckle.

"As if you're one to talk," I say in defense of my best friend.

His amusement turns to annoyance. "I talk to those that are deserving of it. You are not one of those people."

"Good. I'd prefer not to be in your circle."

"You're nowhere near my circle, Mutt."

Hearing the nickname he gave me, I press my lips together. He has no idea how right he truly is. My mother never let me forget where I came from and what I cost her. I feel the heat of anger rise within me.

"Now, Draven," Anders says. "That's no way to treat an employee."

"A contractor," Draven responds.

"Either way, we must not be so rude."

I scoff. "Does Draven have any other mode besides rude?"

The man with the dark eyes scowls. When he opens his mouth with a retort, Warrin jumps between us. "How about that lunch? I have the perfect location."

Calloused fingers engulf mine. Before I can argue, I'm yanked back into the elevator as the other three file in. Anders pushes the button for the private garage with his hands folded in front of him. Draven leans against the handrail, leering at me through the shiny wall. Lex hides in the corner.

Warrin chats away. "Don't worry, Eddie. You can be in my circle."

"Everyone is in your circle," Draven interrupts.

"The more the merrier. But Eddie isn't in just any circle. She's in the one reserved for the best people. Not many people are in that circle."

Draven rolls his eyes but remains silent. I listen to Warrin list the people who are in this inner circle. It seems to consist of family and the other two CEOs. How I fit in it, I doubt I'll ever know. I'm a thief. He was my target. It seems like a weird gesture to put me in his special group.

It turns out that Warrin's perfect place is a seafood restaurant. The three men are greeted at the front desk like royalty, which makes me nervous to see the menu. I drop back to walk next to Lex.

"What are you doing? You hate eating out," I say.

"If I'm going to be forced out of my cave, the least they can do is feed me."

"You have no idea how much this food costs."

He shrugs. "They're buying, so it doesn't matter. I'm not squeamish about bleeding these guys for cash like you are."

Draven looks back in annoyance. I can't figure out why. We're lagging just far enough to avoid being heard. We aren't slowing them down. It's not like they can hear our conversation. Either way, I hurry along, taking the seat Warrin pulls out for me next to Lex. Glancing around makes me feel extremely uncomfortable. Everyone is wearing such rich clothing, and here I am, wearing clothes from the clearance racks to save money.

Annoyed at the impressive meal Lex orders—probably to take home leftovers—I purposely look for the cheapest Item on the menu that will still fill me up. Lex side eyes me, but I ignore him. As he said, I'm squeamish about indulging like this. If he wants to, that's up to him, but I won't. The meal is delicious, if a little fancier than I'd like.

"What do you want for dessert?" Warrin asks.

Lex asks for takeout containers. "We get dessert too?"

"I can't eat another bite," I say in an attempt to get this meal over with.

"Nonsense," Warrin says. "This place has the best chocolate cake. You have to try it."

Arguing does no good, proven by the mountain of chocolate cake, vanilla ice cream, and caramel sauce sitting before me on the table. The cake is rich on my tongue, so moist that it dissolves on impact. It is delicious, but I wasn't lying when I said I couldn't fit much more. Still, I refuse to waste food when starving children roam the streets, so I force as much into me as I can. Lex goes at it as if starving.

Once done, I push away the plate and make a strong effort not to throw up. I won't need to eat for a week after this. Warrin asks me if I want anything else. I hold up a hand in protest because I don't trust opening my mouth. The three men talk of a weekend getaway, one they seem to take every week. I find myself wishing I would have known that. Maybe I could have avoided being caught.

Anders's next words almost make me lose control of the food trying to make its way back up. "We'd like you to come with us this weekend, Eddie."

CHAPTER EIGHT
CHOKING ON AIR

I've heard of people choking on air, but I never did it before. Now, I can definitely say it's part of my experience. I cough and sputter, unable to get a word out because I can't suck air in. Warrin pushes my glass of water toward me while Draven smirks and Anders sits there patiently. Lex is staring at the three men with wide eyes.

"Excuse me?" I say when I'm able to breathe again.

"We would like you to accompany us to our weekend retreat Friday night," Anders says, as if he's merely telling us it's sunny outside.

"You've known her... what... less than a week? And you want her to accompany you on your weekend vacation?" Lex asks.

"Look, it finally speaks to those it's mooching off of," Draven interjects with a snort.

I scowl. "You offered to pay."

"Out of generosity. It's not nice to take advantage of generosity. Or have you never heard that saying before?"

Before I can reply, Anders throws a hand between us and gives Draven a look that reminds me of a parent whose children need to be separated. "Enough, Draven."

Mr. Attitude crosses his arms over his chest and leans back, all his ire now focused on Anders. "They attempted to rob us. You gave them a job. Not once did I ever give you the idea that I approved of this action, but I didn't get the majority of the vote, so my feelings in this don't matter. Instead of listening to my reason, you chose to hire a thief and invite her to our private cabin, which I also didn't agree to. You are stuck on being the most generous businessman, and Warrin is just obsessed with a pretty face."

Anders's brown eyes darken into the first hint of a break in his calm I've seen. I don't blame him. If anyone could break down walls of civility, it's Draven. Instead of interrupting, I decide I wish to watch this display. You can learn a lot about someone from a confrontation. Will Anders lose the collected calm he carries so well? Will Draven's stubbornness win out and cost me a job that I don't really want?

What I'm learning so far is interesting enough. It seems that not all three need to agree on a matter; it's a majority vote. Draven isn't in that majority, so his thinly veiled hatred is bursting free now. Warrin looks at them as if afraid of what may happen next. I'll ignore the part where the dark-haired man called me a pretty face in reference to his companion.

"You know the dangers we face and the reason we need to find out how best to protect ourselves," Anders says with a hiss.

"And we merged to help negate the danger to our businesses. Three is much stronger than one. I'll find a better security firm. We don't need a thief to tell us how to protect what is ours. I don't understand how you feel you can trust someone caught stealing from you."

"Because the stakes for both of us mean compliance. We will hire a better security firm, but I want to see what someone with experience on the other end has to say about it. I even plan on running estimates and plans through her. Stop letting your ego get in the way of protecting what is ours."

Takeaway from this? What the hell did I get myself into? What danger? The note and strange feeling of being watched come to my mind. Are they connected?

"Ego? I'm not the one who insisted on being in charge," Draven says.

"We all agreed it was for the best," Warrin cuts in.

Anders straightens. "Would you like the job?"

Draven looks away with a grumble. From their stances, I'm going to guess this isn't the first time this argument has happened. Draven probably wants the clout to make decisions but not the other responsibilities that come with the position. Despite his earlier position, Warrin doesn't like making decisions for others; I can tell this from the little I know. Anders is the obvious right choice because he seems fair and has the perfect temperament, even if Draven seems to try to push him.

"Let's get over this power play," I say to get this conversation over with. "The fact still stands that I'm a little uncomfortable spending a weekend with three men I don't know while they're enjoying their free time."

"Don't flatter yourself," Draven says. "It's not like we want anything personal from you."

Anders sends the dark-haired man a withering look. "What my less delicate colleague is trying to say is that we need your help there as well. We are looking into increasing security there. I know you can't help with the grounds, but the cabin isn't strong enough to hold anyone out."

Lex sends me a look and shakes his head. I sigh and agree. "Still not seeing the point. Do you have treasure buried out there?"

Warrin laughs as if I said the funniest thing ever. Draven rolls his eyes. It's Anders that speaks. "No, but we have certain people to keep out."

There it is again, the hint that enemies are at large. I chew my lip and look at Lex, who shakes his head again. He doesn't want me to go. *I* don't want me to go. This seems like a strange request.

I decide to put my concerns into words. "You seem awfully worried about someone coming for you. Do we need to be worried?"

Draven laughs. "As if anyone would see you as a threat?"

"Someone sees you as one?" The infuriating man clamps his lips shut, as if I forced his belligerent question out of him. All three men look at each other. The hairs on my arms rise with goosebumps. "You want me to come alone—I'm assuming alone since you haven't invited Lex—to a secluded cabin without knowing the risk behind it."

"There isn't a need for Lex because it's someone we go to escape tech. Cell phones aren't even allowed," Anders explains.

"Excuse me? I can't even take my phone? No thanks."

"You aren't in any danger. In business, we make enemies by doing better than others. This can cause strife and underhanded tactics, which is why Draven thought you were someone you are not. We have to be careful."

I laugh. "You work in finance and banking."

"Which makes a lot of money and sometimes enemies."

Warrin grabs my hand off the table. I turn to face him, almost getting lost in those beautiful blues. I'm not sure why this man affects me as he does. Maybe it's his gentle nature. I'm not used to gentle.

"It's not just our wish. Signal tends to be spotty out there, but if you want to take your phone for safety, I'm sure we can compromise. You having a phone doesn't mean we need to indulge. Most other owners work every second of the day. We want to enjoy some free time in the wilderness. No harm will come to you. It's not a problem, but even if it was, I wouldn't let it. Anders is willing to give you a large bonus for it."

I glance at the main man, noticing his eyebrow raised in question. Draven glares at the hand engulfing mine, so I curl my fingers around Warrin's just to irritate him more. When the fingers respond by tightening against mine, I look at Warrin.

The look in his eyes isn't heated like earlier, but it's definitely warm. I can see the promise in them, and the plea. Deep down, I find myself unable to say no to that look.

Damn it.

"Fine," I sigh.

"Great!" Warrin says. "We're supposed to get snow there, so dress warm."

"Snow?"

"Yeah. The cabin is a two-hour flight north."

"Flight?" These one-word sentences are making me feel like an invalid.

"Yep. We go by chopper. No roads lead that far out."

"Problem with that?" Draven interrupts.

I'll be damned if I let him think of me as a coward. "Not at all."

By his smirk, I feel like he doesn't believe me. It's apparent that they believe the subject is settled, so I'm told to watch my email for details. Conversation moves on to the trio discussing clients and issues. They work well together, and it's easy to see why they chose to combine their businesses. Not all mergers go well, but these three are managing to do it in a way that won't hurt the individual business. I find myself a little impressed.

Glancing at Lex causes worry that him shaking his head back and forth so much will make it fall off. He meets my gaze with his brown eyes and almost grunts. I shrug, knowing I'm in for a lecture later. There is no explanation that he'll accept. My friend will tell me the money isn't worth the risk. How will I tell him it was the plea in Warrin's eyes that made the final decision for me? No way will he understand that one.

It's going to be a fun ride home tonight.

And I was right. He even has me drive, so he can focus on berating me. "What were you thinking?"

I'm not really sure how to answer that because I don't know myself. I press my lips together and take a deep breath through my nose. Lex is worried about me, which I understand, but that doesn't mean I need this right now. There are enough issues fluttering around in my mind, battering off my skull like a bunch of moths against a window. No wonder I can't seem to get rid of this headache.

"Are you going to answer the question?"

I glance at him. "No."

"Why not?"

"Because I don't know what I was thinking, alright?"

Lex sighs and looks out the window. "You can cancel."

"I want to, but..."

"But?"

"I don't want to?"

This time, Lex bows his head and squeezes the bridge of his nose. I count the breaths with him, one through ten. Grumpy Lex is in full swing, and he is not happy about my stupidity. Even I can admit it's stupid. So, why can't I say no? A pair of blue eyes flashes in my mind. Why? At least, that part isn't known right now.

"And don't think I didn't see the way you were looking at Warrin," Lex says.

"Seriously?"

"What?"

"How can you read my mind like you do?"

He scoffs. "Please. He was practically drooling on you, and you were lapping it up."

The image floating through my head at those words makes me gag. "That's disgusting."

"It wasn't literal. Stop trying to deflect."

"I'm not," I say, sulking with clenched teeth.

"Yeah, okay."

Oh, I hate when he does that, and he knows it. Instead of starting an argument over that, I let it slide and turn onto our street. I'm sure he did it simply to rile me. Even though it worked, I won't let him see it. Lex doesn't do smug physically, but I know his mind well enough to know he does it mentally. I won't give him the satisfaction.

Silence is broken only by the roar of the engine. The radio is quiet, mainly because it didn't even work when we bought the car, so there is no respite. I use my ticket to unbar access to the parking garage. The red and white arm lifts, allowing us entry. As I'm rounding the first turn to the second floor, something black runs out in front of me. I slam the brakes, but not early enough to prevent the loud thud. Whatever it is, it runs off toward the rows of cars up ahead.

My breath hitches, and I search for any other furred obstacles to find none. "What the hell was that?"

"It looked like a dog."

"That was a big dog. Should we get out and look for damage to the bumper?"

"You are full of suicidal decisions today, Eddie. One, that thing is probably staring at us and angry at being hit. Two, you drive like my grandma in this garage, so we weren't going fast enough to cause damage."

"You don't have to be an ass about it," I mumble as I put the car into drive.

On the third level, I park in our assigned spot, grateful for the fact it's only a few spots from the elevator. I kill the engine and sit there with my fingers wrapped around the key for a few seconds. Annoyed, Lex reaches over to pull the key out of the ignition, earning a glare from me. Tensions are high. Neither of us is in a patient mood.

"Should we get out?" Lex asks.

"What if it's still out there? If it's angry, it'll attack the first thing that moves. Can you fight it?"

"I'm good, but not that good. A dog that size would rip me to shreds. We can't wait here. The sun will set soon. Our best bet is to get outside before it gets dark."

The elevator dings, opening to release a laughing family. We freeze. What if it attacks them instead? Like the cowards we are, we stay in the car while the kids giggle and pull on their parents' hands. The happiness makes me long for a childhood like that. I feel like I really missed out. Lex grabs my hand to bring me out of my thoughts. We both take a deep breath and nod. We step out of the vehicle.

CHAPTER NINE
DEMONS IN THE SHADOWS

Our shoes slap on the concrete that makes up the floor of the parking garage. We hear a snarl in the near distance and the sound of claws clicking behind us. Lex reaches the elevator first, frantically slamming his fingers on the buttons. The family is already way past us, thanks to my daydreaming, so there is nothing to deter the dog that's determined to get to the people that hit it.

As soon as the doors open, I shove my friend in and follow while he hits the door close button. Something heavier than what seems right for a dog, even of that size, slams into the doors hard enough to bend the steel. I scream as the box we're trapped in lurches downward. It seems like hours before we reach the bottom, and both of us scramble out. We can hear a growl coming around the turn to the second level, so we hurry until we're out in the dwindling daylight.

We walk a little away, then stop to catch our breath. I'm not sure where that animal came from, but I do know it was out for blood. That was one angry canine, and despite all my dangerous work, I've never felt my mortality in that way. It's scary. I'm wondering if I'll be able to go back to our car anytime soon.

"What the hell was that?" Lex pants when he's recovered enough.

"I have no idea, but it had to be rabid. Should we call animal control?"

"Let's wait until we're in the apartment, then you can call. I don't feel safe here."

Concern about the animal getting away nags at me, but his compromise is a sound one. The longer we stand on the sidewalk, the more likely we are to be stuck in the darkness of night, out in the open. That's not something I wish to risk. There's no way the animal would want to leave the cover of the garage for more dangerous prey outside. A nagging feeling tells me I'm wrong, so I hurry to follow Lex back to the apartment building.

Once in the lobby, I breathe a huge sigh of relief. My thighs hurt from the running and speed walking we did, which is a feat since I need to stay in top shape for my nightly activities. I let Lex go for our mail, but unlike him, I wait. Tonight is not the night for a prank that leaves one of us alone.

We return to our apartment, and I search for the number of animal control. It rings five times, but someone finally answers. "I'm calling to report a large feral dog in a parking garage."

I give an account of what happened, as well as the address to the garage. As I hang up, Lex pops his head out of the kitchen, lifting a box of cereal in question. As much as it's not my supper of choice, I nod before plopping down on the couch. My friend brings out my sweet meal, and we eat in silence.

A few hours later, during whatever TV show I let Lex pick, my phone rings. A short conversation leads me to say, "They didn't find the dog."

Lex pops a piece of popcorn into his mouth. "Maybe it slipped out when it got dark?"

"Possible."

My phone pings. When I look at it, I find an email from Warrin. It seems the gentle giant is my personal liaison. It's a time and address to report to Friday night. Since I've done all I can at the office, I plan on working at home to make necessary phone calls, including his list of possible security upgrades for the safe deposit box room. When Lex switches to a horror movie, I decide I'm not ready for that after the dog run-in and head for bed.

Bright sunlight blasts my face with the cool air of morning. Since I'm working from home for three men who can afford for me to dawdle, I decided to take the morning to myself. The leftover cash from our sign-on bonus is in my pocket. I reach the garage, hurrying past it with quick steps. I don't care what animal control says; I'll never feel safe going in there alone. It'll be necessary eventually because I'll still go back to my thieving ways when the day job is done. Doesn't mean I'm in a hurry.

A familiar form at the next corner makes me smile. "Myrl!"

The man in question looks up with dull brown eyes. His ratty gray hair blows back from his face. He's wrapped in three blankets full of holes, so I make a mental note to buy him a new one. Myrl smiles, the gaps in his teeth looking black.

"How are you?" I ask, slipping a hundred from my pocket and putting it into his bucket.

My homeless regular giggles maniacally at the sight of the three-digit bill. "I'll eat well tonight, so I can't complain. Maybe I'll find somewhere safer to sleep. Demons prowl in the darkness."

I purse my lips and offer a noise of agreement. Arguing with the man never goes well. His delusions and hallucinations are too real to him. Trying to convince him what he sees isn't real tends to throw him into a panic. It's best to leave him to his fantasies.

"They're more numerous lately. Best be careful, sweet angel."

Oh, and he thinks I'm an angel. I murmur reassurances that I'll do my best to avoid any demons in the night. This seems to satisfy him, as he hums and picks at the money in his pail. With one more wave, I move on.

My destination isn't far, the woman's shelter. I walk through the doors and up to the front desk. "I want to make a donation."

The receptionist calls back to Patti, who tells her to send me back. She's sitting at her desk when I enter her office, salt and pepper hair pulled into a tight bun. Her gold-rimmed glasses sparkle in the light of the cheap lamp on her desk. Files and boxes litter the entire space; floor, chairs, heating register. I move a few papers and take a seat at her desk.

"Another donation already, Eddie? What did we do to deserve this generosity?" she says with a bright smile that shows worn teeth.

"I recently took on a consulting job. The bonus they gave me is quite generous. I brought it in cash."

She nods and looks for her ledger, filling out a receipt I've told her many times I don't need. Every time I argue, it's the same response. "Formalities."

I hand over what's left of the money dropped on my coffee table not long ago. Her smile broadens when she counts it. "Perfect. Thank you so much, dear. We want to renovate the rooms because they're quite old. This will be so helpful."

"I agree. That's perfect. I'm happy to help."

"Oh," she says, hopping to her feet to dig through some boxes. "Where are they? They have to be somewhere here."

"What does?"

"The shirts. We are giving them to every donor who gives a certain amount. You've surpassed that again and again. I'm going to give you two. What sizes?"

I shake my head. "That's not necessary."

"Nonsense. It's what they're here for, dear. Sizes?"

"Medium and extra-large."

"Excellent. Let's see. Oh! Here they are."

With two pink t-shirts, which I'm sure Lex will love, I leave her office and the building. The receptionist mutters thanks for my generosity around the phone receiver held to her head. I wave and hurry on, stopping at a store to pick up the blanket. Myrl is still in his spot, getting ready to move, so I give him the fluffy blanket. Tears form in his eyes with his thanks.

Returning home, I toss Lex his shirt. He stops typing long enough to look at it and raise his eyebrows. I shrug, grabbing my lists and settling in for work. There are a lot of phone calls to make, so I best start making them.

Stretching, I sit up from my hunched position over the coffee table. I need a desk like Lex has, not that I'm really desk job material. I'm made more for action, particularly at night. The typical nine-to-five is boring to me. Give me action. Give me purpose.

Glancing over, I see Lex rubbing his eyes. "Accomplish anything?"

He nods and takes a sip of his energy drink. "I hacked in again and graded everything on the difficulty it was to break into. Whatever they're paying this security company, they're being ripped off."

"You don't even know what they're paying."

"Doesn't matter. They are definitely on the losing end. I'm going to look into ways to strengthen all the weak spots, which is everything. I can either find appropriate people to handle these areas or try to program my own inbuilt security. I'm done for the night. Cereal?"

I grimace. "Please, no. I have a little cash left. Chinese?"

"Your treat?"

"My treat."

Lex grins. "Two free meals in two days. At least this one won't end with my friend risking her life."

I groan and stand to find the menu in the kitchen. Tossing it at my friend, I settle back on the couch. That menu is ingrained in my brain, so I don't need it. Lex, on the other hand, lives on cereal. With our orders together, I call.

My roommate is typing on his phone. "Jared will be here in an hour."

"Good. The food will be gone by then."

"He doesn't eat that much."

"Remember the bargain packs of hotdogs we had in the freezer for that fundraiser?"

Lex sighs. "That was one time."

"Remember the two dozen cupcakes I bought for the orphanage?"

"Okay. I get the point."

"Remember that three-pound bar of chocolate I bought you for Christmas?"

Lex laughs. "I wonder how he keeps so buff with all this food. He still eats like a teen boy going through puberty."

"He does live at the gym—well, when he's not here."

He scowls at me over the monitor, but I only shrug in response. It's apparent my ribbing of his friend has hit a boundary he doesn't feel like crossing. A knock at the door tells me food has arrived. We keep conversation light. When Jared shows up later, I retreat to my bedroom and look to see what kind of cabin-worthy clothing I may have.

After that, I play on my phone for a while until my yawns take over. I change into a pair of girl boxers and my new tee for the night. I can take a small, but medium covers so much better. Walking over to make sure my curtains are closed, I decide to take a quick glance outside.

The streetlight outside my window flickers a few times. Shadows engulf the other side since that light is out. I feel like I can see something moving. What's worse? I feel like whatever it is meets my gaze. There's no explanation that makes sense. Goosebumps cover me as a chill runs up my spine. I feel eyes on me. Whoever, whatever, it is watches me intently. My heart races. My breathing shallows. I dare not move. I dare not turn away.

Showing your back to a predator would be a bad idea.

Where did that thought come from? If I can't see whatever has my hackles raised, how do I know it's a predator?

Because your instincts tell you so.

Instinct should always be listened to. If life has taught me anything, it's that. Ignoring what your gut is telling you is a recipe for disaster, for pain. When all other resources are removed, instinct is all that's left. Pushing the feelings away dulls them. Survival depends on the razor edge I've always sharpened. There's danger out there. My self-conscience senses something terrible, so I will listen to it.

The note. The strange feeling in the lobby. The dog. Now, this. They're all connected. Something dark is stalking me. I need to make sure it never catches me unaware. My life and the lives of those I care about depend on my watchfulness. Myrl was right. I feel the evil moving in the shadows outside my window.

CHAPTER TEN
BIG EATERS

The whir of the blades slicing through air makes conversation impossible. Below us, the land blurs far below. Not for the first time, I wonder about the idiocy I exhibit by accompanying three men I've only known for a week to their secluded cabin in the snowy mountains. I'm in a flying vehicle far above the ground. I'm traveling to a secluded area, where they've mentioned the helicopter will leave us alone until Sunday. Signal and electronics don't work well. According to Warrin, they have a radio for emergencies. That's the only contact with the outside world.

I'm not sure idiot is an adequate description for me accepting this offer. What have I gotten myself into?

The final days of the week have been incident free, but I've also stayed inside my apartment and away from the windows, much to Lex's confusion. How do you tell someone you've known your entire life that you are sensing Myrl's demons in the shadows? My friend says he trusts my instincts. I doubt it would stay that way if I told him what they are saying right now.

We are in danger. I should warn him, but what proof do I have that I'm not paranoid or insane? He knows I've been off lately. Lex would have all kinds of explanations to why I can't possibly be seeing and feeling what I do. Showing him the letter might freak him out a little. The lack of any other physical evidence makes prank a plausible explanation.

Not all my clues are physical...

This is a mess. I'm already in danger, and here I am, braving the wilderness with three strange, handsome men. For some reason, my instincts aren't screaming at me. Maybe that's why I agreed so easily. My heart tells me it's safe, even if my brain is yelling that I'm a moron.

Warrin's thigh presses into mine, interrupting the turmoil in my head. I look over at the giant sitting next to me. Anders and Draven sit across from us, yelling words at each other that I can't hear. All I know is both look serious; neither look angry. Must be business related. Warrin jumped into the seat next to me the second I chose where to sit.

He leans closer to my side, elbow resting on the armrest between us and a bright smile covering his face. "Ever flown before?"

I can barely hear him, leaving it up to reading lips and matching sounds I think I hear. "Never."

"Nervous?"

"Well, if it was dangerous, I figured you three wouldn't want to be up in the air in this thing. Makes me think it's safe."

Blue eyes twinkle. "Good reasoning."

Looking over, I see the other two watching us. Draven smirks, but Anders's calm expression remains. There's no way they could have heard our conversation, so why are they looking at us instead of continuing their own? I raise an eyebrow in question. Draven shakes as if he's chuckling, and he turns to continue whatever they were talking about.

My gaze returns to the world outside. Snow dots the ground, only broken by blurry trees. As the trip continues, more snow covers the little I can see amongst the blur until even the trees are submerged in white. A little further, the chopper begins to descend. The bump that happens when we touch down makes me grip Warrin's arm. He pats my hand to signal all is well, and I feel slightly embarrassed.

We all climb out. I watch the pilot lift off, taking away my only form of escape, which causes my logical part to scream in panic. My heart remains steady, sure I will be safe. As usual, I choose to listen to my heart. Someday, maybe my brain will give up trying to make me see sense.

"Coming?" Warrin calls from behind me.

Turning, I see him with his bag and my duffle. I nod and hurry after—as much as I can in snow that comes up to my knees. I'm thankful for the broken trail in the fluff that the guys left.

Cabin is not a fitting word for the log mansion in front of me. My feet pause as my jaw drops. It's easily two stories of interlaced logs and dark red shingles. The porch surrounds the front and side, making me wonder what's in the back. Wooden chairs sit on the floorboards outside the walls. Wind chimes jingle. The railings of the porch are carved in swirling shapes. It's beautiful.

"Eddie?"

Warrin's voice reminds me of how cold it is out here, and I rush to climb the perfectly shaped steps. I glance at the lock and knob as I walk through the front door out of habit. I sit on a chair made of branches to remove my boots. Warrin takes my coat, then disappears with my bag. That's when I get another shock.

Looking up shows me that even my ideas based on the outside don't hold a candle to reality. This time, my mouth doesn't simply fall open; my jaw hits the floor. Everything is, of course, made of wood. The back wall holds a double glass door. A fireplace sits on the right wall, Draven working on starting a fire. The dark gray stone of the frame continues into a chimney that climbs through the roof. Wildlife figurines cover the mantle. The huge living space is littered with couches and recliners, a rustic coffee table in the middle. Light glows from lampshades with images of bears and trees on them.

I take a few steps into the massive room to see a stainless steel kitchen with stone counters off to the side. A bar separates the two rooms, stools lining the stone wall. The wall not occupied by appliances and wooden cupboards features shelves full of expensive liquor. Above the kitchen is a loft area, accessed by a rich staircase. Warrin is taking my bag into one of the five doors upstairs.

The entire place is rustic with a touch of modern. It's stunning. I can only imagine the wealth that went into building this hideaway.

"Impressed, Mutt?"

Blinking, I turn my eyes to Draven, who is still crouched in front of the fireplace with his arms resting on his knees, flames flickering behind him. The position emphasizes the litheness that makes up his muscles. He has a grace to him that's almost surprising. Those dark eyes bore holes into me, as if he knows what I'm thinking. I swallow and look away.

"Impressed by the amount of money you three throw around? I think you have a lot more to learn about me," I say.

"I believe I know everything important there is."

"Oh, yeah? Enlighten me," I challenge, bringing my gaze back to him.

"Well, you don't like that some people are more well off than you and feel the need to dictate how they spend wealth that isn't yours. You don't understand that what people do with the money they earn isn't any of your business. But you have this vision of the 'greater good' and take it upon yourself to take what isn't yours to give away to where you think it should go. You'd rather lump together every person that has more money than you, label them as evil to assuage your guilty conscience."

My fists clench. "All that only proves how little you know and how selfish you really are. Having excess doesn't make you better. It doesn't mean you deserve more. It's easy to climb on the backs of others to get what you want. Isn't it?"

He stands, fury sparking in his eyes. "And that proves *you* know nothing about *me*. You don't know my journey. You don't know what I deserve or if I even feel entitled to it. You have no idea what my life has been like, instead painting me as dark and evil because I have more than you. Not everyone fits in the tiny boxes you want to shove them in."

I open my mouth to argue, but Warrin interrupts. "Is everything alright?"

When I look at him, I can see stress creasing the area around his eyes. It's easy to tell Warrin doesn't like conflict. To keep the peace, I press my lips shut. Draven watches me, daring me to turn it all on him. I don't need this drama. I walk over and plop down on a leather couch. "Everything is fine, Warrin."

Anders walks in and looks at the mood of the room. He sighs. "Let's try to keep peace for this weekend at least, please? Since it's late, who is up for some subs? We have all kinds of lunch meat and cheese. Come to the counter."

Ignoring Draven, I stand to follow along because I feel the pit in my stomach that says I'm starving. Once again, Warrin takes the seat next to me. I can tell he wants to be near. It doesn't bother me because he's a sweetheart. The beauty in his features doesn't hurt either. All three men won the genetic lottery, and none of them understand how lucky they are.

I put some cheddar on my bun, then load it with a few different types of meat. Like typical of larger men, they all cram as much meat as possible in their buns. When they go for seconds, I'm only slightly concerned. Thirds make me wonder if they have eating conditions. How can one person eat that much?

Instead of moving when I'm done, I watch with wide eyes until the last sandwich is in Draven's stomach. Anders announces the three of them want to check the borders of the property and make sure there's nothing out of place. I narrow my eyes, wondering what could find them here and again, why I need to work on their security. I guess if we can reach here by helicopter, someone else can too.

Warrin cleans up the mess before they leave, and I watch them exit the house in no more than their dress shirts. Shaking my head, I decide they can't stand the cold for long, so they'll be back. Standing, I stretch my arms above my head. Warrin barges back through the door while I'm still in this position. His eyes travel up and down my prone body, leaving a trail of heat in their wake. I can move, but I choose not to. He licks his lips, and I find myself wondering what else that tongue can do. It's been a long time since I've partaken.

Heat rises between my thighs and up into my core until I feel a desirable ache. His light blue eyes darken to the shade of a stormy sea again. Taking a deep breath, I watch his gaze follow the movement. Even this is pleasurable enough that I need to hold back a moan. What would this man's hands or mouth feel like on the objects of his current obsession?

To clear the thoughts from my mind, I shake my head and let my hands fall. This man is one of my bosses, so we need to remain professional. Even if he wasn't, Warrin is one of the rich elite, the enemy that I've made people like him. Somehow, I can't see Warrin as a vile creature to be despised. Maybe I've been spending too much time with him.

He reaches over and grabs a flashlight. "Um, sorry if I startled you. We wanted to check one of the trails that leads from behind the cabin. I thought it would be a good idea if you had a flashlight and a direction if you would happen to need us. Just come to the end of the trail and shout. We'll return."

Smiling at the innocent intentions, I walk over to grab the light from him. Our fingers meet, and I feel his moving in a way to caress mine. I stop, looking into his icy eyes and taking a deep breath as warmth from his attention courses through me. I'm definitely spending too much time with this man if my inhibitions disappear with a simple touch.

"Thank you, Warrin."

He smiles, releasing the flashlight into my possession without breaking our gaze. "Um, I'm sure the guys are wondering where I've gone."

I nod and let him go without protest. Taking a few deep breaths calms my racing heart. I need to keep myself in control. I am definitely not the type of woman to sleep with her boss. When I get back, I need to find some way to get laid. Anything to keep me from making such a huge mistake because it's obvious to me that Warrin wouldn't object.

CHAPTER ELEVEN
SEEING TOO MUCH

The morning sun brightens my room just enough to wake me from dreams that make me blush. I rummage through my bag for warm clothing and my bathroom supplies, then head out my door and down the hall. The downstairs bathroom only holds a toilet and sink, so I'm hoping for something more in the upstairs one. It's at the end of the hall, and I tiptoe past the rooms of my companions.

The volume of each snore as I pass the doors makes me wonder if I should suggest the men see a sleep specialist. Very few people don't snore, but the loudness I'm hearing in these rumbles is concerning.

When I enter the bathroom, I almost drop everything in my bag. Here, the floor is covered with stone tile. The counter is the same as those in the kitchen. A marble sink with gold-plated plumbing sits in the middle of it. A claw-foot tub takes one corner, larger than I've ever expected one to be. In the other corner, the shower is enormous and lined with a brownish kind of brick. All plumbing looks like what's in the sink.

My feet carry me over the cool tile until I reach the shower that looks big enough to fit three. Maybe not three men of the size I'm "vacationing" with. Normal men, definitely. I feel like I could fit four or five of me in here. I open the glass door, step in, and arrange my shower items on one of the inbuilt shelves. That's when I notice a bench built into the wall and two separate showerheads.

I'm not sure if this place is going to stop surprising me. I'm also not sure why I'm surprised. It's clear these three are loaded, so pooling their money together would afford lots of opulence. My shower is quick, helped along by a very strong stream of water. When I exit, I come across a new dilemma. None of the cabinets or cupboards hold towels.

Mortified, I pop my head out of the door, careful to keep everything hidden. "Is anyone awake?"

Draven pops his head out of the closest room. Anyone but him. Why is he the only one awake? After calling for help, I can't just slink back away and wait for the next one to wake.

"What do you need, Mutt?"

I sigh. "Where are the towels?"

He points to the closet at the end of the hall; close but too far if I don't want to streak. I chew my lip and weigh my options. I could put my pajamas back on and walk over. I hate wearing dirty clothes when I'm clean. Besides, they'll get soaked. I sure as hell am not going to give Draven a walk of shame.

My eyes meet his again. "Can you maybe get one for me?"

Draven's dark eyes twinkle. "Why? Afraid I might see something."

His smugness makes me glare. "Forget it. I'll air dry."

"Stop being so dramatic. I was teasing."

As Draven walks by, I stare at his shirtless torso. Without covering, his muscles flex in front of my very eyes. He's thin, but he shows me thin doesn't mean weak. Not that I thought that to begin with. It's just so apparent right now. My teeth are driving pain through my bottom lip by the time he turns back with a dark green towel. Something in my gaze makes him pause.

Seconds later, his smirk reappears. As he hands me the towel, he says, "Might want to learn to hide your emotions better, Mutt. It's almost like you like something you see."

His eyes follow my arm until they meet the wooden door. With a squeak, I pull my arm in and slam the barrier between us. I really need to get a hold of myself. Lusting over one boss is enough. Now I'm batting two out of three. Wrapping the towel around me, I lean against the door and slowly slide to the floor. Going home means I need to put Operation Lay into effect. I can't be acting like this around these men. My position is too far beneath them.

I'd like that distance closed.

Squeezing my eyes shut, I gasp and force the thought out of my mind. I need to focus. I need to stick to doing my job. And I definitely need to get laid before my urges get the better of me. I just have today and tomorrow to get through, then I'll be good. I can do this. What else can they throw at me besides their handsome looks? At least they're open books. No surprises.

At the sink, I grimace. My dark roots are showing in my long blonde hair, showcasing my shame. I should have bleached them before leaving. That's definitely being pushed to the top of my list when I get home. I can't let my failure show.

By the time I'm groomed, out of the bathroom, and dressed, the smell of bacon and eggs sends my stomach into a rolling grumble. Draven is working in the kitchen as I walk down the stairs, and I find it odd to see him cooking. I didn't peg him as the type.

Anders looks up from where the coffee pot is brewing. "Breakfast will be another fifteen. Coffee in five. Would you like some?"

"Please. Cream, no sugar."

"Will do."

While two bustle around the kitchen, Warrin readies plates and silverware. I consider offering to help, but even in the big kitchen, three of them are a crowd. I slip my boots and coat on before walking out into the crisp air. Wisps of breath curl and rise with each exhale. I walk toward the back to find a large deck with a grill and something else I can't figure out in the corner. A few lumps in the snow showcase unknown objects buried. I'm careful to navigate around the possible pitfalls and find the trail that their footprints lead to.

Bending down, I run my hand over a giant paw print. The base is wide, leading to five indents that look like short fingers. At the end of those, I find impressions of claws. I'm nowhere near an avid outdoorswoman, so I'm curious as to what I'm seeing.

"Bear."

I jump up to find Anders standing behind me with a small thermos. He holds it out, and I take the offering. The liquid is still hot, but I take a few sips and ignore the burn on the top of my tongue.

My eyes find the impression in the snow again. "Should I not be out here alone? Aren't bears dangerous?"

"I wouldn't worry. Bears are solitary creatures and don't attack without provocation. Besides, the bears around here are pretty docile."

"Are you sure?"

"No bear is going to hurt you, Eddie. You have my word."

I nod and take another sip. Anders stands close enough that I can feel his warmth. It's alluring enough that I find myself leaning toward him without thinking. I straighten, but he catches the movement.

"We aren't the men you think we are," he says.

"Then who are you?"

"We weren't born into this life. I'm sure you know Warrin's story because he's quick to trust and tell everyone. Just understand we all have our stories, and they're nowhere near what you think they are."

"Warrin trusts, but you don't?"

"Me and Draven have our excuses. Also, excuse Draven's rough edges. There are not many people he lets in."

"Especially a thief?"

Anders grunts. "There's more to it than that. All I ask is that you don't stereotype without learning who we are. We fought to get where we are and would fight to keep what we've earned, but there's much more behind the money that you can't understand."

I purse my lips and turn, but Anders is already walking back to the cabin. After a few more sips of coffee, I follow. No matter what he says, I really don't wish to encounter a bear. I've heard stories and watched documentaries. It's best not to trust a large predator.

By the time my feet cross the threshold, breakfast is being set on the table. Warrin looks up with a smile. "Just in time."

I return his smile and settle again. The food is still scalding hot, so I blow on each bite. Anders does the same, but Draven inhales it with the steam rolling off it. I flinch, thinking that it has to be much too hot. Anders seems to like his food just right.

Warrin focuses on his coffee, leaving his food untouched. I watch him from the corner of my eye until the food on my plate grows cool. When it does, Warrin touches his before finally eating. Why does he wait for his food to get cold first?

He notices me watching. "I don't like it too hot."

"He prefers it too cold," Draven says.

Anders shakes his head. "We all like our food different. To Warrin, it's just right. There's no reason to judge each other."

I stay out of this argument, finishing my coffee while all three consume an inhuman amount of food in a short time, Warrin of course finishing last.

After breakfast, the giant of a man grabs my arm and pulls me toward the doors to the back deck. He pauses only long enough to let me get my boots and coat. We travel onto the deck, then down the steps. Warrin plops himself into the snow.

"Make a snow angel with me," he says with a belly laugh that makes me think of a child's merriment.

How can I say no to that? So, to be a good sport, I throw myself into the white fluff. My arms and legs move back and forth.

Warrin appears above me. "It's perfect."

The way he looks at me sends fire through my veins and into my cheeks. I doubt I'll need this coat much longer if he keeps this up. His words indicate the snow angel, but his eyes are locked on me. I have to be reading too much into his gaze, but I secretly find myself hoping it's true.

I sit up to get a better look at my angel, and immediately get hit in the face with a snowball. Draven's laughter echoes in the air as I wipe snow from my eyes. The mirth on his face is too much.

"Oh. It's on," I growl.

Standing, I grab a few handfuls of snow to turn into balls. I launch them at him, but Draven is too quick for me. Every throw is dodged. Any retaliation from him hits its mark.

"Draven, this isn't a fair battle," Warrin says from the other side of the yard while I run the other way.

"Who says I have to play fair?"

Watching Warrin pick up a massive armful of snow, I lose the almost nonexistent tactical advantage I might have. A snowball hits me in the side of the head. Draven barely starts laughing when Warrin's snow cannonball knocks him down. Anders laughs from the deck, earning a glare from the slightly smaller man. That only causes Anders to laugh harder. Draven hits him in the face with a snowball.

Anders jumps over the railing, making my heart stop. He lands as if the distance to the ground is nothing. There's now four in the game, three against one. Draven is so stubborn that he fights on for a few hours before surrendering.

By this point, my clothes are soaked, and I'm frozen. Warrin suggests a hot bath. That sounds wonderful. In the giant tub, I let the warm water wash away all the chills. After all these days of fear and uncertainty, this day feels like heaven. I sink up to my nose and let the water wash all my worries away.

Upon returning downstairs, I find Warrin out on the deck without a shirt, checking something on the grill. My eyes widen. "He's going to freeze."

"Believe it or not, Warrin doesn't really get that cold. He thrives on it."

Anders hands me a mug of hot cocoa. I sit and sip until the steaks are done, enjoying Warrin's display. As I guessed, he doesn't have the well-defined bulk of the other two, but he's not squishy either. He's solid. I purse my lips and wonder what he'd feel like under my fingertips.

Warrin also grilled some corn on the cob. It's a bit large for lunch, in my opinion, but it's delicious. While eating, I go over what I found with my examinations last night, and we discuss what to do next.

Draven takes the dishes and rinses them for the dishwasher. Warrin turns to me. "Hot tub?"

"You have a hot tub?"

"On the deck, yes. What do you say?"

"Isn't it a little cold out?"

"That's the point of the hot part of the name, Mutt," Draven says. "Afraid you're not strong enough to handle it."

"I can handle anything you can."

"I doubt that."

Warrin grabs my hand. "Meet you out on the deck."

"I don't have a bathing suit."

"You can wear whatever."

When I return in my sleepwear, I see all three men already in the bubbling water. Looking at the three of them relaxed and bare chested, I feel warmth that no cold can penetrate fill my veins. All three of them are different. All three of them are spectacular.

Draven has his dark hair tied in a bun on top of his head. He's in a corner between the other two, his strong biceps wrapping around the frame containing the pool of water.

Anders sits to his right, tall enough to show off his impressive pecs. The hard muscle shines in the sunlight. His usually styled hair sticks up as if he ran wet fingers through it.

Warrin smiles. His light hair is wet, and the only thing above the water is his eyes. He looks a bit like a child playing submarine in the bathtub.

"Planning on getting in or freezing out in the open?" Draven says.

The spot between Anders and Warrin is open, so I climb in while glaring at Draven. Warrin surfaces to allow me more leg room. I'm comfortable between these two, except for the fact I'm face to face with Draven, who wears the signature smirk.

All three chiseled faces are calm and relaxed. I settle in to allow myself to enjoy the warm jets. I could get used to this, which is why I need to take care that I don't. This isn't my life. I'm here as a consultant and enjoying the perks of my environment. This isn't who I am. It never will be. Excess leads to and comes from greed.

Draven lays his head back, and I find myself hypnotized by his Adam's apple. When he's not talking, he's easy on the eyes. Warrin splashes a little while Anders smiles at him like a father watching his toddler explore the water for the first time. Conversation starts slowly. The men are large, but the talk is small. This is what I need in my life.

The men went out again. I sit by the fire and feel bored, so I pick up my flashlight, dress appropriately, and walk outside into the darkness of night. I hear voices to the right, so I turn that way. As much as I feel keeping my distance is best, I find myself missing their companionship—even Draven.

I follow the sounds and find a path to follow. My hesitation only lasts a moment, brought on by Warrin's instructions last night. Voices stop, but I keep moving. Thoughts of the bear print flash through my mind. I shake them away. If there was danger, the men wouldn't be out here. I'm not even sure why they feel the need to patrol the grounds so often and so late.

I find Warrin and let out a relieved sigh. The light beam startles him. He turns. The flashlight falls to the ground. In front of me stands Warrin, but it's not.

Where his nose and mouth are supposed to be, a muzzle opens to reveal sharp teeth. Before my very eyes, white fur grows all over him until he's standing in front of me covered and on all fours.

It's a freaking polar bear. No, that's not right. They aren't native here. My mind keeps pushing out the fact that this bear was once my gentle giant. My mouth opens and closes. When it takes a step toward me, I turn and flee back to the house in hopes that enough of Warrin remains not to attack this stupidly fleeing prey.

WARRIN

I watch Eddie flee for the safety of the cabin and call for the other two bears that I know are near. Shifting, I wait for them to return to my position. My clothes are hanging from a nearby tree, so I pluck them down and dress while I wait. I have to get to Eddie. I need to explain.

The terror in her eyes is too much for me to stand. I never wanted her to be scared of me. In fact, it's the last thing I could ever want. Why didn't I sniff around to make sure the area is clear? I never thought she'd come out here in the cold darkness. Why would she? Why did she?

Anders ambles over in grizzly form as I pull the shirt over my head. I don't wait for the question I know will come in the form of a chuff. "Eddie saw me changing. She's freaked out. We need to fix this. I don't want her to be scared of me."

Draven returns as I finish telling Anders what happened. He's smart enough to get what I'm saying without hearing all of it. I think he's the smartest out of all of us. Anders is the unspoken leader because of his calmness and fairness, but he listens a lot to what Draven says. He just goes about things in a better way while the black bear shifter reacts in anger and annoyance. Anders is a bear to look up to.

I'm at the edge of the woods before I hear the other two running behind me. Eddie is already inside, so I hurry across the clearing and up the stairs. I slide the door open and burst through. My feet eat the short distance to the stairs, and I'm taking them two at a time.

Anders catches me at the top and grabs my arm. "What happened? We can't rush into this."

"I was just starting to change when she walked up behind me. It was too late to stop the transformation. She looked terrified, screamed, and ran away. I don't know what to do."

"I'm going to go speak to Draven. Don't break down her door. If you want to try to talk her down, that's fine, but don't do anything sudden or rash."

"Okay." I knock on her door. Of course she doesn't answer. "Eddie?"

Nothing. By her panicked scent, I know she's in there. How do I get her to listen to me? How do I explain this without scaring her more?

"Please. I need to talk to you," I say.

"Go away," comes the answer through the door.

Sighing, I sit with my back against the wall. I won't go away. I won't let her be here alone, even if she doesn't want me. I'll try to be a calming presence through the door. Anything she needs to feel better, I'll do, but I won't leave her.

"You should have let me take care of her when I caught her robbing us," Draven says downstairs.

I look between the door and the direction of the voice, worried about scaring Eddie more. The concern vanishes when I remember humans don't hear as well as a bear does, and I let out a breath of relief.

"You are not harming her," Anders says, to which I agree. "We will figure this out."

"No one will ever know. It's not like anyone can find anything in this wilderness."

I feel a growl rumble out of me. When I feel Eddie's panic increase, I fight it down. Until her reaction, I didn't realize how loud my growl was. Even Draven and Anders pause their conversation at the sound. I don't care. Draven needs to understand that I won't let him touch her.

Settling in, I ready myself for a long night. I'm not leaving this spot until the problem is solved, even if it means I sit here all night. I certainly won't let Draven hurt her. Whether anyone knows it or not, I consider her mine. I will protect her from everyone, including my own bonded brothers.

CHAPTER TWELVE
EXPLANATIONS

"Eddie, please let me in to talk."

Desperate, I walk around with my phone in the air, looking for a signal and ignoring Warrin's pleas, like I've been doing for hours now. I need to get out of here. My intuition failed me. There is danger here. I've walked right into the bears' den, pun intended. Like an idiot, I let my guard down. I trusted when I shouldn't have. I'm doomed.

Murmured voices talk beneath my feet. Since the polar bear is at my door, it has to be the other two. The other two? Oh my god. Are they bears as well? What have I gotten myself into?

Calm, Eddie. Breathe. You never panic.

I've also never met a person that can turn into a bear. What am I saying? That's not possible. People are people. They're not animals. I mean, we technically are, but we aren't salmon eating, hibernating wild animals. He's a person.

That's not what you saw last night.

Ugh. It's bad enough arguing with others. Arguing with yourself is a whole new level of crazy, particularly with these specifics. I can't get the sight of sweet Warrin turning into a monster out of my head. What am I going to do?

Lex was right. I should never have agreed to this. Was this their plan the entire time? Hire me as a consultant, lure me out to a secluded cabin with no chance of escape, then what?

Kill me to keep my mouth shut? Feed me to their bears? I hope not. I don't want to be eaten by a bear. Shot, stabbed, strangled, run over by a car, thrown into a lake with cement shoes. All terrible. All preferable to being gored and digested by a freaking bear.

No, none of that makes sense. That's awfully complicated when they only had to give me to Draven when I was caught. Also, there's still Lex to consider. If I don't return, he'll go to the police. Even if it implicates him, he won't let the big guys get away with mauling me to death. So, what was the point?

This isn't fair! Yesterday was so much fun. Snow angels, snowball fights, barbecue, hot tub. Was it all a way to lull me into a sense of complacency? Even Draven wasn't as much of an ass yesterday. None of this makes sense. Why am I here? Why didn't my intuition tell me about the danger?

After my twentieth circle around the room, I realize I'm not getting a signal. Growling, I throw my phone across the room. It bounces off the wall, then ricochets into the other before falling onto the floor in the corner. No, no, no. I rush over and pick it up. The screen is cracked. I press the button, and nothing happens. Everything I try leaves me with the same result. It's dead.

I can just hear Lex in my head right now. "I told you to get a case that is actually functional. You always pick cases because they're pretty." Turning it over, the glittering unicorn is cracked as if mocking me for my poor choices. My only source of rescue is smashed beyond relief due to my impracticality and temper tantrum.

I rub my eyes with a sob. "Damn it!"

Warrin pounds on my door. "Are you okay, Eddie? Do you need help?"

"No, I'm fine! I'm just going insane by seeing things that can't possibly be true!"

"Let me in, please."

"So you can eat me?"

"I'm sure he'd like to, but not in the way you're implying," comes a sarcastic reply from Draven. They must be done discussing downstairs.

Anders speaks next. "Eddie, I'm coming in. I have a master key, so you don't have to come close. I just want to talk."

Oh, no. My eyes fly around the room, looking for any type of weapon as the lock clicks. I unplug the lamp and move back to the corner. I'm not sure how much whacking someone on the head with a lamp will do, particularly with two more strong men outside the door, but I won't go down without a fight.

As the door opens, the rocking chair I put in front of it slides across the floor until it hits the carpet. Anders grunts and pushes harder. Draven and Warrin try to peek in, but Anders closes the door before they can get too much of a glimpse of the frightened human threatening a bear of a man with a tiny bedside lamp. Bear of a man. That thought makes me snort.

The man cornering me in my room looks at the rocking chair, then back at me with an eyebrow raised. I knew it was a stupid blockade. It's not a heavy piece of furniture, but I had to work with what I had.

"The dressers and bed were too heavy to move," I say in my defense, hackles raised at the insult my mind is illogically telling me Anders thinks.

Anders lifts the seat I struggled to put in place, as if it weighs as much as a pillow. He draws closer, and I press further into the corner while raising my lamp in threat. He holds up his free hand, places the rocking chair a few feet away from the foot of my bed, and sits. His hand motions for me to take a seat on the bed. I merely shake my head for an answer.

"How do we fix this, Eddie?"

I chew my lip, unsure of what he wants from me. "Did I really see what I saw?"

What a stupid question that is. Who talks like that? Oh, yeah. Someone who just found out her entire life is a lie. There are bearmen among us.

Anders sighs and leans back. He folds his hands in his lap. "You did. You weren't supposed to see that?"

"Why? So you could feed me to the bears without telling me? Not a surprise I wish to encounter. Was that print outside yesterday morning Warrin's?"

"No, it was Draven's. Warrin has much bigger paws. He's the largest of us."

My eyes burn and beg for me to rub them. I won't offer that moment of weakness to a predator. Sweat is making my grip on the lamp slick, but I dare not let go. "Do you often bring young women up here to feast on? Or am I special because I was able to break into your poorly secured office building? Now that you got what you needed from me, this is your way of doing away with me to keep from being forced to pay me for the life of your business. I won't be easy prey."

Anders shakes his head. "I meant what I said yesterday, Eddie. No bears here are going to hurt you. Even Draven won't eat you. Please sit. You can bring your lamp. I just want to talk."

"I'm fine right here."

"Suit yourself. All three of us are bear shifters. Our weekend retreats are mainly to give our bear sides the freedom they need. A caged bear is a cranky bear."

I can't help myself. "What's Draven's excuse?"

Anders chuckles. "Excuse him. He's not exactly fond of humans."

"But he works with humans."

"He does, but he doesn't let them close to him. Draven is also the reason we come so far out to get away. He gets nervous closer to human population. He has his reasons, and it's not my story to tell. If you sit, I'll tell you what I can of the rest of it."

Indecision brings my lower lip between my teeth. Sitting brings me closer to the bear in human skin, one that can lift a wooden rocking chair with his pinky if needed. My legs are getting tired from standing still for so long. Besides, I don't think my lamp is going to do too much damage in a fight. Sighing, I resign myself to my fate of possible bear chow. Anders says that's not my purpose, but how can I trust someone not entirely human when I don't even trust my own kind?

Inching forward with small steps, I skim the edge of my bed to keep as much distance as possible from the man relaxing in my rocking chair like it's a normal day. The soft mattress feels good, and my knees scream thanks. In a show of faith, I sit my useless weapon behind me. I hope I don't regret this.

"Good," he says with a deep breath. "I want to solve this issue as peacefully as possible."

I like the sounds of that, but I need to make sure. "So, no Eddie buffet?"

"We don't eat humans, Eddie. I've bitten one in defense, but I didn't eat them. You don't taste as good as you think you do."

"Self-defense?"

"It happens sometimes. Can I start from the beginning?" My nod satisfies as an answer, so he continues. "First, I want to explain bear shifters. We aren't many in number, and we're spread across the globe. Bears are solitary creatures, only coming together to mate."

"But the three of you are in business together."

Anders nods. "Out of necessity. Our bear natures crave solitude, but the human side softens that. Family is important to us. There used to be a few more of our kind in the city, but we've been preyed on by an enemy wishing to increase their territory. Many have left or been killed, which is why the three of us are staying under one roof. We are part of a war we don't want. I'm not sure what started it, but something made our enemies angry with us. It's been a long feud, so I'm not even sure if they know why they're fighting. I had a mate once."

The sudden change in subject makes me jerk straight. "What?"

"Our people mate for life. If a mate is lost, we will sometimes take another, but it's hard on a person. Not all survive the loss. At that point, I was a small business owner. I sold business supplies while working toward my CPA. When the enemy started their bid to take over more territory, I was seen as an obstacle. They attacked us. I held my own for a while, but they eventually knocked me out, using numbers to overwhelm me. When I came to, my store was in flames, my mate nowhere to be seen. She was found bound in the bathroom, burnt alive. I was left alive as a warning. None of the humans would listen to me when I swore it wasn't an accident. They didn't even pay attention to her being bound."

My hand flies to my mouth. "I'm so sorry."

Anders looks away, his mask of calm slipping. Despair and rage are visible. The shimmer of tears glimmers in the corners of his brown eyes. My heart breaks.

"I was supposed to move on. They sent me a letter later that stated that. I was a lesson to the others of my people, one most of them took. My life was in shambles, and I almost gave up. I couldn't do it. They killed my mate in a hostile takeover. Instead, I finished my certifications and degrees, climbed to the top, and opened my own business. This one wasn't easy for them to take down with fire. I made sure of it."

Hostile takeover. I'd say he's right with that term. Although, I've never known it to be that hostile. I've suspected big companies play dirty with the competition, but I never imagined this. Brings new meaning to the label.

"Once I established myself," he continues, "I found a small polar bear shifter who lost his father. His mother was struggling."

"Warrin."

"Yes, Warrin. He is such a gentle soul, and I feared for what the world would do to him. Instead of leaving him at the mercy of the cruelness we live in, I took him under my paw and taught him what I knew. I even gave him the capital to start big. Most of the profits he keeps are used to make sure his mother is safe. She's human."

That startles me. "You don't have to mate with other bears?"

Anders shakes his head. "Not at all. Most tend to stick to our kind, but sometimes one of us strays. The only difference is that the children have an equal chance of coming out as human or shifter. There is only one way to negate that effect of mating outside our kind."

"What's that?"

"It's something most humans don't approve of. Even those of us that mate with a human simply accept the risks of human children. Not that they don't love those children. It's just that they tend to feel left out by not being able to shift. It's like a secret society full of wonderful perks they can't take part in. It causes resentment and divide."

I lick my lips, wondering if I really want to know. Curiosity gets the better of me. "What's it take to ensure shifter children?"

"One human female has to accept two or more shifters."

A lump forms in my throat to make the next words difficult. "I thought bears were solitary creatures."

"We are, which is why many of us can't handle that. Some bears form a bond that feels like family when forced together, but I'm off track. You have all the time in the world to ask questions about our nature. Let me finish the story. There isn't much left.

“Our enemies became angry at my defiance and success. They hated that I was helping others. Draven already had his own successful firm, and we got together to discuss our options. Pressure was mounting. Merging saved us and made sure we remain thorns in our enemies' paws."

Threat forgotten, I sit back with my hands against the mattress to take it all in. "So, it wasn't greed that brought you together."

"It was survival. There were some kinks in the process, but we work well as one unit, more like brothers than business partners."

The bond needed for successful human mating. I shake my head. This isn't what I need to be thinking about. "While I accept your reasoning and assurances of safety, I'd rather go home. This is a lot to handle."

"We're still under contract. Listen, I didn't take you on because you look like a tasty morsel. We really need you to stay ahead of the competition, who also happens to be the enemy."

"I won't renege on the contract, but this isn't part of the deal. I agreed to come here outside of the contract. Home is where I want to be to process everything."

Anders shakes his head. "We can't because the only thing we are to use the radio for is an emergency. Despite your fear of us, there is no danger of harm. Our pilot has eaglets to care for. He can't just up and leave without a good reason on short notice."

Of course, leaving is too good to be true. Well, if I'm in no danger, I'll have to accept that answer. I trust his words, but I'm still nervous about learning everything. Nothing to do but make the best of everything. My mind balks at the thought. This is going to be hard.

Something else he said hits me. "Eaglets?"

"Our pilot is an eagle shifter."

Of course he is. This just keeps getting better and better. Anders stands and walks to the door while I process, asking me to come out when I'm ready. A memory flashes before my eyes. It can't be. Can it?

"Anders, are dog shifters a possibility?"

The man freezes with his hand on the doorknob. "Why?"

The intensity in his gaze scares me a little. He realizes I'm nervous again and forces a calmness back over his features, but I can still see the tenseness in his muscles. I explain the incident at the parking garage, then throw in the note and strange feelings as well. If he wants to think I'm crazy for relying so heavily on these instincts, he's free to do so. I won't accept judgment from a man that can turn into a bear.

At the end of my explanation, he turns the doorknob. "I'm going to make breakfast and talk to the men. What you told me is unsettling, so I need to talk to the others about what this means. Get yourself a shower, then join us. We'll discuss it when you're downstairs."

Before I can argue, he slips out of the door. What has him so out of sorts? I guess there's only one way to find out.

CHAPTER THIRTEEN
HEAVY COMMITMENT

The mirror makes me grimace again, and I tie my hair up into a messy bun. Bags droop beneath my eyes. Sleep isn't possible when you see something you shouldn't. My skin is pale. If anything, my roots aren't something I need to focus on right now; neither is everything else I just pointed out.

Worrying about my looks is simply a way to stall what I need to do. Yes, I've given Anders my trust. Nothing in anything that has happened proves all my crazy theories. In fact, everything that has happened after Draven knocked me on the head says that they don't mean to harm me. But how do I get over everything I just learned? Also, if they mate for life, what does that say about Warrin's obvious pursuit of my attention? Would he want to share me?

That thought sends a thrilling shiver over me, and I can't explain why? Sure, I've never conformed to traditional relationship dynamics and expectations. I've also never had a serious relationship. Trusting someone with the nature of my mission isn't something I've ever felt comfortable doing. I've had flings and one-night stands, but I've never committed myself to someone. I doubt a bear is my best bet for that, even if he's in awe of my night job.

First of all, I'm not an animal. I'm not one of his kind. Second, he's part of the target demographic for my alter ego. It wouldn't be right.

With those thoughts strengthened in my head, I roll my neck and stretch my shoulders. Let's do this. Pancakes lend the air a sweetness that I can feel deep down. I guess they decided I need something less meaty on a morning like this. At the bottom of the stairs, I take a few deep breaths to fortify myself. I can do this. I take the required steps forward.

Cautious, I crane my neck to look into the kitchen. Figures one of the toppings is honey. Some clichés are true it seems. Maple syrup and a huge tub of butter sit next to the amber jar. Here goes nothing.

Straightening my shoulders and holding my head high, I walk into the living room and observe the three men moving like a well-oiled machine. They do work well together. My mind goes back to what Anders said. What would it feel like to have three men focused on me at once? Warrin would be game. I think Anders would come around eventually. Draven, I'm not so sure. While he can be an insufferable ass sometimes—most of the time—he showed a less severe edge to his personality yesterday.

Now, Draven leans on the counter, tosses a blueberry into the air, and catches it on his tongue before consuming it. What else can he do with that tongue? What the hell is wrong with me? This man is rude and selfish. Besides that, I just learned that he's part bear. I blame Anders because his words bring pure fantasy.

Motion pulls my attention to the stove as Warrin flips a pancake in the air. It spins over and over until it lands in the pan. People can actually do that with pancakes?

Anders pours four mugs of coffee. He looks up and smiles before motioning me over. Warrin turns, sees me standing there uncertainly, then rushes over to engulf me in a bear hug. "I was so worried you wouldn't come down."

Eyes wide, I find myself wondering if bear hugs can be lethal. My lungs are screaming for air. I push on his shoulders, and he finally realizes that this may not be the best time to squeeze me to death. He places me back on my feet and murmurs apologies. Draven watches with his eyes emotionless. We're back to contempt and distrust from him. Who is he to act this way toward me? He's not the one who just found out supernatural creatures actually exist.

I meet his gaze, scowl for scowl, before turning back to Warrin. "I guess I kind of lost it there."

"I'm so sorry. You were never supposed to see me like that. It must have been terrifying. If I would have known you were there, I wouldn't have gone through the change."

Patting his arm, I take a deep breath, floored by the fact I have to say something like this. "It's okay, Warrin. I'd like some time to process, then I want to talk to you alone at some point."

The play of emotions on Warrin's face is interesting. Hope and fear. Anticipation and trepidation. Excitement and nervousness. All those emotions transitioning on his face are giving me whiplash. I can't watch anymore, so I walk past him to find the counter.

I take a seat, my gentle giant pulling out the stool next to mine. He pauses, and I can see the uncertainty as he looks between me and the place that he wants to hold his rear end. After my initial panic, I realize that Warrin would never hurt me. Sighing, I pat the stool and nod. He settles in with a smile warm enough to melt the snow outside.

Anders looks at me. "Buttermilk or blueberry?"

"I like chocolate chips, but Anders forgot to put them on the food order," Warrin says.

That's such a normal Warrin thing to say that I feel a little of the remaining tension melt from my muscles. "Can I have one of each?"

"Of course!" Anders says, prepping my plate and handing it to me.

I smother both in butter and syrup. We eat in silence, with me ignoring the mountains of sweet breakfast food that they devour without thought. I guess it makes sense now. Bears need to eat more. Don't they?

The desire to ask nags at me, but there are more important things to worry about right now. "Listen, I appreciate the normalcy of what's happening here, but I really need to know what freaked Anders out about the giant dog."

"Wolf," Draven says around his mouthful.

"Excuse me."

"It wasn't a dog. It was a wolf."

"In the city?"

His dark eyes heat. "Bears aren't typically in the city either, but here we are."

I snap my mouth shut and bring my attention back to my pancakes. "Well, what is a wolf doing stalking and threatening me?"

"It's probably more than one."

"Draven," Anders says, "don't make this worse than it needs to be."

"She brought herself into this situation."

"Apparently, not with all the facts," I say with a roll of my eyes.

I spear a triangle of pancake and shove it into my mouth, washing it down with a sip of coffee. As I set the mug next to my glass of orange juice, Anders decides it's better if he answers. "I do apologize for that, Eddie. We didn't think they'd target you because you're simply an employee. Either our enemy feels making no one want to work with us will be our downfall, or they've targeted you because they know you can help us."

"Your ancient enemy is a wolf?"

"Wolves."

"Werewolves?"

"Wolf shifters, yes."

Great. Not only am I working for a trio of sexy bears, but I'm also stalked by things straight out of a horror book. "Can this get any better?" I mumble.

"We're sorry," Warrin says. "We didn't want to put you in danger. We really didn't expect this complication. We will make sure you're safe."

"And Lex?"

Anders grabs my attention with a sweep of his hand. "We will keep both you and your friend safe, but you can't tell Lex what you saw last night and anything else I've told you. Our kind are only safe by hiding in the shadows."

As much as I expected this, it still makes me cringe. I hate keeping secrets from the friend that's basically my brother. He knows me better than I know myself. This is a monumental ask on their part, but I understand. "Your secret is safe with me."

"Good," Anders says with a sigh. Warrin looks as if he expected my answer. Draven appears distrustful.

"You guys owe me a new phone," I say, pushing my empty plate forward and sliding both drinks closer.

"With what we're paying you, you want more? Use the bonus you get from this trip," Draven says.

"I broke my phone while on employment business and due to the shock that comes with learning your bosses are actually bears. You owe me that much for the scare alone."

"I'll buy it!" Warrin says as he takes my plate to the dishwasher. "It's the least I can do for almost giving you a heart attack."

"Thank you, Warrin."

Draven rolls his eyes, but everyone ignores him. Anders tells me that the pilot will be here around one, so I should pack now. He starts the dishwasher. With a nod, I turn and make my way to the bathroom to collect my grooming utensils and shower bottles, then move to my room to fold my dirty clothes and pack them.

When I exit my room with my bag, Warrin steps from his door and rushes over. "Let me take that."

"I can carry my bags."

"I know, but it's the least I can do."

Figuring I won't win this argument, I follow him down the stairs to be met with silence. "The other two packing?"

"No. They already packed before Anders spoke to you. They went for one last run. I don't really want to though, not after last night."

Guilt slithers into my head. Warrin is afraid to be who he is because of my reaction to seeing him as half a bear. Granted, I think any sane human would react the same, but I feel bad for making him stay in on his last day at the cabin.

I touch his arm with my fingers. "You don't have to be ashamed of what you are. I'm sorry for the way I reacted. You caught me really off guard. You can be a bear all you want."

"I scared you."

"Only because I decided to come looking for you instead of staying put like I should have. Besides, once you were done changing, you were a very handsome polar bear."

He smiles. "Really?"

"Yep. If I wouldn't have panicked as I did, I would have been mesmerized."

He doesn't need to know I'd still scream and run. A handsome polar bear doesn't make him any less dangerous, particularly in an area they aren't supposed to be. There is no polar bear population here.

My gentle giant embraces my head with two very large hands. "Thank you. It means a lot to hear you say that."

His ice-blue eyes hold mine, and I feel the temperature of the room rise a few degrees in less than a second. His thumb brushes my cheek before fingers tuck a piece of hair behind my ears. I lick my lips, which he takes as a signal.

Before I know what's happening, his lips are on mine. I don't waste time on shock, taking his gentle caresses and turning them into something hungrier. His tongue begs for entrance, so I part my lips. A greedy tongue reaches for mine, looking for guidance. Strong arms wrap around my back to lift me and carry me to the wall. My hands make his unruly hair even messier.

Careful hands brush the skin under the hem of my shirt. I arch my back, pressing into his chest and abdomen while one of his hands cups the back of my head. Anders's words come to mind, forcing me to push away.

"I'm sorry," Warrin says, panting to catch his breath. "I've been wanting to do that since the first moment I laid eyes on your beautiful face. The desire has only grown as I've gotten to know you. You're hard to resist, but I should have tried harder."

"It's not the kiss, Warrin. That was wonderful. Anders told me your people mate for life."

"Mhmm," he hums. His forehead rests on mine.

"I'm not ready for a commitment like that. I don't know if I ever could be."

My gentle giant chuckles, moving his head until I feel his breath on my ears. "We can do plenty without me claiming you as mine forever. All you have to do is say the word."

Warm shivers run over me, and I gasp at the thought of what he could possibly mean. I didn't expect this out of innocent Warrin, but I guess everyone has their wild side. "What are you proposing we do?"

He pulls back, shyness taking over his eyes. "I'm not entirely sure. I just know how to make a mate, but I know there are other things we can do too. We can experiment."

Okay, so not so surprising. He's inexperienced, but the thought of experimenting with him sends a tingling through me. I'm about to respond when a familiar annoying voice cuts in.

"Are we interrupting anything?" Draven says.

I look over to see the other two men standing shirtless in the doorway. Squeaking, I push Warrin away. He moves slowly, as if not caring what the two have walked in on. Maybe he wouldn't mind the sharing part. I push the thought away. Now is definitely not the time to consider that.

Anders decides to drive me home. They're not willing to leave me alone with their enemy possibly stalking me. "We didn't mean to interrupt anything back at the cabin."

I find myself wishing for the passenger seat to open up and swallow me. "I'm sorry about that. I didn't mean..." I'm not sure how to finish that.

"Don't worry, Eddie. Warrin is a grown man. He can do as he likes. Just remember my words." I nod, and he adds, "All of them."

My mouth goes dry. All of them? All three of them? Can I handle that much sexy? He can't mean that because he's barely spent any time with me. I glance over to see him watching the road with his usual calm. Was I expecting a smirk? That's Draven's specialty.

By the time we reach my building, my mind is swirling in so many different directions. I thank Anders and walk through the doors to the lobby. He waits until I enter the elevator to drive away.

Jared and Lex are on the couch, but I don't say more than hi. I feel out of sorts and desperately need some me time. "How did it go?" Lex asks.

"Fine. Great. I'm tired."

"Okay," my friend says, drawing out the word. "Um, I tried to call your phone when you said you'd be back in town."

"Yeah. Sorry about that. You were right. I have very terrible tastes in phone cases. I need to unpack and lie down. Goodnight."

I rush for my room and hear Jared whispering, "Is she alright?"

My door closes on Lex's confused answer. All my dirty clothes are dumped into my hamper, along with the unworn clean clothes. I'll just wash them all. The ache is still nagging at me, so I practically run to my nightstand, digging all the way to the back. My hand wraps around the smooth surface of my prize. When I pull it out, I make sure the batteries are still good.

Great. A woman's best friend.

CHAPTER FOURTEEN
HONEY

Breakfast features tons of questions to dodge. Lex seems suspicious. I can't tell him why I needed to rush to my room last night because he wouldn't understand. Never once have I ever seen him with a girl. Dating or intimacy never seem to interest my roommate.

"Did something bad happen? Did they hurt you?" Lex asks while sniffing to see if his shirt is clean enough to wear.

We're going into the office to handle the weekly check-in. They have no objections to us working from home, as long as we check in once a week and make sure we are doing as promised in our contract.

"They didn't hurt me," I say without mentioning my early Sunday morning terror fest where I locked myself in my room and didn't sleep the night before.

"You seem quiet and edgy."

I reach down and grab my shoes, sitting down to slip them on and tie them. Not once have I ever dressed up for anyone. I don't even own dress clothes. At times, I feel out of place, but I remind myself I'm a consultant hired as a contractor. Professionalism isn't needed or part of the deal. It's not like we need to do this, but I still feel odd at times.

"Lex, I'm seriously fine. They didn't hurt me. They didn't come onto me." That last part may be a bit of a lie if I remember the kiss properly. "And they certainly didn't threaten me. I went there to do a job, and I did it. The free time was spent in front of the fire, out in the snow, or in the hot tub."

"Hot tub?!"

"Yes. Hot tub. How many rich people do we know that don't have a hot tub?"

Lex raises an eyebrow. "Since we don't know any rich people besides these three, none?"

"Exactly. None. Every rich person we know has a hot tub."

"I swear if I find out they laid a hand on you in any way, I'll make them pay."

Well, there was the snowball fight, the closeness, and the kiss. I wonder how Lex would feel about all that. All those qualify as a hand on me. Trying not to smirk is hard, so I do my best to push the memories away. At least he's not asking me if they're some supernatural beings that can turn into bears or anything. No lying going on. No revealing secrets. Just a little deflection and omission.

"You'll what, Lex?"

"I know how to fight."

I laugh. "You do, but they're heavily protected."

"No one is completely safe. There's always a vulnerable point somewhere. You're best at that with your hands on thieving, but I could figure something else."

"Well, you don't need to worry about getting dirty. They neither hurt me nor threatened to. Even Draven was somewhat not an ass all weekend."

"Somewhat?"

I shrug. "What more can we expect from Draven?"

Certainly not being part of a love session with a human. I feel my cheeks heat and turn away before Lex can notice, using putting on my coat as a way to divert attention from my likely red cheeks. Anything to keep my best friend from noticing how thinking of that trip makes me blush.

A knock echoes through the thin wood of our door. "He's here. Time to go."

Lex freezes. "Who's here?"

Did I forget to tell him? I must have. "Warrin sent me an email this morning saying he would be picking us up. I told them about the dog, and they don't want us mauled."

Half-truths are my friend right now. They keep the discomfort of an uncomfortable subject with the person I trust most in this world. I hate lying to Lex, but I certainly can't tell him about the bears. For one, he'll probably have me committed. I wouldn't blame him either. I still think I'm crazy when I replay everything in my head. Then we have the promise I made. As much as I want to confide in the friend who has been with me since the beginning, it's not my secret to tell.

Yes, I'm an honorable thief.

"Well, it would have been nice to know ahead of time. And I thought animal control said they didn't find a dog."

"I know," I say, grabbing my wallet and keys. "I forgot. It was in my email when I checked this morning. My phone is toast."

"How did you break it?"

More lies. "I dropped it."

"I told you to get a proper case."

"Yes, Lex. I know."

To forestall further arguments and lies, I open the door to find my gentle giant about to knock again. Smiling, I brush past him, wishing I could linger against him for a little longer. We have an audience that won't approve. Nothing will be said to Warrin. When I'm alone with him, all bets are off. We need to keep distance between us for now. Sometime between our kiss and now, I must have decided to take him up on his offer to experiment. No guilt here.

The elevator is cramped with the mountain of the man in between us. Now, I can enjoy the closeness without giving anything away, which I do. His warmth is nice, even through my puffy coat. I'm glad Lex is staring straight ahead into the door that no longer shines from all the rust and fingerprints. Warrin leans a little into me, and I don't do anything to pull away.

Our boss startles as the elevator jerks but doesn't react further after seeing us not panic. When he leans closer, Lex looks over. Warrin digs in his pocket, carrying himself nearer to me by necessity. He pulls out a cell phone. "I hope this one is okay."

My eyes go wide. "You didn't have to get me the most expensive model."

"Least I could do. It was my fault the other broke."

Lex looks over at me, bending to clear his vision away from the large man between us. My mind works fast. "I dropped it because Warrin slipped on ice. He hit my hand, and it went flying."

I'm thankful to see my friend accept my excuse. Warrin makes sure to play along. "Yeah. I'm really sorry about that. I'm clumsy on ice."

The thought of a polar bear sliding around on ice makes me smirk. I look up to see him grinning as well and wonder if he has the same thought. With his second nature, ice shouldn't be a danger. Again, I'm happy Lex is oblivious to our secret thoughts.

I sit in the back seat with my roommate, much to Warrin's displeasure. Glancing at the phone, I realize it already has my number and contacts programmed in. I don't even want to know how he did this. If they can program a phone without me present, I can only imagine the resources they have at their disposal. No wonder the wolves find them such a big threat. I can't believe I just thought that. I'll never get used to this new world I find myself in.

Flipping through all the features, I stop on favorites. *Mr. Gentle Giant* is at the top of my favorites, even above Lex. I lift my eyes to see Warrin watching from the rearview mirror. He must know what I'm looking at because he sends me a wink.

My cheeks heat again, and I decide that's enough exploration for now.

"Why is your face red? Are you too warm?" Lex asks.

"It is a little warm in here with this coat on."

"We can crack some windows," Warrin says. The moment has passed, and it feels like he is really trying to solve the issue. He has no idea how hot I really am right now.

"No, I'm good. No use freezing anyone else out."

"I don't get cold very easily."

The bastard. I have so many smart ass answers to that, and I can't utter any of them with the one I'm not supposed to reveal secrets to right beside me. "Lex does."

"I'll just turn the heat down a little."

Can I feel any more on the spot than I do now? I really don't think so. Clueless, Lex seems happy with the solution. Warrin is making it hard for me to keep my emotions and secrets behind a thin veil of innocence that is extremely hard to hold on to right now, for so many reasons. This is going to be so freaking hard.

Silence feels heavy, and I do my best to breathe normally. I'm saved when we pull through the gate of the private parking garage. As soon as we are parked, I open the door and hop out. I need some cold air on my face. Anything to take the flames from my ears. Under the building, a breeze isn't really possible, but it's considerably cooler. I'm able to calm my racing heart and steady my mind. Ready for the day.

Lex is in the security room again while I roam the hall, showing Warrin how my unprofessional proposal can be best utilized. After days of making phone calls, asking questions, and getting quotes, I have plans that I think will best secure the building. I'll even try to break in to test it when everything me and Lex have looked into is implemented. I'm itching to do a little thieving, even if it's simulated.

We reach the same supply closet as before, and I turn the knob. It's locked, which makes me happy. I turn it hard again, and we hear a loud thunk on the other side. The door pushes open with a mere touch. On the floor, the other side of the doorknob rolls around.

I walk in and pick it up. "This makes the lock a little useless now."

Warrin steps in, takes the useless chunk of metal, grabs a screwdriver from one of the shelves, and gets to work. I stand back, looking at the boxes lining the shelves. My gaze travels back to the muscles that flex with each twist of the screwdriver. I lick my lips.

"Done," he says, making me jump.

The polar bear twists the knob. It doesn't budge. He fiddles with the lock and tries again. The knob won't turn. Warrin grunts in annoyance.

"Can't you just take it off?" I ask.

He nods and tries just that. "I think the screw is stripped. We're stuck."

"Do you have your phone?" When Warrin shakes his head, I pull mine from my back pocket. "I open my contacts."

"I'm the Mr. Gentle Giant, right?"

I laugh. "You're very tall, almost intimidating, but you're really, really sweet. Soft."

Warrin pats his stomach. "I know I don't have all the creases Anders and Draven have, but I wouldn't call me soft."

"Not in that way. I meant in your personality. Your body is perfect."

Realizing what I said, I freeze and try to look up at Warrin through my lashes to gauge his reaction. A strong hand grips my chin to gently pull my gaze to his. My lips part, and my breathing becomes shallow. Warrin takes my phone out of my hand to place on one of the shelves, then his lips are on mine.

No protest comes. Instead, I wrap my arms around his neck. He pushes me back against the wall that isn't taken by a bunch of shelves. Our tongues dance a dangerous dance. Warrin presses against me, careful not to crush my smaller frame. Both hands move from the sides of my head and down. One of his fingers brushes over a nipple, sending heat coursing through me.

My sexy polar bear pulls away. "I'm sorry. I didn't mean to do that. Should I have asked?"

I groan, wishing he would stay caught up in the moment. For an answer, I pull my shirt above my head and remove my bra. The sight of Warrin's pupils dilating and his irises darkening from ice to a stormy sky sends tingles all over. I grab his large hands before placing them directly on my breasts. He grunts while licking his lips.

My lips are on his again. Strong hands knead into the sensitive flesh of my breasts. Fingers pinch and twitch nipples. His mouth migrates to my throat. My hands run up and down his back while I arch further into his touch to guide his efforts. When my fingers tangle in his hair, his tongue stops tracing circles on my neck.

"Do that elsewhere," I say through my pants.

"What?"

I use my grip in his hair to guide him down my chest. Arching my back more, I wait for him to get the hint. It takes only a moment. His warm mouth around my nipple makes me moan, trying to keep it quiet to avoid drawing attention. The sound makes Warrin bolder, and his tongue runs up and down over my nipple. The tingling sensation I had originally becomes a burn that spreads down to the spot between my thighs.

Warrin pulls away. "No mating? Where should we start?"

"No mating," I agree.

My hand moves to his pants, working the button and zipper without need for eyes. Slipping my fingers into his boxers, they wrap around a very large shaft. Just the feel of it turns my burn into an ache of need, but we can't do that yet. I'm guiding my innocent polar bear. I'm sure he'll be willing to reciprocate.

"Your hands feel good," he moans.

"It's not my hands you need to worry about."

"What else can we—"

Words die as I drop to my knees and take his cock in my mouth. By the noises rumbling out of him, words are no longer possible. My tongue circles his tip and travels down. Warrin grabs my hair but avoids pulling. I move my head back and forth while he hisses his pleasure. It isn't long before he unleashes.

As soon as I stand, he devours me again. Who would've thought I was terrified of being devoured by this man just a little over twenty-four hours again? Where my fingers were nimble, Warrin's has issues with my pants, so I help him free my lower half. Before I can ask what he's planning, I find myself lifted until my thighs are alongside his ears. My hands shoot out to steady myself on the shelves to either side.

His tongue finds my clit, and he remembers my lesson with the nipples. Deft movement creates a moan that I can't stop. My fingers grip the shelves so hard that my knuckles turn white. Supplies rattle as I gasp and whimper. The ache turns to agony for the need to release, but I don't release it. I let myself climb higher and higher.

My body tenses and shudders, begging for me to let it jump off that edge. My back arches, successfully holding my body enough that I can stuff one hand in my mouth. I bite hard to hide the guttural sound that issues as I give into what my body wants. I clench and shake until spent, and Warrin slowly sets my unsteady legs under me.

Unable to hold myself up, I lean against his chest, coming down from the high. I needed that. It's been a while. Despite his lack of confidence, Warrin sent a wave of pleasure through me that I almost didn't survive.

"You taste like honey," he says.

"You can't be serious. There's no way I taste sweet."

"You do to me."

"Do polar bears eat honey?"

"This one does."

I chuckle, pushing away when I feel more stable. Together, we get dressed. "Should I call for help now?"

"Yes, please. That workout made me hungry."

I call Anders for help, and we wait for him to release us. Within minutes, the knob is jiggling. After a couple of attempts, I hear something hit it a few times. The knob falls off, and Anders yanks the door open. He takes a few deep breaths and pauses. Brown eyes turn almost black as he looks at me.

"Well, Warrin," he says, "it seems like you already had dessert. Did you save any room for lunch?"

My mouth goes dry. There's no way he could smell that on us. There has to be another way he knows. That's when I remember what Draven said when he found my car. He does smell it because his inner bear makes it easy.

CHAPTER FIFTEEN
CHEAP FOOD

As we walk to their car, I ask, "No Lex?"

"He wanted to stay and work on some kind of programming issues," Anders says. "I know very little about computers, so nothing he said made sense. I can work my programs and email, but don't expect me to dig deeper."

Draven scoffs. "Not that we need another mooch."

As he says it, he eyes me from the corner of his eye. I roll my eyes, fed up with his insults to me and my best friend. "One, I never asked you guys to take me out to lunch. In fact, the amount you three spend on food makes me uncomfortable. Two, Lex hardly eats anything more than cereal. Your lunch last week fed him for three days. While I will admit to him taking advantage, I cast no blame on him. In his eyes, you three are money-hungry rich guys who don't care about the little people. Three, I didn't ask for this weekend. I was asked, almost begged, to attend to help you out. Any cost incurred is your own fault."

The annoying man opens his mouth to retort, but Warrin jumps in. "Why does Lex eat so much cereal?"

"Truthfully? He has a lot of mental health issues, which are not for the ears of those he doesn't trust. He deals with anxiety and depression on a regular basis and hates leaving the house. Neither of us had the best time growing up, but his childhood was worse than mine. He prefers to avoid people whenever possible."

"That's sad." Warrin's tone implies he really feels it is, which I'd never doubt. The polar bear has no issues whatsoever dealing with his emotions, unlike the man glaring at me with dark eyes.

I long to see Draven's softer side again, the one that is willing to laugh and play in the snow, even if I'm his main target for snowball practice. The grin and teasing side he showed me when I needed the towel. With our return, it's gone. Even before, when I spied Warrin changing into his other form. What's Draven's story?

Mirroring my thoughts, Anders says, "What's your story then?"

"Listen, I appreciate your explanation yesterday morning, but I'm not sure I'm ready to share that information. Not until I trust and am trusted completely by all," I answer, sending a knowing look at Draven.

He pretends to ignore me, but I see his jaw tick. On the other hand, the two calmer men utter understanding. Once we reach the car, Warrin opens the back door. I slide in while Draven takes the passenger seat. My gentle giant slides in next to me, taking my hand in his. Draven glances back, which makes me blush.

He rolls his eyes and turns back to the front. "Relax, Mutt. The only way you could smell more like my colleague is if you actually mated with him. With the way he's been drooling over you, I'm surprised it took this long."

Anders slides in, shooting Draven a warning glance. I press my lips together to hold in the angry growl that wants release. "Are you saying I jump any man that throws himself at me?"

Dark eyes look back. "I can only know what I've learned so far. I know it's too soon for love."

I let the growl out. "What's it to you? I'm allowed to find joy in any way I accept."

"Let's put it this way, Mutt. You hurt Warrin, I'll make sure you regret it. He's not a fling type of guy."

The man beside me squeezes my hand. "I can protect myself. Even if it's just for fun, I want to have this time with Eddie."

"We all know how you throw your heart into everything, Warrin. I'm only looking out for you because I doubt this woman has any care besides her own libido."

"That's enough, Draven," Anders says.

I scoff. "Let him throw a temper tantrum. I think he's just jealous that Warrin can get what he can't."

Watching his hands curl into fists, I stare at the man sitting in the passenger seat, challenging him to keep this ridiculous argument going. Warrin decides to break the tension once again. "Since Eddie feels uncomfortable where we eat, maybe we should try where she wants to."

Draven relaxes, and Anders sighs in relief. Fine. Not that I expect them to not spend a lot, but I'll be more comfortable in my own setting. Pizza.

The men sit with two large pizzas each, which is less than I'm used to seeing after the cabin. There are breadsticks, salad, and wings galore. Warrin insisted that I get my own pizza with the reasoning that I can take it home, so Lex can eat something other than cereal tonight. I can't deny that reasoning, but I feel gluttonous sitting here with an entire large sitting in front of me, not to mention the wealth of other food I'm encouraged to try.

To my surprise, none of the men care about the downgrade in food. It reminds me that Anders said they weren't born with a lot of money. Nibbling at a piece of pepperoni pizza, I reach my free hand for a garlic parmesan wing. The men systematically destroy the food in front of them. It'll never cease to amaze me how much they can put away. Any one of them eats enough to feed me and Lex for a week.

I'm asked how much more I have left to do. When I say I'm about finished with anything I have to be in the office for, Anders says, "Good. We have some meetings later. It's either we take you home right after lunch or you'll have to wait until late tonight. We don't want to keep you that long if we don't have to."

I agree, hoping I can use the time to bleach my roots and get my laundry done. After the weekend, I don't have much that's still clean. I should have done laundry before the trip, but my mind wasn't on it. Now I'm in danger of dirty hamper diving. My clothes need to be washed.

On the ride home, Anders decides he can drive us. That's fine because I'm not sure I'll be able to keep my dealings with Warrin a secret from Lex. I feel like I'm drowning in the lies and half-truths. It feels like each new deception leads me into another until I feel buried in them. I wish things could be normal.

Lex is excited that we have pizza for supper again, and he eats a piece before putting it into the refrigerator for later. I walk to the bathroom and take out my bleaching kit. Time to eradicate the dark roots that make me less likable.

I allowed Lex to eat most of the pizza, feigning eating too much at lunch to make sure he gets to fully enjoy the treat, so my stomach growling fights with the noise of my washing machines. I sit in one of the blue plastic chairs, looking through social media and emails until I receive a text.

Mr. Gentle Giant: Hi. Whatcha doing?

Me: Laundry.

Mr. Gentle Giant: Did Lex enjoy the pizza?

Me: Yep.

Mr. Gentle Giant: Great!

The polar bear shifter sends a winking emoji.

Mr. Gentle Giant: I'm so sorry. I meant to use a smiley face.

I laugh, chewing my lip to determine if I have the guts to send what I want to next. We're way past this shy stage. This is fun, nothing serious, so I need to stop acting like a teenager with a crush.

Me: I thought maybe it was because you were thinking about the supply closet.

Mr. Gentle Giant: No!

Realizing he's probably panicking that he said something wrong, I laugh. The sound bounces off the walls and metal machines. The poor man's innocence is going to be destroyed.

Mr. Gentle Giant: Or did you want me to?

Me: It wouldn't bother me.

A man walks in while I grin at my screen like the little girl I promised myself not to become only seconds ago. Something about this man warms my heart until it's ready to melt. He's perfect, and not at all corruptible by his good fortune. The new occupant reads over the bulletins posted. It's strange that he doesn't have any laundry, but maybe this board is closer than the lobby for him.

My machines all buzz at the same time, so I jump to my feet and move my clothes into the dryers. I hear my phone chime, which brings another dreamy smile to my face. I'm an idiot right now. As soon as I insert my quarters and start the dryers, I pull out my phone.

Mr. Gentle Giant: What should we try next?

As my thumbs ready to tell him exactly what I'd like to do, a heavy weight slams into my back. My phone falls from my hands, sliding between the two dryers in front of me. I gasp and turn, only to find a strong hand gripping my throat.

Breathing becomes difficult as my back slams painfully into the machines. If I escape this, I'll feel that in the morning.

The man who was looking at the bulletin board brings his face close to mine. One side of his lip pulls up in a snarl, revealing fangs that don't belong in any normal human being. His eyes are crazed and full of rage, and his breath smells of rotten meat. I push at him but gain no distance. He's too strong.

"Do you have any idea what kind of trouble you cause?" His voice is a rumbling growl that grates on the sensitive canals in my ears.

I open my mouth to speak, but my words can't get past the constricted area created by his fingers. He loosens them enough to allow words to pass through. "I am only doing my job."

My voice is a raspy whisper, thanks to the bruises that I'm sure are going to cover my throat. I know he can hear me just fine. I know exactly what I'm dealing with here.

"We had the systems all figured out. We were ripe for sabotage. Then you and your partner come in and change everything."

Lex. Oh, I hope there isn't one of these bastards attacking him right now. "Do you even remember the reason for the war between you and them anymore?"

"They told you about that? I shouldn't be surprised; I can smell ursa all over you, bitch. The reason doesn't matter. We don't let our enemies free without a surrender. Anders decided it's best not to surrender and chose to fight. We never should have let him live."

"Wait. Were you the one I hit with my car?" Do not ask me why I ask that question. My mind isn't working well in this situation.

"No. The entire pack watches all of you. And we're ready to bite."

His thumb closes on my windpipe again. Oxygen flow halts, and I beat at his hands in an effort to free myself. My fists and nails do absolutely nothing, so I try kicking him, but this man must be made of steel because none of Lex's moves helps me. Blackness edges my vision, sight fleeing with the burning in my struggling lungs. He lifts me, putting even more pressure on my throat. My feet kick his gut as weakness moves in.

Voices break through the encroaching darkness of death. I can't make out the words, but I feel myself fall onto the hard floor. A scuffle accompanies my desperate gasps for life-giving air. By the time my vision clears, I see two men with tattoos lying on the floor in front of me. The man that assaulted me snarls by the door, not a scratch while these strong men roll around in pain.

Wild eyes promise to complete my death, but one of the men on the floor pulls a gun. The man growls, not perturbed by the gun pointed directly at his face. He still hesitates before turning and disappearing into the hall. One of the men helps me up into a sitting position. It's now that I recognize the bandana of the ruling gang that considers this block their territory. They tend to leave me alone, so I'm not the least bit worried.

Sure the wolf is gone, I roll onto my back, spotting my phone. I reach my arm in, but it's not skinny enough to squeeze between the rumbling dryers. The machine to my right shifts, and I see one of my rescuers moving it to allow me access. The other is slowly climbing to his feet, holding his stomach and wincing in pain.

I pull my phone out. The one that helped says, "We can't have the cops here."

"That's fine. I'm not calling them. The asshole is gone, and I have no idea who he is. We both know no cop will help us in this area, even if they show up."

He grunts agreement while I look to see three missed texts.

Mr. Gentle Giant: I'm sorry. I probably shouldn't have said that. If you're not answering, I probably made you feel funny. I didn't mean to.

Mr. Gentle Giant: Talk to me. Pleeeeease!

Mr. Gentle Giant: Okay, I'll leave you alone now. I'm sorry.

Coughing through my sore throat, my thumbs move over the screen. I keep it short.

Me: Wolves

Mr. Gentle Giant: What?! I'm coming over.

At this point, I don't have the strength to argue. I let my phone drop onto my chest, rest my head back against the dryer, and drop my arms. Everything hurts. The two men offer to take me back to my apartment. I accept the offer, but I need a minute to breathe first.

ANDERS

"This is a disaster. How could you tell her everything? She'll say something to that hacker friend of hers. Who knows who he'll spill the beans to with his skills," Draven says.

I sigh and rub my eyes. This is not the first time we've had this argument. I've actually lost count of how many times we've had this same discussion. My head is starting to throb.

"The only other option was killing her, and I wasn't going to allow that. Warrin is already attached. Eddie is trustworthy. I know you don't trust any humans, but you need to realize that not all are the same. She's kind, sweet, and selfless. Let it go, Draven."

"You don't understand how dangerous humans are."

"Eddie isn't dangerous, and I know you know that. I've seen the way you look at her. You seemed to enjoy the snowball fight."

He scoffs. "I was purposely trying to hit her as much as I could because I don't like her intrusion."

I laugh. "If that was the case, she'd have bruises. Let it go."

Draven plops down on my couch with his arms crossed over his chest. If anything, I wish he'd return to his own suite. The longer he stays here, the more likely we are to rehash this again. I'm tired of the same crap over and over. My phone rings.

"Yes, Warrin. What do you need?" I say.

"Eddie's been attacked."

Even Draven sits up at that. As a bear, I'm sure he can hear the other side of the conversation perfectly. He can deny it all he wants, but the woman is growing on him—as she is all of us. I will admit to having thoughts along the lines of the mating ritual. My discussion with her after I entered her room as peacefully as possible wasn't just for her benefit. I was hoping to plant the seeds of thought into our young thief.

"What do you mean, *attacked*?" I ask.

"We were texting." Warrin pauses here. The blush I hear in his voice tells me what kind of texts they were. I feel a slight spark of jealousy, but I squash it down. Warrin can help ease her in to the idea. "She stopped replying for a while, and I was worried I overstepped myself. When she finally answered me, all she typed was 'wolves.'"

"But she's okay?"

"I think so. I'm already on my way."

"We'll follow behind."

I hang up. Draven jumps to his feet. We rush for the elevator and to one of the company vehicles. He slides into the passenger seat while I start the engine. "If they damaged her too much, they'll rue the day they were whelped."

Without replying, I throw the car into drive and speed out of the garage. Draven can blubber all he wants. He isn't impervious to what happened this weekend. The arguments are as much to convince himself as me.

CHAPTER SIXTEEN
WARNINGS

I'm huddled on the couch, Lex and Jared staring at me. Jared sits with a stupefied expression on his face, unbelieving of what occurred tonight. Lex looks concerned. My friend is sitting beside me on the couch, twisted to sit facing me, while *his* friend sits in the armchair staring off into space. While I'm thankful for Lex's presence and comfort, I can't say I was happy to see Jared upon my return.

Of all nights Jared has to come while I'm out, it has to be tonight.

A knock sounds from the other side of the door. Lex stands to answer it, knowing who it is already. Part of recounting the incident was telling him Warrin was coming. As soon as the door is open, the big man rushes in and kneels in front of me. "Where are you hurt?"

Lex raises an eyebrow, sending me a look that promises we will be having a discussion later. Well, as much as I know he won't approve, whatever is blossoming between me and Warrin doesn't need to be kept a secret. One less thing to hide from my best friend. There's a little relief in that thought, enough to negate the dread I feel at his incoming reaction.

"I'm fine," I say. I wince when I hear how raspy my voice still is.

The sound brings his attention to my throat, and he stands to grab my head with his usual gentleness to examine the bruises forming. I checked a minute ago. There are visible handprints. His icy blue eyes shoot cold fire when he sees, so I turn my gaze away to avoid seeing it. That means I'm looking at a smirking Jared. I don't dare look at Lex right now.

"It's fine," I say.

"It's not fine. Wait until I get my hands on them."

The anger in his quiet voice pulls my attention back. Fury resides in those icy pools. I swallow the air sticking on the lump caused by both his anger and possible inflammation. My gentle giant is ready to take on an entire pack of wolves for one hurting me. I place a hand on his cheek in an attempt to ground him. His expression instantly settles into the gentleness that makes my heart flutter. Clancy comes out to weave between Warrin's ankles.

Lex clears his throat, and I jump away from Warrin as if burned. My gaze meets his. "We will talk about it later."

With a resigned sigh, he shakes his head. I'm sure he understands exactly what's going on between the two of us. I don't want to talk to him about it in front of others. This is a conversation best had between the two of us.

Warrin touches my arm. "You flinched when you moved. Where else are you hurt?"

"My back hit the edge of one of the washers when he cornered me."

His jaw clenches. Before anyone can say anything else, another knock sounds. Lex walks over to let Anders and Draven in after fighting with the door a bit. I look up at Warrin, asking the question with a mere look.

"I called them on the way," he says.

Anders walks over without a single glance around the room. Draven takes in his surroundings, letting his lip curl up in distaste. The look he gives puts my back up, so I drop my feet to the floor, straighten my spine, and scowl at Mr. Attitude. I dare him to say something about my living arrangements. Just give me a reason to lay into him right now.

Unlike his normal disdainful need to comment, Draven remains silent. He looks between Lex and Jared, taking a long inhale. Being the subject of that intense stare, Jared begins to squirm. Lex's friend excuses himself and rushes for the door. After closing the door, he opens it again to grab his car keys from the hooks by the exit and hurries out again. Of course, it doesn't stick for him.

Another knock sounds. "Who else is coming?" Lex asks.

"Don't look at me. The only person I said anything to was Warrin."

Grumbling, my friend walks over to open the door. I hear voices, and Lex returns with my hamper. "Looks like the men that stopped the attack removed your clothes from the dryer and even folded them for you."

"That was nice of them. Definitely not what I'd expect from gang members."

Silence holds for a few moments. Anders looks over at me. "You're sure about who attacked you?"

"I am."

For the first time ever, I watch Anders become less than cool. Caution turns to guilt. Guilt turns to anger. Anger turns to rage. I've seen him frustrated with Draven, but I've never seen the pure fury in those brown eyes.

"What do you know of the man who attacked Eddie? Is this your fault?" Lex asks, brown eyes cold and leveled on all three of them. "Did you put my best friend in danger?"

"Not on purpose," Anders says with a hot sigh. "None of us thought they'd target an employee."

"What kind of business uses thugs like this?"

"You have no idea what the business world is like," Draven says. "You and your friend signed a contract for employment. You made the choice."

"But we weren't informed of all the risks it seems," Lex says with a scowl.

I cut in, unable to take the stress of an argument right now. "Drop it, Lex. They didn't mean for this to happen. No one is to blame but the prick who tried to strangle me."

My friend throws his hands up in anger before stomping out of the apartment to cool down. I take a few deep breaths, turning my attention back to the men. Draven's focus is on the dark marks on my throat. His eyes blaze, but I turn away from him. Whether he's angry at me or my attacker, he can shove it. He doesn't deserve to care either way right now.

"He told me that they were getting ready for sabotage, but my presence and help is getting in the way," I say.

All three men stop focusing on the visible handprints under my chin, looking between each other in question. I can tell they're disturbed, despite their attempts to hide the emotion from me.

Anders turns his gaze back to mine. "When are all the people we scheduled coming to work on things?"

"The first of my people won't be coming until the end of the week, but Lex's cyber security choice will be there tomorrow."

"We should increase the number of guards stationed," Warrin says.

Draven looks my way. "Why did he tell you something like that?"

"How am I supposed to know? It was right before he almost killed me, so I'm guessing he didn't expect me to survive. My attempted murder was interrupted by the gentleman that dropped off my laundry."

"They didn't smell like gentlemen. I smelled the sour scent of drugs."

I look up at his dark eyes. "Better than some of the present company."

Warrin jumps in to prevent another argument between me and his angsty companion. "Did he say anything else?"

"I revealed that I knew he was a wolf," I say, hurrying on before any can react past the winces I see, even Draven. "He said he figured I knew because I smelled of ursa, whatever that is."

"It's a word for bear," Warrin says. "He can smell me on you. I've put you in more danger."

"It's not your fault. It's not like I tried to stop what happened."

"Whether you tried or not isn't the issue here," Draven says. "What is the issue is that it isn't fixable at this point. Your hormones added danger to this situation."

"If you don't remember, the wolves were stalking me before this. It's obvious they think I'm a threat to whatever plan they have for you."

We talk longer until Lex returns. He looks less stressed out, but I can still see the lines surrounding his eyes that tell me he's tense. Our bosses file out, asking us to come in tomorrow to oversee things. We agree—Lex reluctantly—and are told someone will pick us up at seven.

Once the coast is clear, Lex drops onto the couch. "I'm trying to not feel betrayed, but why didn't you tell me about this threat? It's obvious you knew if you called them into it."

"I in no way betrayed you, Lex. It came up before we left on Sunday. I went to bed when we got home, then we went to work in the morning. It's not like I've had a lot of time to tell you our bosses have enemies."

"Most businessmen don't have people coming after their employees."

I lean back on the couch, feeling my throat getting sorer with each sentence I speak. I'm going to need to rest soon. It's late, and I was attacked by a wolf shifter for helping bear shifters. Lex has no idea what we are in the middle of, and I have no way of telling him without betraying the secret I promised not to. Withholding information from the best friend that has seen my very soul is painful.

Lex reads my silence but not the true reason behind it. How could he? "You need to be careful, Eddie."

"I will. You should be too."

He runs his hands over his cheeks, pulling his glasses off to pinch the bridge of his nose. "I'm always careful, unlike someone else I know. Why are you sleeping with your boss?"

I bite my lip and try not to flinch away from the question. It's not like I didn't know it was coming, so I should have braced for it. "It sounds so crude when you say it like that."

"Because it *is* crude. Eddie, he's a boss. He's someone you tried to rob less than two weeks ago. He's a rich guy that you should despise."

"I know. I know. And I know. Warrin is different."

"Just Warrin?"

Blinking, I pretend not to know what he's asking. It's not like the thought hasn't been running through my mind since Anders dropped it there without a care in the world. I'm not even sure why I'm considering it. Three men? One of them Draven? He must have hit me on the head harder after catching me than I thought.

"No, Lex. It's just Warrin. If you were a woman, would you want to sleep with Draven? What kind of woman do you think I am?" I say.

"Well, he does carry pleasing physical characteristics that I've caught you staring at pretty often."

I glare at him. "I do not. Besides, one man in my life is enough. You guys are a pain in the ass, as you're proving right now."

"You're infuriating. You know that, right?"

"The feeling is mutual, but I love you anyway."

He shakes his head. "Since we have to go into the office tomorrow, I'm going to bed."

I watch him walk to his room and take a deep breath. My fingers press into my eyes, trying to dispel the burning from them. My life went from normalish to rattled to dangerous.

Men that can change into wolves are threatening to kill me. One almost succeeded today. I'm having steamy moments with one of the bosses I never expected to even have while having daydreams of the other two joining us. I don't even know who I am anymore.

Am I still Eddie? Or am I someone that doesn't deserve to carry my name?

Shaking my head, I decide I'm too tired and shook up to contemplate that question. I'll figure out who I am tomorrow. After my run in, I feel dirty, like the wolf left fleas jumping around on my skin. I stand and make my way to the bathroom for a shower. Even the steamy water isn't enough to make me feel clean, but I'll feel at least a little better after.

When I come back out, with a towel wrapped around my body and another on my head something catches my eyes. An envelope lies on the floor, right next to the door, as if someone pushed it under. Taking a few deep breaths, I walk over and lift it. I flip it around in my fingers to find no marking on it anywhere.

Glad Lex didn't find this, I walk back to my room. I can't keep this from him anymore, so I'll show him. Tonight is not the time. Not after all that happened so far. We both need a break. Despite this, I sit on my bed and flip open the envelope.

Heed my warning. Stay out of things that don't concern you, or a bruised throat will be the least of your worries.

CHAPTER SEVENTEEN
ELEVATOR RIDE

"What have you gotten us into, Eddie?" Lex groans while waving the note around.

"It's not like I knew this was going to happen. I can't research a business for crazy stalkers who are violent against those helping."

My phone dinging stops him from arguing further. I don't know what he wants from me. I didn't know supernaturals existed, let alone that my alliance with three bears was going to bring freaking werewolves down on us. At least he doesn't know this part. If Lex is acting the way he is now, I would hate to see if he knew the truth. My freak out would be eclipsed by his.

Mr. Attitude: I'm here, Mutt.

I leave the text unanswered and tell Lex it's time to go. The ride down is full of tense silence, making me hate the sharp turn our lives have made. Well, we'll do our jobs and walk away. After that, we can go back to what we once were; a pair of friends that sometimes go days without proper speaking but are still happy.

Draven honks the second we exit the building, as if we are going to make him late. I look at the clock to see he's fifteen minutes early and scowl at him. Once settled in the back, I reach forward to hand Draven the note. Let them deal with the drama. All he does is shake his head and grunt. I'm not sure if his annoyance is directed at me or the wolf shifters, so I'll assume both. Either way, I know he'll make sure the other two see it.

To break the tension, I ask Lex, "What are the specialists you chose coming to do today?"

It works. Anything dealing with computers will blow everything else out of his mind. My roommate chatters away while I listen and not understand a word. I'm decent with computers and electronics, but I have no idea what he's talking about. It doesn't matter. Lex being happy instead of mad at me is worth listening to a bunch of terms and processes that mean nothing to me.

By the time we reach the office, silence takes over again. Lex hops out and rushes for the elevator before I can even open my door. With a sigh, I shake my head.

"He really lets you know when he's unhappy, doesn't he?" Draven says, looking at me in the mirror.

I shrug and push down the sadness that always comes when we have a disagreement. "He has the right to be upset. My decisions have put us both in danger. It'll blow over once this is all done. We've been together our entire lives, so it'll take more than a little danger to pull us apart for good."

"In a hurry to be done with us, Mutt?"

Sending his reflection a glare, I get out of the car, walk to the elevator, and press the button to bring it back to us. Draven walks up behind me, standing so close that I can feel the heat radiating off him. My breath freezes in my chest with his proximity. This man riles me up like no other can, but I still find my heart racing at his near touch.

"What's it matter to you? I figure you'll be happy to see me gone," I say, hating myself for how unsteady my voice sounds.

"You disappearing will hurt my colleague."

"One, I don't plan on hurting Warrin. I quite enjoy spending time with him, and I'm not just talking about what happened between us yesterday. Two, I'm glad your only worry when it comes to me is about your bear buddy."

The doors slide open, and I rush in to push the button. Draven follows with a slow swagger. As soon as we move up, he reaches over and pushes the stop button. The small, crowded space jerks to a halt. I find myself wondering if I maybe pushed him too far.

A strong hand grips my upper arm, spinning me to pin my shocked body against the side. My bruised back touches the handrail, so I hiss and create some space, which brings my hips against his. I can feel the bulge in his pants pressing into sensitive areas. Is it better to deal with this torture or the pain of the bar pressing into my back? I can't decide.

Draven leans close, fanning my face with his warm breath. "What else would you like, Mutt? You've pulled Warrin in with your beauty and selflessness. Even Anders is falling for your wit and strong sense of honor. Would you like me to be there with them? I know Anders told you about us, what solitary creatures do when they form a bond with each other. Is that what you want?"

My breath leaves me unable to speak. I gulp and feel my racing heart enter my throat. An ache builds between my legs, spreading to my lower abdomen. Draven growls and pulls my face until I'm meeting his gaze. His dark eyes are pools of blackness.

"Watch that scent, or I may need to devour you," he whispers.

Tingles travel from my gut and into my breasts, settling in my nipples. "You smell me?"

"Your arousal smells delicious, Mutt. Seducing me won't work though because I don't wish to be some random fling of yours."

He steps away, back straight, and pushes the button. We lurch upward. My knees feel unsteady, so I grip the railing to hold myself up.

"Don't think I'm falling for your aloofness, Draven. I wasn't the one that acted seductive just now. The tent in your pants tells me what I'd smell if I could."

He looks back at me with a smirk. His hand slips into his pants to readjust and hide his desires. "Unlike many, I have the willpower not to go for a bad idea. You don't know me well enough to consider me anything but a walking sex toy. My brothers' desire for you spikes my own, so don't get ahead of yourself. Unless you prove to me that you're willing to commit to us, my tent pole stays in my pants. Enjoy your day."

The door opens at the end of his small speech, and he slips out without a word. I place my feet on the hard tile, looking around before I head to the bathroom. In a stall, I lean my head against the metal door to catch my breath. There's no way I'm letting anyone else catch me this frazzled. I go over everything he just said. Despite his disdain, he desires me. Also, Anders is falling for me as well. I should back away from all three, but I'm starting to care enough for Warrin that I don't wish to hurt him. Maybe this whole thing is a terrible mistake.

What if it isn't?

Part of me says that the true mistake will be running from what we can have if I stay. Is the danger of the wolves worth it? It's possible for us to find a solution to their canine problem without it involving me disappearing into the sunset with a job well-done. Can we? I'd maybe like to try.

Shaking my head, I make my way to the security area. What am I saying? Have I decided I want this? That's crazy. I barely know these men, and I'm already considering giving myself to all three of them for eternity. That's quite a large commitment, one that takes a lot of consideration. I need more time to think, but I'm in danger of letting myself take the plunge on intuition alone. Instinct is a powerful tool. Yet, I need to try to remove emotions from my current intuition to avoid making a colossal mistake.

Entering the hall where security waits, I pause. Jeff stands in the hall with his potbelly straining the buttons on his uniform to the point I wonder how much he's bloated out since he got the shirt. He's glaring into the room with his arms crossed over his stomach. Sweat beads the bald spot on top of his head.

My feet carry me the rest of the way. "Is something wrong, Jeff?"

The aging man turns his angry eyes on me. "I hate being treated like me and my men aren't good enough for security."

"You're still going to have a job. We are just making that job easier. I would think you'd want to make sure everything was the most secure."

"Everything was fine until you showed up. It's not just our job security."

"What else is it?"

He looks away, clenching his jaw. After a few breaths, he says, "You broke in and made us obsolete."

For a second, I could have sworn he was going to say something else. Something nags at the back of my mind, but I brush it away. I'm under a lot of stress and jumping at my own shadow. Walking past the glowering security chief, I stick my head in the door. Lex is standing by the computer and discussing things with two other men while gesturing wildly at the monitors.

There's no way I'm getting into the middle of whatever is going on in there right now. I'm saved by Warrin hailing me from down the hall. I walk toward him to meet my polar bear halfway. "Were you looking for me?"

He grins. "Maybe. I don't have anything important going on, so I want to take you somewhere."

"Where?"

"The first part of it is lunch. The second is a surprise."

I'm not a fan of surprises. His smile keeps me from telling him that because I don't want to make him unhappy. Maybe

I am already on the way to making a decision. That thought causes me to grimace. Am I that easy?

"Oh, okay. It's not lunchtime yet."

He shakes his head. "I already talked to Anders and Draven. I'll get you when it's time to go."

"Are they coming?"

"Just me and you. That's why I told them, so they wouldn't be too disappointed they won't be coming along."

I laugh. "I doubt it would bother them that much."

Warrin looks down at his feet. "Anders was definitely sad."

Anders is falling for your wit and strong sense of honor.

I push Draven's words from my mind. In the heat of the moment, I believed those words, but I can't see such an intelligent businessman bedding down with the thief caught pilfering from his office building. My thoughts strain to him telling me about how multiple bears will take on a human if they're close enough, strengthen the gene pool. Am I being looked at like someone to breed with? No. Anders wouldn't think like that after losing his mate. If he's interested in me, there has to be another reason.

I clear my throat. "Probably not Draven."

"Draven has many layers, most you haven't learned enough to understand. He enjoys our lunches too, even though he always complains."

My big bear leaves me alone with that thought. If anyone would know Draven, it's him. The three seem so close, which only brings back the explanation Anders gave me in the cabin. What have I gotten myself into? Worse than that; why does the thought send pleasant chills over me?

After a quick lunch at a local deli, we are on the road for whatever this surprise is. As we drive, the chill seeps into the vehicle. I consider asking if we can turn the heat up, but I figure polar bears are probably more comfortable with the chill. It's not that cold anyway.

We head out of the city to a rich little suburb. The streets are perfectly maintained. Smoke rises from chimneys of the large houses we pass. Leafless trees line pristine sidewalks. After a few blocks of this, we pull up to a locked gate guarded by a man in an olive-green uniform.

The man sees who's driving and lets us in without question. In silence, I feel my heart skip a beat. Whatever the surprise is, we must be getting close. Driveways like this usually end at a house and nowhere else.

"Where are we?" I ask.

"My mother's house."

My heart drops into my feet. He brought me home to meet his mother. Sole surviving parent. Human mated to a polar bear.

CHAPTER EIGHTEEN
MAMA BEAR

"Are you alright, Eddie?" Warrin asks as we circle the driveway to the house that's smaller than the others in this neighborhood.

Smaller doesn't mean less grand. The house is made of white and tan stone, dark gray shutters framing the windows. The porch wraps around one side of the house. Skeletal shrubs line the driveway, probably filling the yard with color in the warm months. A small gazebo sits off to the side, overlooking a small orchard. My mouth drops open.

"Eddie?"

Oh, yeah. Warrin. "I didn't expect you to bring me to meet your mother."

"I told her all about you. She's wanted to meet you for a while."

My brows furrow. "We haven't known each other that long."

"I tell my mother everything. She has known about you since you broke in."

"She knows I'm a thief?"

"Sure. When I told her why, she instantly decided you're as awesome as I think you are."

That's nice, but it doesn't stop the panic I feel deep inside. His mother. Warrin brought me to meet his mother. This is huge.

My thoughts must be written plainly on my face. "Eddie, is something wrong?"

"This is a big step, Warrin. Most people don't bring the person they're seeing to meet their parents until they're serious."

"Why not? My mother is a wonderful person. I think you'll love her."

"I'm not saying she's not. After all, she raised a gentleman. I just thought we weren't seriously dating yet."

"Yet?"

Sighing, I look up at the big house in front of me. "Yes, yet. Even with everything I've learned, I'm not going to put us going further in our relationship as unachievable. I really care about you, Warrin, but it's a lot to take in."

"All the more reason to meet my mother. She's been where you are. I'm not saying I want to push you, and I feel terrible if I did something wrong. If you're uncomfortable, I can call her and cancel the visit."

Taking in his words, I let out a large exhale. We could go, act like this never happened, but then it'll always be hanging over our heads. Friends meet parents, right? That's all this is.

"No, don't call her," I say. "I'll meet her."

Warrin beams with the brightest smile ever, and all my worries are swept away in the warm waves that come from him. He squeezes his way out of the small car door, rushes around the car before I can contemplate opening the door, and opens it like the gentleman he is. Taking his offered hand, I slide out.

As we walk toward the porch, I ask, "Isn't she in danger from the wolves?"

He shakes his head. "Since she's human, they tend to leave her alone. After my father's disappearance, she refuses to let them scare her, but I make sure she's protected. If they want me, they'll come after me. Humans are below their notice unless they cause problems."

"Good."

We reach the steps. "Don't think this means I expect to meet your parents now, Eddie. It can be when you're comfortable."

My feet stop on the first step. Warrin doesn't notice until his arm pulls back with my grip on his hand. He looks back at me. Smile turns to concern.

"Did I do something wrong again?" Warrin says.

I shake my head and continue up the stairs. "I don't know if you'll ever meet my mother."

"Why not?" He looks hurt by my admission.

"It's not you, Warrin. I barely even see my mom, and I don't go out of my way to."

"Why? Mothers are the best."

"Not mine. She blames my existence for her miserable life."

"That doesn't make any sense. Mothers love their children."

His sweet innocence is almost too much. "My mom blamed me for my father leaving, and she was kind of right."

Before he can ask more, the door swings open. A black and white dog runs out between the feet of a tall older woman. Her hair is dyed black, but her eyebrows are brown with lines of white. Although her back is hunched, her green eyes are alert and bright. A smile stretches over her wrinkled lips while the dog jumps all over Warrin.

"Pancake! Get down," Warrin says when the animal decides it's my turn for hellos.

I give him a scratch before turning my attention back to Warrin's mother. "Hello, Ma'am."

When I raise my hand for a shake, she grabs it and pulls me into a hug. "Call me Caroline, dear. Come in! I've been watching you two, and you were taking way too long. I was hoping you weren't going to make a run for it."

Warrin follows as I find myself dragged inside the house. Pancake follows. He's a happy dog, but he doesn't bark much. Once the doors are closed, Pancake runs across the shining white tile with his nails clicking. Caroline leads me to a livingroom and directs me to a white couch with flowers on the fabric. Inside, the house has a homey feel to it. The fireplace crackles with real logs, not the fake flames many of the modern fireplaces have now. The walls are wooden. Hardwood floors are covered in fluffy beige rugs.

A tea set already sits on the coffee table. Tea has never been my hot drink of choice, preferring coffee, but I accept a cup with some sugar. I take a sip, feeling a familiar burn on my tongue with a different flavor than I'm used to. Warrin's cup looks like a child's in his large hands, which makes it hard for me not to laugh.

"Warrin has told me so much about you, Eddie," Caroline says.

"He told me he did, even the seedier parts of my life."

"Oh, no need to be embarrassed. I think it's wonderful the less fortunate have someone like you to look after them."

My cheeks feel warm. Sure, this is what I want, to help others. That doesn't mean that I'm comfortable being recognized and adored for it. I spend my nights operating in the shadows, not out in the light for others to see. It's always been expected that others would despise me for my career choice. Instead, I've been hired as a consultant and am now sitting in a room with two people who think I'm some sort of hero. I'm not sure how to respond.

"You have a lovely home," I say to change the subject.

"Thank you, dear. My son felt I deserved such a wonderful place to live because I raised him. I only did what a mother is obligated to while loving him as a mother should."

My heart skips a beat, longing for what I never had. What would it have been like to grow up in an environment full of love and laughter, instead of shame and anger? I've never envied the rich for their treasures, but I'm a bit jealous of this one. It's not his money that I wish for, but the love of the one person in this world that should love most. A true mother.

Caroline has stopped speaking. "What's wrong?"

"Nothing. It's such a blessing for Warrin to have a mother that thinks the best of him as you do. He's lucky."

"I'm the lucky one. He's been a great son. Speaking of... Warrin, can you take Pancake out? He hasn't had outside time in a while."

"Sure." Warrin jumps up and gives his mother a kiss on the cheek. Pancake chases after him, tail wagging like crazy.

"I guess your dog doesn't have a problem with bears?"

Caroline laughs and takes another sip of her tea. "Not at all. They grew up together. Warrin is the one to name him Pancake. There probably isn't a lot of time left in his life, so Warrin does his best to spend as many of his free hours as possible with him."

I nod, knowing Warrin feels big and would want the same. It's clear the dog loves him. After a few seconds of silence, Caroline says, "It's a pity you found out the way you did. It must have been quite a shock."

"Understatement of the century. How did you find out?"

"Warrin's father eased me in. When he decided I was the one, he left hints before telling me. I didn't believe him until he showed me. It's definitely a shock."

"When did *you* decide?" Topic of the day, the one that's been on my mind.

"That took a bit longer, dear. More tea?" I look into my cup and shake my head. "It's a huge commitment, one that you can't make without serious consideration. Although, you can enjoy the perks of a bear lover before making the final decision. I've heard you might have three! I can't imagine."

The tea I just tried to swallow gets stuck in my throat, and I find myself coughing and spewing it back into the teacup. Unsteady hands put the cup down before I stain her nice couch with it. Caroline hops up to pat me on the back. The fact that this sweet old lady said something like that caught me off guard. Not something I was expecting from her.

"No need to be embarrassed," she continues. "Bears are very passionate creatures. Loyal too. You won't find one better."

This isn't helping. The tea is gone, either sloshing in the cup on the tray or unsettled in my belly. It takes a few more seconds to relieve the coughing. My lungs are sore by the time I'm done.

"Are you alright, dear?"

I nod, not trusting myself to speak. Caroline dumps my regurgitated drink into Warrin's cup and pours more into mine. She stirs in sugar before handing it to me. I drink the hot liquid, letting it soothe a throat sore from hacking. A few more deep breaths.

"Now that you're calm," Warrin's mother says, "I want you to know that I wasn't trying to weird you out there. It's something you need to know. When a bear has their eye on you, they can be pretty relentless. Warrin told me of your beauty and ethics the first day after he met you. He's infatuated. If you decide this isn't the life for you, you can walk away. All I ask is that you're gentle. He won't give up easily, but he won't push something you don't want either."

"I care for him; I really do. This is just pretty big, and I haven't known him very long."

"Do you trust your gut?"

Blinking, I look up in surprise. "Yes."

"So do I, but I waited too long to follow it. I lost months of being a bear's mate because of it. Give yours the attention it deserves. Even now, my instincts are telling me you deserve the regard my son gives you. It's up to you to listen to your heart. That doesn't mean you can't have a little fun until you decide. Three will keep you rather busy, but once you do decide, you know for a fact your children will be shifters."

Another coughing fit takes over at the thought of her already planning on me giving her grandchildren. Instead of being alarmed or offended, she only laughs. Warrin walks back in, eyes bouncing between the two of us. "Is something wrong?"

"Eddie is just a little overwhelmed by her possible future."

"Mom."

"Don't use that tone on me, young man. I've been where she is, so she deserves the truth about what she's in for. Why don't you give her a tour? I'm going to check on supper and see what I need to start."

Caroline disappears down the hall. Warrin does as commanded and shows me around the house. It's all beautiful and amazing, but my mind isn't on what I'm seeing. All I can think of is what his mother said. She seems a little envious over my three bears while I'm trying to get used to one. Her words bring heat to my cheeks though, and I find myself wondering if she's right.

CHAPTER NINETEEN
CONSIDERING THE FUTURE

"And this is my room."

I enter the large room to find white carpets and light blue walls. Posters of animals hang by tacks. Stuffed animals and figurines litter the area. Even his comforter is full of dogs and cats. While I admire Warrin's innocence, this seems to be a bit much. He closes the door behind me.

"What do you think?" he asks as my eyes follow all the fluffy brightness.

"Really love animals?"

"I used to want to be a vet when I grew up. Thinking of sick and hurt animals always broke my heart. I wanted to help."

Now, that makes sense. It's a totally Warrin aspiration to grow up and help sick animals. Did his future take a huge deviation from his childhood dream or what? "Why didn't you become one?"

"It was brought to my attention that to help animals, I might have to hurt them; like shots and stitches and things. The worst was when I found out I may need to put them to sleep too. I couldn't do any of that."

Sighing, I plop down on his bed, my legs crossed under me. Warrin sits, and I grab his shoulders to signal that he should lie down. My fingers stroke his messy blond hair once his head is in my lap. "Is that before you met Anders?"

He nods. "When I learned that my dream job wasn't for me, I decided I needed to find a way to support my mother. She worked so hard for us and deserved a break. Anders found me and knew I was a bear shifter right away. He took me in and mentored me. Now, my mother will never go without for me, and I have two brothers. It was lonely growing up, but I guess it was for the best."

"Why?"

"Well, with my mom being human, shifter genes aren't for sure. Since I was born a polar bear, any other child that didn't receive the gift may have become bitter."

"But they could have received the gift?"

"Yeah. It's just that each child is a chance of being either."

"Unless the mate takes more than one?"

His cool blue eyes look up at me. "Anders told us he explained that to you, but it's your choice if you want one of us, two of us, all three, or none at all. The choice is completely yours, Eddie."

"But you hope for..."

"I want you. I have since we first met, but it gets worse with each day I spend with you. My new brothers are very much a part of me, so it would be nice. Even if it's only me though, I'd be very happy."

Warrin's mother's words run through my mind. The longer I fight the urge to give him what he wants, the more I'll regret the time I didn't give him. I'm still not ready. As I said, I follow my instincts. Right now, they're pushing me into Warrin's arms and bed; into his future life. For once, I fight my intuition.

"Give me a few more days to think about it, then we can revisit the idea," I say.

"Really?"

"Yeah. Maybe you can take me out to dinner Thursday."

"Like a date?"

"Yep."

"I would like that. Can it be a fancy restaurant? Do you have a dress?"

"Maybe nothing that fancy, but I'll make it work."

Warrin opens his mouth, probably to offer to spend more money on me. Instead of allowing him to do so, I run my fingers over his chest and down. He lifts onto his elbows to invite me in for a kiss. In a flash, he's up and has me on my back. With his body pressed against mine, I wrap my arms around his neck.

My hips rise to rub against his cock through his pants. It's stiff with desire for me, which sends a shiver over my spine. What would it be like to give everything to him? Feel his entire bulk inside me? Anticipation threatens to undo our earlier discussion. Patience for now, even if it's as much torture for me as it is for him.

Between my motion and the friction of our bodies, Warrin is growling like the great big polar bear he is. There's something to say about having a gentle beast pressing down on top of you, poking you with a dick that's standing at the ready. Despite my desire to ignore her words, Caroline's point feels like it's being made right now.

There's nothing like a bear of a man.

Frantic fingers slide under the hem of his shirt until I'm able to pull it over his head. Before he can return for a kiss, I reach up to nibble at his throat. The sounds that reverberate out of him are outstanding, fueling my rising heat even more. The ache between my legs grows into the neediest of hungers, ready to devour anything presented to it.

My fingers run over his chest, thumbs rubbing over his nipples. Warrin decides I need the pleasure reciprocated. Shirt and bra are on the floor in seconds, his mouth remembering the joys it gave me last time. As his tongue circles my nipple, I feel a tingle settle in before it travels deep to my core. Goosebumps grow larger with each shiver. When he gives the nipple a slight nip, I gasp and dig my nails into his back.

Grasping hands work between us. I manage to undo the button and zipper with little difficulty. The groan that vibrates my breast makes my breath stop and my heart race. Agony gives way to wetness in my panties.

Warrin freezes, burying his head in my neck as I pump along his smooth shaft. His muscles tense, and I feel him bite down gently on my neck as his cock twitches and releases. The warm spurts on my belly slow.

Stopping, Warrin takes the time to clean me off with tissues while I beg for my own release. Just when I'm starting to cool, he rips my jeans down over my hips and thrusts his fingers inside me. It happens so fast that I cry out in pleasure and shock. My surprise keeps me from holding back, and I shudder and release almost immediately.

"Don't stop," I say when he slows.

Reaching down, I direct his thumb to my clit. He rubs a few times before drawing lazy circles. The pressure slowly builds again with each round.

"Faster," I gasp.

Warrin complies. My throbbing returns, aching for more and more of this delicious man. Both hands grip the dog and cat comforter so tight I'm not sure it'll be easy to let go. When he thrusts two fingers in without stopping the circles, my entire body tenses with pleasure.

The large polar bear has pleasingly large fingers.

It isn't long until I'm fighting the pull to let go. Instead, I torture myself to feel as much as I can. My willpower only lasts another minute or two before I'm stuffing my fist in my mouth to muffle the scream bursting from me while I feel my body clench around Warrin's fingers.

My polar bear relaxes over me, keeping most of his weight from smothering me by bracing up on his elbows. He gives me a slow kiss, full of tenderness that makes me melt.

"Dinner," comes a call from the base of the stairs.

I startle. "Do you think she heard us?"

"If she was a bear, she'd hear it. Age and humanity will make me say no. She'll probably still know though. Nothing gets by her."

Groaning, I roll out from under him while he chuckles. "She was a bit adamant about things we can't do."

"I'm sure she was. Mom is pretty blunt, but she's a sweetheart too. We better get dressed before dinner cools."

After dodging all the "told you so" looks from Caroline throughout our seafood dinner, we are now getting ready to leave. Warrin helps me into my coat, Pancake weaving around us. His mother chatters away about how nice it was for us to visit.

"Come back please, Eddie. It doesn't matter what you decide. It's nice having female company that doesn't involve being nagged to go to bingo," Warrin's mother says while squeezing me to death one last time.

I pat her back. "I promise I'll visit no matter what."

"Good."

She returns to watch us from the warmth of her windows. Warrin opens my door, then closes it once I'm nestled inside. Heat blasts me, all vents turned my way while Warrin drives with his window cracked. It's dark, and I stare at the streetlights as we drive by.

Back in the city, everything is more brightly lit. My driver reaches over and takes my hand. Smiling at him, I twine my fingers with his. The acceptance of his gesture makes him beam.

This feels so right. My brain fights the feeling, but when have I ever listened to the wrinkly organ in my head? My heart always leads the way, and right now, it's leading me to Warrin.

This isn't infatuation, but it's not quite love. Something tells me Warrin is where I belong. Something calls him home.

For the life of me, I can't understand why I'm fighting this so hard.

Because not fighting it would be a stupid move. There's my annoying brain again. A quiet sigh slips out of me, and I realize that I'm worried my intuition is wrong for once. It doesn't happen often, but it does occasionally. A mistake like this would have terrible long-term consequences.

We drive past the park. Howls rend the air. Loud enough to be heard through the exterior of the car. I jump, squeezing Warrin's fingers tighter. A glance shows me he's tense as well. The carefree expression is gone, replaced by lines around his eyes and mouth. He doesn't stop, forging ahead as the light turns green. We leave the howls behind us.

Is that another warning? They're watching us and know where we will be? Our schedule is not hidden from them? I'm sure they know by now I haven't backed away yet.

I've thought about it. For my safety and Lex's, I should ask for release from the contract now. We did our job. Systems are being upgraded. It shouldn't be a problem.

My eyes move back to the relaxing polar bear. It's more than a contract now. It's more than testing the system for them. Warrin keeps me there. He's wormed his way into my heart. Anders pulls to me as well, and I wonder what's in store for us in the future. Even Draven has his appeal. Three sexy men that have hinted at being willing to let me claim them.

That's not something easy to walk away from.

Lex would be happy if I would; no doubt about that. I can't. Too much holds me here. Can I continue to keep Lex in danger? I can ask them to release him, but I doubt the wolves won't still use him to make a point. These thoughts sour the carefree nature of our day. I can't seem to push them away.

Warrin parks along the curb and insists on escorting me to my apartment. At the door, he leans down and consumes my mouth. Our tongues dance and tangle. His hands reach back and boldly squeeze my ass hard enough to make me yelp.

He smiles as he pulls away. "Thursday night? Since you're working from home, I'll pick you up at six?"

"Sounds good."

One last peck, and he walks away. I stand still to watch, admiring his strong backside as he moves. When he's almost tripped by a bleeding poodle being chased by Betsy, I can't help but laugh. I watch until he's in the elevator.

Lex barely looks up from whatever game has his full attention. I get a grunt and wave that tells me we'll be alright. Otherwise, I wouldn't have gotten that much. Of course, we'll be okay. We're found family, and nothing will break us apart. A sign of a lasting friendship is to never run away from each other, no matter how much of an idiot they're being.

I head straight to bed, ready to spend my night thinking of everything and barely sleeping. As I slide my jeans down, I feel something heavy in my back pocket. An envelope comes out with Warrin's writing on it.

For a nice dress. Think princess perfect for the formality level. Whatever you don't use, feel free to donate wherever. I know that's where the sign-on bonus went. Just make sure you feel like the queen you are.

Sighing, I look in to find what has to be a few thousand. My fingers leaf through the large green bills as I shake my head. I lift my phone and type a message.

Me: I hope naughty princess is okay. I don't do sparkly.

Mr. Gentle Giant: I look forward to it.

His line of winking emojis makes me smile. My heart lifts, and I fall back onto my mattress. Warmth floods me. "What are you doing to me, Warrin?"

CHAPTER TWENTY
NAUGHTY PRINCESS

My hands smooth the black fabric over my hips and thighs. I went with modern day naughty princess while shopping yesterday. The little black dress hugs my form in all the right places. One strap goes over my right shoulder, leaving the other bare. The bottom reaches to just above my knees. A gold braided belt accents the dress nicely. There's just one issue.

Picking up my phone, I send a text for help to Lex, asking that he leaves Jared behind on the couch. When my friend enters, his jaw drops to the floor. I rush over to shut the door his lax hands have forgotten.

His reaction is making me feel self-conscious. "Is it bad?"

"Not at all. You look gorgeous. Why didn't you tell me that you clean up this well?"

I laugh. "You went to prom with me, Lex."

"Yeah, but you've grown up since then. Besides, once in how many years isn't enough to spark memory."

"I thought you never forget."

"I don't," he says with a scowl. "I file away older memories until needed."

Turning, I show him the reason for my request for help. He steps over, pulling the zipper up. My roommate takes care to move slowly and avoid snags. I let my hair fall once he's done and stare at myself in the mirror. Everything took the utmost care. My bleached hair bounces with slight curls. My makeup highlights my best features, which took a while since I don't wear makeup often. No man has ever gotten this treatment from me before.

"You know I don't approve of whatever is going on, but *I* know I can't stop you," Lex says with a sigh. "I worry about what's in store for you at the end of whatever you're doing with this man. I really don't want you to get hurt. But, while I don't approve, damn you look fine."

Tears threaten, and I blink to try to dispel them before they fall. "Damn it, Lex. It took me forever to get my makeup right. Don't ruin it, please."

He places his hands on my shoulders, looking into my eyes in the mirror. "Be careful. I've never killed before, but I will for my best friend. He better not hurt you."

Laughter chases away the mist in my eyes. "You've never even pinched someone before."

"I never had a reason."

I want to laugh again, but the seriousness in his eyes tells me he's not joking. Knowing my best friend would make that threat for me is a sobering thought. I know I'd do anything to protect him. It's both heartwarming and terrifying to know he'd risk himself for me as well. If something would happen to me, the last thing I would want would be Lex sacrificing himself.

Turning, I take his hands in mine. "One, no. I don't want you getting hurt for me. Two, it's not an issue. Warrin is one of the softest people I've ever met. He's not going to hurt me. I can promise you that."

Lex sighs. "I kind of got that impression from him as well, but it's not just him. Being close to Warrin puts you close to the other two. I don't trust Warrin. I trust the other two even less. They're hiding something, some secret. I can feel it."

My breath stops. I know exactly what that secret is, and I wish I could tell him. Telling him would only make him worry about me more though, so I won't break my promise. I can only hope the secret doesn't come out at the worst time like they usually do. My instincts are screaming at me to tell him. I can't. I promised.

"I'll be fine," I say after my internal debate.

"I trust you, but you can't blame me for worrying."

A lump forms in my throat right as my phone pings. Trust I'm breaking. Worry is warranted. I'm a terrible friend, who is putting my desires and men I barely know above the only friend that's always been there for me. How will he react if I tell him the truth? While my instincts want me to say something, they also tell me to practice caution. This isn't some run-of-the-mill secret. It's huge. My reaction is nothing compared to the breakdown Lex is capable of.

"Aren't you going to check your message?" he asks, breaking me from my thoughts. "Probably your date."

He walks out the door, and I catch a glimpse of Jared eating takeout on our couch. I shake my head. Even if I decide to break my promise, which I haven't, it can't be in front of Jared. Lex, I trust. Jared, not so much. Taking a deep breath, I answer Warrin's text and walk out of my room.

Jared whistles. "Nice, Eddie. I still think some color would be better than all the black you wear, but no one can complain about that dress." Lex elbows him with an eyebrow raised. "What? I can't appreciate a well-put-together woman? It's not like I'm hitting on her. Although, Eddie, try smiling a little more. Men like that."

I drag my eyebrows together, pinch the bridge of my nose, and walk for the door. Lex yells, "We won't wait up."

Before I can make a very unpleasant gesture that would probably only make him laugh, I decide to leave. The door picks this time to jam shut again. Growling, I yank, then stumble backwards when the door releases. No decision has proven to be right as much as my decision to ignore the clerk's suggestion I wear ridiculous heels. I can't even walk in them, so that would have been a rolled ankle for sure.

Outside, I ignore Jared's laughter, sliding my phone into my new purse with my keys and wallet. Never thought I'd ever carry around a black leather bag like this. I hate purses; just something else to risk forgetting somewhere. Dresses this fancy don't come with pockets. Neither does the suggested sweater. The shoes are the only part of my wardrobe I didn't let the lady at the desk talk me out of. For some reason, I want to live up to the rich standards tonight. For Warrin.

I'm happy not to meet anyone on the way out. Warrin opens the door as I approach the curb. His mouth drops when I get closer. "You look beautiful."

I glance over his black suit and smile. "So do you."

He stands taller, making me laugh. I've never seen a bear preen before, but Warrin definitely is. Sliding into the passenger seat, I offer him a smile as he closes my door. Not because Jared told me to. Being with this man always makes me smile. I can't help myself. The car dips as he climbs in, squeezing through the door without mussing his suit too much. We're off.

The restaurant is a fancy place, all red and gold. Each table has an elaborate candle centerpiece, and the overhead lights are dim. The walls remind me of the cabin. The scent of fish is heavy. I can see why this is a Warrin kind of restaurant.

The hostess offers a huge smile and leads us to a table in a corner. Warrin waits for me to choose my seat against the wall, then pulls out my chair. Before I can answer what I want to drink, he asks the waitress to bring us a bottle of wine. I also ask for water because I don't want only alcohol. As much as I trust Warrin, I like to keep my wits about me.

I open the menu. "There are no prices."

"Nope. And it's bad manners to ask, so you'll just have to let it go for tonight."

Sighing, I flip through the pages. The dishes are hard to pronounce, and I have no idea what the ingredients are. I bite my lip, closing the menu. My eyes watch Warrin look over the laminated pages with a thoughtful look.

Blue eyes look over the open booklet. "Something wrong?"

"I have no idea what I'm looking at. What would you suggest?"

Warrin starts rattling off dishes with an excitement that makes me smile. I listen to the ones he thinks I would like best. By the time the waitress returns with our wine, I have a few choices to choose between. Warrin orders an appetizer.

I purse my lips in thought. "These places never give you the food I've seen you eating elsewhere, and you three never ask for multiple meals. Not that I don't blame you with these prices, but you're not hungry after?"

"I'll eat again when I get home. We also always keep snacks in our desks."

That makes sense. The appetizer arrives, our orders are taken, and Warrin digs into some kind of seafood dip with crackers. Even the crackers look fancy. I eat a few but leave most to him. I'll fill up on the meal. I don't want him to be hungry when he's paying for everything.

Once my polar bear devours the appetizer, he asks, "When did you get into your night job?"

I bite my lip, looking around to make sure no one is close. One thing I've learned is that these men can hear really well, so I feel it's safe to talk. "I didn't have a lot growing up. My mom didn't like spending more on me than she needed to keep herself out of jail. If I wanted more than the barest of necessities, I had to get it myself. Unfortunately, I couldn't work until I turned sixteen. So, I had to find other means of procuring an extra pair of socks or underwear."

"You started in school?"

With a wince, I nod reluctantly. "Wasn't the proudest time of my life. Yes, I'm still a thief, but it was done for me and Lex, not for the overall good. I also only stuck to the rich kids who were always breaking their expensive things or throwing them away for something new. Anything left was given away though, so there was a little toward the greater good, I guess."

"You did what you had to do. Why didn't your mom get you what you needed?"

I sigh, looking away. While I'll tell him of my hooligan years, I'm not ready for that much. The darkest part of my soul isn't ready for the light. The food comes to save me from awkwardly telling him I'm not ready to speak of it. Either Warrin senses my reluctance, or he's just hungry, because we eat in silence.

After a much too large dessert that I give him half of, we sit and talk over wine. I learn of his childhood and hear the pain he and his mother went through when his father disappeared. While I keep my darkness in the shadows of my mind, he exposes his with the ultimate trust. Each new thing I learn about him swells my heart bigger.

By the time we're back in the car, I'm ready to trust my intuition. "Can we go back to your place?"

Warrin's eyes widen. "Really? Are we going to experiment more?"

I laugh before taking his hand in mine. "I'm ready for the commitment you offered, Warrin."

His wide eyes get even bigger, which I didn't think was possible. "Are you sure? I really want to, but there's no going back. I don't want you to regret this."

"Your mom told me some things that made the decision easier. As much as I never thought I'd say this, I've fallen in love with you already. You're sweet, charming, and generous."

He smiles with each word. "I feel the same about you. I admit I was fascinated with you before, but it's so much more now. That's why I offered to move slowly. I've loved you for a while."

"You love easy."

"I do, but you made it even easier, which is why I wanted you to be my mate."

"Let's do this then."

We hold hands the entire drive to the office building, and he explains which floors at the top of the building belong to each bear. A security officer lets us into the garage without question. The elevator takes us up to a level locked by the key Warrin keeps on his ring.

My jaw drops open when the doors slide apart. Beige carpets lead directly into a spacious living room. A large TV hangs on one wall, surrounded by brown couches. A spotless kitchen with black appliances sits to the right. I walk over to the large window and gawk shamelessly at the view. The entire city rests before my eyes, glowing bright with lights.

"It's beautiful," I say.

"Not as beautiful as you."

"You're just saying that because I'm your soon-to-be mate."

"No view is more gorgeous than you are."

Turning, I see him staring at me with excitement in his eyes. Even with his size, he's almost bouncing on the balls of his feet like a little boy who got the car set he wanted for Christmas. My mouth goes dry at the love and adoration in his light blue eyes.

Of course, my phone decides now is a good time to chime. "Are you going to get that?" Warrin asks.

"It's probably just Lex checking in."

"This can wait. We have all night."

All night. Those words form a lump in my throat, and I find myself wishing I could open this stupid bag faster. As expected, it's my roomie.

Lex: I know I said I wouldn't wait up, but I want to make sure all is good.

Me: I know you won't approve, but don't wait up. I won't be home tonight.

Before he can send a lecture, I turn my phone off. No more beeps. No more check-ins. No more interruptions. I toss my phone on the couch.

My feet leave the ground before my phone even completes its bounce, making me squeal. Warrin's strong arms carry me into a door to the left, and I find my mouth dropping open once again. That's a big bed. I bounce like my phone did on the couch before settling in.

Warrin fumbles with the zipper while kissing me. He growls. "How did you even get this thing zippered?"

"Lex helped."

"Well, I'm certainly not asking him for help. No one gets to see what's under this but me right now. I guess you don't want me to rip it?"

"It's pretty expensive, so no."

After an infuriating couple of minutes, Warrin exclaims success. It takes just as long to get all his pieces off before he's pinning me on top of his fluffy comforter. We kiss, soft and gentle until he pulls away.

One strong hand brushes my hair back from my face. "You're so beautiful."

"So are you, but let's talk about that later."

My patience for what's coming is thin, so I wrap my fingers in his hair and pull his lips back to mine. This time, our kiss is hungry. No hesitation threatens. I don't care if this means I'll be his as long as he still lives. All I care about is making him mine.

Practiced, his hand glides up my naked side to my breast. His thumb brushes over my nipple, forcing a moan from my throat. Soft lips move to my neck, but my attention is all on the fingers pinching the hard nipple. My hands run over his back, resting on his ass for a good squeeze. He nips my neck.

Warrin's hard shaft rubs against my lower thigh, and I find myself angry at the height difference. I want to touch it, but my arms don't reach. Determined, I surprise my polar bear by pushing him over. As soon as I'm straddling his hips, my hands are wrapped around the length of him.

Warrin groans. "Keep doing that, and I'm not going to last very long during the actual mating." Before I can argue, he flips me back over. "We can go back to that position later if you'd like, but I need access to your neck."

To prove that point, he buries his lips in the space between my jaw and shoulder. Warrin turns out to be more flexible than it seems when he manages to arch his back to put his tip at my entrance without moving his lips from my neck.

"Last chance to back out," he pants. "No going back from this point."

Instead of using words to answer, I wrap my legs around his hips to slide his length into my warm wetness. He moans, almost collapsing on top of me. I continue pushing him into me until I'm as full as I can get.

For a few moments, we simply enjoy the feeling of our bodies connected as they are. The stretch is perfect, and Warrin is in no hurry. After a bit, he starts moving in and out. Pleasure explodes through me with each gentle thrust. The fact he's a gentle lover doesn't surprise me. I'll relish the care he takes in making me feel good.

One of his hands moves to my breast as his lips continue to add warmth to my neck. I gasp and arch my back as my body tenses. This time, I don't hold back, remembering Warrin's earlier words.

I release my torrent of pleasure, riding the wave over the cliff. I cry out, shuddering and gasping as my body gives way to the pleasure of having my polar bear inside of me. Warrin releases, and I feel him bite down on my neck. It doesn't hurt. Instead, stars flash before my eyes as my body takes the plunge again. I have no idea what he just did, but I'll accept the burning running through my veins any day.

Warrin rolls off. "My arms were feeling weak. I didn't want to crush you."

"That's all it took?"

"Yep. You're mine now, and I'll treasure you for the rest of my life."

I take a deep breath, inhaling the scent of my polar bear. He's mine, and I'm his. There are no regrets. Love floods every corner of my body and soul. This bear is mine.

WARRIN

My hand travels up my mate's side and back down. She moans in her exhausted sleep. Eddie's skin is so soft. Her entire body is perfect and warm. Mating was more than I ever imagined, and I can't believe how lucky I am to have her.

Soft snores escape her throat. I stare at her, unable to look away. I've wanted this since I first saw her in the cell. Every part of my body screams that it's my duty to protect her, now and before. She's mine.

Eddie's dark eyes flutter open. "Anyone ever tell you it's not polite to stare?"

Worried I erred, I turn away. "I'm sorry. You just look so beautiful that I couldn't help myself. I didn't mean to offend you."

A soft hand touches my cheek and pulls my face back to hers. "I'm only teasing, my gentle giant."

"I like that nickname."

She laughs, a sound I long to hear for the rest of my days. "It fits you perfectly. Did you see the other two when you programmed my phone?"

I chuckle. "Yeah. Those fit them perfectly too."

"Can I ask you something? I feel weird asking."

"You're not at all weird. You can always ask me anything."

"Did you bite me?"

My mind cycles through what she's asking. "Yeah. That's part of the mating process."

"Oh. I thought I felt it, but I wasn't sure. I was in the middle of a euphoric event."

My heart skips a beat. I satisfied her as much as she did me. There is a lot more to learn, but I know some of the things that make her gasp and moan. I was so worried about not doing this right. I apparently did better than alright.

Eddie starts kissing me greedily again. My length instantly hardens. I moan and pull her tight. She pushes me over to straddle my waist. "Let's try this way."

"Yes, please."

This time, I truly understand what a euphoric event is.

CHAPTER TWENTY ONE
SEARCHING FOR SAFETY

Bright sunlight heats the inside of the car enough to make my sweater feel like too much, even in the chill of the season. I crane my neck to look out over the bright blue sky above. The yellow orb turning the darkness into a world of light is clear of the fluffy white clouds covering other parts of the sky. My breath mists on the glass, but I don't bother to wipe the fog out of my way. I rest my head on the window.

A large hand wraps around mine. Blinking, I lift my head and look at the polar bear I gave the rest of my life to. Warrin's typical bright smile radiates more warmth than the sun beating down on us. His blond hair is even messier than his normal fluff. Blue eyes shine with happiness.

"I wish I didn't have to take you back," he says. "We're basically married by human standards."

"I know, and I want to stay with you. Lex needs to hear it in person, and I need to pack. It may take a few days for me to be ready."

My happiness sours. Lex isn't going to like this. I don't really want to leave him either. I'm not sure what I should do. Warrin is right; we're basically married—something I never expected to happen in my lifetime. How do I explain that to my best friend and roommate? I can't just say that I had sex with a bear and now belong to him. Humans don't act like this. We date for years, get engaged, and maybe move in with each other, then we get married. I haven't known Warrin that long. Explaining the need to follow my intuition is never enough.

"You seem sad. Did I do something wrong?" Warrin asks.

I take a deep breath. "No. It's just the end of one stage of life and onto the next."

"Do you regret it?"

"Not one bit, but I'll miss Lex. We've been friends since we first learned to ride bikes. We're all the other has ever had. I feel bad deciding to leave him so suddenly. It's terrible that I never even thought about him before I made the decision."

"He can come too. We have extra rooms he can stay in. You can even stay with him and just spend your nights with me, or us if you decide to go that route."

"You have extra rooms in an office building?"

"Sure. Draven took the top floor. Anders has the second from the top. I have the third. The floor under is empty. It can be set up to have two bedrooms easily."

I bite my lip and turn my gaze back to the people walking around on the sidewalk. "How do you expect to keep your secret with him so close?"

"We are close to humans all the time without giving ourselves away. It would be fine."

Warrin doesn't get how hard it is for me to keep lying to Lex. His compromise is sound, but I can forget about the bears when they're not right in my face. Putting us on the next floor down from the three of them will be a constant reminder, which can make it harder to resist the urge to tell Lex. The weight of all three bears will weigh down on me from above.

Not like you didn't have the weight of one bear on top of you multiple times last night. What's two more?

I close my eyes to the thought. What would that be like? Warrin is as gentle with lovemaking as he is with everything else. Anders seems like he would be bossy, maybe a little dominating. He's used to being in charge. Draven might be a little rough. The thoughts of both those traits in bed with me and Warrin send pleasant shivers up my spine.

"You really wouldn't mind if I invited the other two into our bed?" Well, I didn't expect to ask that question, but it's out now. I look at Warrin from the corner of my eye, noticing the question takes him by surprise but doesn't make him angry or jealous.

"Of course. We became allies, then brothers. Bears may prefer to be alone, but when we attach ourselves to another, it's a deep connection. All we need is for you to want more. As long as I have plenty of time with my mate, I don't mind if she chooses to take on the rest of my brothers. Just more to make you happy."

Make me happy. It's clear to me that Warrin is focusing on that part. He wants a happy mate. Happy wife, happy life doesn't fit here. Would it be happy mate, happy fate? Either way, I want him to be happy too. Still, the thought of all three giving me attention all at the same time sends a thrill through me. I've never thought of anything like this, but the possibility is panty-wetting material.

By the time I push the thoughts away, we pull up to the front door of the apartments. Warrin grabs my hand and pulls to get my attention. "Think of it this way: if you and Lex live in the rooms beneath mine, you won't have so many expenses to worry about, so more of your payments from us can go to the charities of your choice."

"Master manipulator," I say with a grin. When Warrin's smile turns to concern, I squeeze his strong hand. "I was only teasing, my gentle giant. You would never manipulate me. Let me talk to Lex. Give me a few days because he's going to be distraught that I told him I was spending the night with you before turning my phone off completely. It'll take some convincing."

"Actually, we're a bit nervous about leaving you two for the weekend. We'd like to invite both you and your friend to the cabin."

My heart soars at the thought of spending unprofessional time with all three. It sinks when I remember why. Danger waits in the shadows—and my laundry room—and they can't keep an eye on us while they're away. A sour taste in the back of my throat makes me grimace. While going away with the men seems like a great idea, I'm not sure I can talk Lex into it. There's no wifi.

I don't want to be in danger though. "I will talk to him. For sure, I'm coming, but Lex is... hard to convince at times. He's not a huge people person."

"I've noticed. I'll call you later."

Warrin leans across the center console to give me a kiss with a small taste of tongue. I savor his flavor and breathe in his musky scent. Ever since last night, I feel like I could pick his scent out of a crowd. It's exhilarating. Is this what he feels when he smells me near? I'm intoxicated.

After our goodbyes, I slip out of my seat. Warrin refuses to move until he sees me into the building and then the elevator. The steel box lurches upward, catching and jerking only twice on the way up. I step onto the dirty hallway carpet. Mrs. Barlow is going at it with Mr. Elsher again. Neither animal is in sight, so I squeeze between the man and the wall behind them. Something sticky grabs the fabric of my dress, and I wince at the thought I won't be able to sell or donate the garment if it stains.

Once past, I leave the argument behind and use my keys to unlock the door. Of course, when I turn the knob, the cheap slab of wood decides to stick. I press harder, grumbling a threat to Lex if he used the chain. The door gives way. With a yelp, I find myself flying forward until I faceplant on our rough carpet. Mrs. Barlow exclaims from my doorway, apparently giving up her rivalry to check on me.

"You shouldn't lay on the floor like that while wearing a dress. You're showing the world everything," the old woman says.

Glancing down shows me that the bottom of my dress hiked almost to my hip. The old woman glares at my state of undress, not caring about my welfare over my wardrobe malfunction. Her stained robe hangs open. A purple nightgown reaches from above her collarbone to her ankles but seems oddly crumpled at the bottom.

"I apologize, Mrs. Barlow," I say, climbing to my feet. "It was an accident."

"Ladies don't have accidents that reveal themselves to the world. You should have worn a more appropriate dress. I thought better of you. Always so sensible."

The elderly woman turns to stomp away, revealing that her nightgown is tucked in her underwear as the robe shifts. I did not need to see that. If accidents don't happen to ladies, I think Mrs. Barlow needs to check herself a bit better. When I turn around with a small wobble, I find Lex glaring at me from the couch.

My fingers wiggle in a wave. "Hey."

As I close the door, I listen to the silence. Lex waits until I turn back around. "What the hell is wrong with you? You barely know the man."

I roll my eyes. "I've had how many one-night stands without you nagging me, Lex."

"This is one of your bosses that you tried to rob not long ago."

"I think I may recall that. After all, it's highly possible I was there that night."

Lex huffs. "You left with a strange man that happens to sign very large paychecks that we give to others. You went home with him, sent me a cryptic message that was easily decipherable, then turned your phone off. I've been worried sick, so leave your sarcasm out the door."

"Cryptic and easily decipherable don't seem like adjectives that should be used together."

"Eddie..."

I sigh, plopping down on the couch without a thought for flashing my best friend. My purse thumps onto the table. Using my toes to kick off my shoes, I lean back against the couch with my arms out. Clancy jumps up onto my lap. He sniffs, then purrs. I wonder if he smells Warrin on me because the cat seems to like him a lot. He's usually pretty indifferent.

"Warrin would never hurt me," I say into the tense silence. "If anything, he's dedicated to protecting me. I can take company with whoever I wish to. Speaking of, where's the friend that's usually attached to your hip?"

"I told Jared to go home because I need to test some of the new systems put in place. If you have forgotten, you have people trying to kill you for these men. They go away every weekend. How safe do you actually think you are?"

"Well, I'm heading back out to the cabin with them this weekend. You're invited." Silence answers me, so I open an eye and look over at Lex to see him staring at me with his mouth and eyes wide. I purse my lips and allow him the time to process what I just asked before continuing. "I think you should come with me. These men are threatening me, but I'm sure they consider you an obstacle as well. Come with me."

He shakes his head. "Unlike you, I won't put myself in a position where no one can hear me scream. You could be murdered and buried in the snow. No one would ever find you."

"They're not going to kill me, Lex."

Not that I didn't think the same before I left last weekend or when I stumbled upon a half polar bear man. He doesn't need to know that, particularly not while he's trying to convince me that being alone with them is dangerous. No need to give him more ammo to freak out over.

"I'm not going," he says.

"Please? I really want to make sure you're safe."

"Likewise, but you don't listen to me." I sigh and give him an exaggerated pout. He only shakes his head. "Not going to work any better than the time you tried to get me to risk breaking my neck on that monster during Christmas when we were ten."

"It wasn't a monster, Lex. It was a horse. Your aunt was kind enough to take us both horseback riding, and you ran away screaming."

"I don't scream."

"Not how I remember it."

"I don't," he says with a glare. "And I'm not going to go to a strange cabin with you."

If I can't even get him to go to the cabin, how will I talk him into the safety that comes from our new offer for lodgings? I'll need to consider this. "I will worry over you endlessly."

"Then you'd know how I feel. Don't look at me like that. I'll spend the weekend with Jared. His mom will let me crash on the couch."

I open my mouth to argue before closing it with a pop. He's not going to budge on this. At least at Jared's, he won't be alone. Safety in numbers. Not only does Jared live with his parents, but his older gun-toting junky of a brother does as well. If my friend will be safe anywhere, it will be there. I'll have to trust him. With a groan, I stand to make my way toward a hot shower before starting my day of calling experts to confirm next week's appointments.

CHAPTER TWENTY TWO
MAKING PIZZA

My mind keeps returning to watching Lex walk from our apartment before me. It was clear he thought my precautions and anxiety were over-the-top, but I couldn't help it. I need my best friend to be safe. I'd feel better if he was here with me. He's not, and I can't dictate what he does. I can only hope he's safe with Jared for the weekend.

Silence stretches beneath the thrum of rotating blades. Warrin grabs my hand, sensing my inner turmoil. I hate that I've brought danger into Lex's life—more than we already had—but I hate upsetting Warrin more. Sighing, I lean over and place my head on his shoulder. He lets go of my hand to wrap his arm around me. I breathe deep, taking comfort from his musky scent and once more wondering why I didn't smell it before.

Glancing at Anders shows me warmth in his brown eyes. The desire I see makes me swallow. It's not enough to make me break eye contact. As foreign as the idea is, I can see myself giving into him as well. My forwardness makes him smile, and he releases me by looking out the window.

My gaze travels to Draven. He watches me with a sense of curiosity. The usual disdain is gone from his dark eyes. Instead, I see an emotion similar to what I'd guess deep consideration would look like. Can he tell I'm committed to Warrin now? It's what he said he wanted in the elevator that day. Does that mean he's considering me worth giving attention to?

Why can't I keep my mind from having the three of them all at once? Isn't Warrin enough? Looking up at my gentle giant swells my heart. No. The polar bear is definitely enough. That doesn't mean I can't crave more.

The chopper landing jars me to my bones. We're here. The danger is there. Lex is there as well. I need to push my worries from my mind. Otherwise, I'm going to have a miserable weekend with no sleep.

When I ready myself to the exit, Warrin lifts me to place my feet steadily on the snow-covered ground. The men pick up all the luggage, including mine, and make their way toward the fancy cabin. I have to admit; I am happy to be back. While I'm not much for settling in environments that are opulent, I enjoy this large cabin. It feels good to be back. Is it strange that it feels like home?

Hurrying, I follow Warrin's broad back, hypnotized by his clenching backside. The thought of being mostly alone with him for the weekend twists my stomach in knots and weaves an ache through me. I have a feeling that I'm going to enjoy this weekend so much that I'll have no choice but to try to find a reason that will make Lex understand and agree to us moving. Maybe the saving money part will be a good way to go.

Draven watches me from the porch with a knowing smirk on his face. It's wicked and delicious. Heat climbs in me, not at all from embarrassment. Why can't I get control over my body? This is going to be a long weekend, even without Lex to worry about. What have I gotten myself into?

As I pass the dark-haired man, he inhales as if sniffing me. My mind goes back to other things said, both in the laundry room and Draven himself. Since I accepted Warrin's proposal of mate, do I smell different now? Did Warrin tell them, or do they just automatically know I decided to let him call me his for the rest of our lives?

Once again, I'm stunned at the beauty and rustic feel of the cabin, enough to shake me from my thoughts. Warrin leans in close while I stare with my mouth open like this is my first time here. "Would you object to me putting your bags in my room?"

The insinuation that he would think I don't want to spend the night with him breaks me from my childish stupor. "Of course, I want to stay with you."

His smile is reward enough, and I give him a soft kiss on the lips. "Tonight then?"

I nod, unable to form words. This feeling is unfamiliar to me. It's not like Warrin is my first partner, but I find the thought of sleeping in bed with him thrilling. It makes no sense. Whatever the reason, I don't care. I'm going to enjoy my time here and let myself drown my worries in an attentive polar bear shifter.

While the men set up their rooms, I'm told to make myself comfortable. My knees are weak, so I decide it's great advice. I can help when I stop acting like some innocent schoolgirl. The first armchair I plop into isn't very comfortable. The cushion is too firm and digs into my tailbone. My ass will definitely go numb on this thing. I try another to find the opposite problem. I let out a squeak as I sink so far into the chair that I'm not sure I'll be able to climb out again.

Warrin's laughter precedes his return. "That chair belongs to Anders."

"Whose is that one? Because I can tell you it's not very comfortable."

"Draven's. Here, try mine with a little extra support."

He lifts me out of the chair that I swear is trying to digest me, carries me over to the one I haven't sampled yet, and sits me on his lap. Since he doesn't take the initiative, probably because he's afraid of upsetting me, I pull his strong arms around me. I can sit here all day.

"This seat is just right," I say, looking up and kissing the bottom of his jaw.

My polar bear growls, a sound that I'll do anything to hear more. I contemplate what else I can do to hear it again when Draven walks past. "Get a room, you two."

"We have one," I counter. "It's called Warrin's room."

I refuse to act shy with my affections for this man. With everything they've said to me about their people's sexual habits, they don't deserve perceived innocence. Warrin is mine, and I'll claim him however I want. If anything, I hope to make the others a little envious tonight.

Anders lifts a cooler into the kitchen to put things away. When he gets ready to make supper, I hop off Warrin's lap. "Let me help."

The muscular man looks back at me. "No need. Let us treat you."

"You've treated me enough. You can make me happy now by letting me help."

Draven coughs out a chuckle and places a few bottles of liquor in the cabinet. "How much do you know about feeding bears, Mutt?"

"Well, from what I've seen, you eat what I eat. The only difference is the quantity. I didn't say I wanted to cook it all. I'll work beside you."

"Suit yourself."

I rub my hands together. "What's on the menu?"

Warrin walks up behind me, as if being too far from me is hard on him. "Inspired by you. Homemade pizza."

"Yum. I am totally on board with that."

"Surprise. Surprise," Draven says.

Ignoring him is becoming easier as the days go by. Instead of responding, I set in to help measure ingredients for multiple square pans. I turn and toss flour at Warrin, which leads to

Anders taking over when I'm tackled. Thanks to our shenanigans, it takes twice as long as needed to get the pizzas in the oven. None of the men complain that we don't sit down and eat until the sky is dark.

Afterward, I'm not allowed to help clean up, even though the vast majority of the mess on the floor is mine. I settle on my stool to watch them work. As usual, watching the way they move and work together is fascinating. These are three men who are so comfortable with each other that they're willing to share anything. Warrin has told me many times that he'd be honored to share a mate with his brothers but no one else. I'm still having issues wrapping my head around it all.

That doesn't mean I don't daydream as I watch muscles flex under shirts while they clean for me. It's like I've hit the jackpot.

It isn't long before the kitchen is sparkling. Warrin hops onto the stool next to me, laughing when I giggle and brush flour from behind his ear. "Would you mind if the three of us go for a run in our other form?"

"Of course. Bears will be bears." Never thought I'd say that.

"Since you know what we are," Draven interrupts with a drawl, "I'm assuming we can go ahead and shift in the backyard instead of hiding away in the forest."

"Your property." My shrug makes him grin. I've had an entire week to get used to the fact these men have an animal side. I'm still unbelieving at times, but I know what I saw and trust what they tell me. "Do I get to watch?"

"Window shopping?" Draven asks.

"If you flaunt it, you can't deny me a look."

Draven shakes his head while Anders laughs. Warrin kisses my cheek. "We want you to fully understand us, so you're free to watch. I hope you realize that means you'll see all of us naked."

Images swirl, and I feel my cheeks heat. "I can handle it. You all don't mind?"

"One, you have already seen me naked and will many more times. Two, shifters don't view nudity the same as humans. It helps that we've grown up getting naked to let our wild side out."

"Makes sense."

The men stand to move to the back sliding door, and I jump off my stool to follow. They wait patiently while I put my boots and coat on. Of course, they don't need any of it. Excitement at what I'm about to witness overwhelms me; not just the bear part. I must be crazier than I thought.

At least it's by choice this time. The men walk out onto the deck and down the stairs. I stay up high, white puffs of breaths floating up into the darkness. The lights on the side of the house leave a small ring of brightness that fights off the shadows of the night.

The men make sure to stand where I can see the transformation. Warrin strips first. Like that night last weekend, I watch his face grow a snout at white hair springs all over his body. The familiar shapes disappear beneath fluffy hair.

Once Warrin is done, Anders strips. I can't help but wonder if they always transform one at a time or if this is a show for me. As his clothes come off, I find my eyes hungry for the sight of him. His muscles gleam in the low light. I drink it *all* in and wonder what it would be like to become his mate as well. His transformation is faster, leaving a large grizzly bear standing where he is.

Draven strips slowly, as if he's giving me a show to watch. And watch I do. His lithe muscles twitch and tense. Bend and soften. I'm mesmerized. Like he knows what I'm thinking, he turns to give me the full nude view. My breath stops. His chuckles reach me over the quiet air before a black bear stands in his place.

My feet move as if they have a mind of their own. The other two hang back, but my polar bear walks over to me. He chuffs, and I reach out a cautious hand while wondering how wild he is in this form.

Warrin's broad head bumps into my palms. I run my fingers through his thick hair. Familiar icy eyes close as a rumble sounds in his chest. Feeling brave, I lean forward to plant a kiss on his nose.

The rumble sounds again. I step back to tell him to join Draven and Anders, who are almost to the tree line. Maybe this interaction is a mate thing. I hope to share it with all of them someday.

Long after they disappear, I stand and watch where they vanished until the cold pushes me back inside. I'm determined to stay awake, so I snuggle into Warrin's covers and play a game on my phone while I wait. In the end, the excitement of the last week and the warmth of his covers drive me into a deep slumber.

CHAPTER TWENTY THREE
THE PERFECT BED

I stretch big in the bright sunlight streaming through the thin white curtains. A yawn bursts free from me, louder than I wanted to let it be. I can't remember the last time I've slept so well. Blinking clears my vision enough to make me remember where I am, and rolling over shows me an empty other side of the bed. I frown.

"He didn't wake me when he came home," I mumble into the emptiness.

Warrin's side is messed up, so I know he came to bed last night. I was hoping for a pleasant waking in the middle of the night. Plans were made. Disappointment is heavy in my chest. He is going to need to make this up to me, which should be fun. I guess it's a win.

A heavy bladder forces me from the warmth of the covers. I straighten the sheets and comforter, change from my shorts into sweats, then throw a sweater over my tank top before rushing to the bathroom. In the bathroom, I also run a brush through my hair. I should shower, but I want to see what kept my polar bear from initiating a little fun before I clean myself.

Exiting the bathroom, I inhale the heavy scent of bacon and eggs. Even better, the bitter coffee smell is beginning to interlace itself in the food. I could use a little caffeine. As I pass the next room—belongs to Anders, I believe—I hear voices. I pause and peek around the half-open door to see Warrin poking around at the owner of the room's back. I take a moment to watch the glory of bright light shining over the bulky muscles under Warrin's hands.

"They're healing well," Warrin says, "so not a shifter."

"Confirms the scent then."

Anders glances over to see me staring. I jump and feel my cheeks grow warm. "I'm sorry. I didn't mean to spy on you. The voices drew me to look."

"It's fine, Darlin. Why don't you come in?"

My heart thumps at the new nickname Anders calls me. He's never used anything other than Eddie when speaking to me, besides Edith until I explained that I don't like my full name. I lick my lips and take a step in at his invitation, leaving the door half closed.

When I walk over to them, I notice long red marks running down his back. "What happened?"

"Mountain lion got brave last night," Anders said.

I look up at Warrin. "You mentioned something about a shifter?"

He shakes his head in answer. "It was a regular mountain lion. Our kind heals faster than humans, but wounds from another shifter can cause issues. He's healing like he should, so not a shifter."

"Good." I reach out, running my fingers down the almost healed wounds. Anders sucks in a sharp breath. "Does that hurt? I'm sorry."

"Not pain," Anders says. "Your delicate touch just sent chills over me. It takes more than a cat to hurt a bear."

Walking around the men, I plop down on the soft bed. When I sink down, my legs come off the floor. "This is as soft as your chair."

Anders chuckles. "You should try Draven's. It's hard as stone."

I scrunch my nose. "No, thank you. I like Warrin's bed. It's perfectly in between hard and soft. Just right."

The grizzly shifter leans down, pushing my hair behind my ear before bringing his fingers down to run along my jaw. "You don't like being in my bed?"

My breath hitches. I look around Anders to see Warrin watching us with a smile. No matter how many times he tells me about his willingness to let me have the other two as well, I find it hard to believe. Men tend to be possessive, in my experience. This is a whole new feeling for me, one that's not at all unpleasant.

"I didn't say that," I whisper, unable to make my voice louder.

"Does my touch bother you?" All I can do is shake my head, which makes him grin. "How about this?"

His lips touch mine in a commanding embrace while his hand cups the back of my head. My hesitation is momentary, only until I remind myself that Warrin says he wants this for us. His tongue pushes to demand entrance, and I allow it. Anders takes control, guiding my tongue with his. Heat builds in me, threatening to burst at any moment.

As he pulls away, I feel the bed dip. I find Warrin sitting next to me, his smile consuming his face. I open my mouth to make sure he's okay, but he takes over where Anders left off to silence any questions. Anders moves to nibble my neck, and I gasp into Warrin's mouth. Strong hands lift my sweater. Warrin moves enough to pull it off, then goes back to consuming my lips with hunger as soon as the obstacle is gone.

Strong hands that I can only assume belong to a grizzly run over my sides over the tank top. He moves his hands up, stroking the sensitive skin under my breast. A whimper escapes without permission. The next time Warrin pulls away, it's to let the thin cloth covering me be pulled up. An ache builds when wet warmth embraces my nipple. My head falls back, so my polar bear moves his gentle kisses to my throat.

When a hand kneads the unattended breast, I can tell for sure the previous touch belonged to Anders. I would know the feel of Warrin's fingers blindfolded. Where his touch is gentle, the other's is firm and commanding. The sensation of having both is almost too much, forcing a moan out of me.

Warrin pushes me gently down onto the mattress. He gazes into my eyes with such love that I feel tears prick at the corners. As the grizzly bear tugs on my sweatpants, my polar bear caresses my cheeks and runs his fingers through my hair. All my attention is focused on the love I see in those icy blues. I've never known love before, so it's a little overwhelming.

All thoughts are blown away when Anders positions my legs on his shoulders and runs his tongue from my entrance to my clit. My back arches, and Warrin brings his mouth down to a hard nipple. His one hand continues to cup my cheek as his other pinches the other pebbled peak. Thanks to our foreplay and the double attention, I already find myself on the edge. My body fights for release, but I grasp the edge as if my life depends on it.

Anders circles my clit with his tongue and thrusts two fingers deep. My body trembles with the sensation, the warmth flooding me until I feel like I'm melting. A whimper escapes, and I can hold back no more. I cry out, digging my fingers into Warrin's shoulders as he continues to give my nipple needed attention. My body clenches around Anders's fingers as my body shudders. Moans turn to gasps as I crest over the wave of pleasure, crashing down.

Warrin rolls on top of me when Anders moves. "Would you like more?"

"Please."

His hands run up my thigh, and my ache rebuilds within seconds. Anders moves to kneel beside his bed. The bulge in his pants pulls my attention. I reach for it, but he grabs my hand to kiss it the same time Warrin's fingers make me moan. "No, Darlin. As I said last night, let us treat you."

"What about you?"

"This is all about you." He kisses each fingertip.

"But—"

The words are forgotten when Warrin positions his head at my entrance and gently fills me. My fingers curl around his hand while the others fist the comforter. Anders turns my head, leans over, and kisses me as Warrin thrusts in and out. My body tightens again. Anders allows my death grip on his hand to remain, but the other moves between our writhing bodies. His finger reaches down to circle my clit, and white flashes through my vision. I'm seriously seeing stars.

I can't hold back this time. The moment my body clenches around Warrin's cock, he grunts and lets go with me. I call his name, only muffled by the grizzly's mouth. Once my second orgasm finishes, Warrin lies down and pulls my back against his chest. Anders crawls into the bed in front of me. His hand runs down my arm as I try to catch my breath.

"I can tell you enjoyed that," Anders says with a pleased growl. "There's plenty more where that came from when you're ready for it."

Panting, I can't speak. Instead, I reach out and run my fingers over the hard planes of his chest. Both of these bears are perfect in every way. If Lex doesn't approve of me and Warrin, what would he think of me now? In the end, I decide it's none of his business. I want this. I want to be loved by two men, three if he'll let me. My loveless life is now full of men that want nothing but me. It's perfect. I no longer harbor any inhibitions. No reluctance. No shame. These men want me and only me.

"If you three are done, breakfast is ready," a cocky voice calls from the doorway.

Looking over, I see Draven watching me with a hunger that isn't for the food cooling downstairs. When he catches me looking at him, he flashes his signature sneer before ducking back behind the door.

"I guess he probably heard that," I say.

"Bears have excellent hearing," Anders answers. "Not to mention a great sense of smell. Both probably alerted him to what was going on up here."

"He could smell that?"

"Don't worry." Warrin nuzzles the back of my neck, sending chills over me. "It's a pleasant smell, one that's hard to control ourselves around."

"He looked interested," I say. "Until he didn't."

Anders chuckles. "Don't worry about Draven. He knows what he wants. He's just stubborn. Most black bears are."

"So his attitude is a black bear thing?"

"Among other issues. He'll come around, and I predict it won't be long. Should I assume this means you accept us as a whole?"

I chew my lip, nodding after a few seconds. "It's odd thinking I'm going to be partnered with three men. It's not something I ever expected."

"Just imagine what three of us can do."

A shiver runs up my spine at the thought. "Do we have to go all the way to cement it?"

"There will be time for that to come. Right now, enjoy the attention we give you," Warrin says. "Ease you in, so to speak."

"I like to plan ahead," I say.

Anders brushes a sweaty tendril behind my ear. "Yes. You will need to have sex with each of us, then all of us, to finish the bond."

My eyes widen, which makes him chuckle. He assures me it won't happen until I feel ready, then climbs off the bed and slips a shirt on. I rush to get dressed and take a very quick shower. My food may cool, but something tells me they'll still be eating by the time I get down there. I need to clean myself before eating.

The mug warms my hand as I sip the hot coffee. They managed to keep my food warm for me and are now cleaning up while I finish my coffee. Draven avoids looking right at me. I hope we don't build up tension and ruin the relationship these three have between them. Why is he still fighting me? What more proof does he need that I'm in this for the long haul?

Snow falls heavy outside the cabin, so the men decide that it is a good morning to sit in front of the fire and watch some movies. We're too far out to have any form of cable or streaming service, but they have a nice collection of DVDs. It's a wonderful way to spend the morning. Although, every time I look at Draven, I find his eyes on me instead of the TV.

CHAPTER TWENTY FOUR
TARGETS

After lunch, the sun shines bright once again. The men tell me it's typical for the weather to change this much in such a short time. It was sunny when I woke up, a blizzard when I got out of my shower, and sunny again. It's so different from the city. Almost magical. Alright, now I'm sounding like some animated princess. I need to back off the magic thoughts.

Maybe it's the delicious chocolate cake the men brought. That must be what's turning me mushy. There's nothing magical about life. There's something special about having the devotion of these men, but nothing magic.

Well, maybe a little supernatural. After all... bear shifters.

When I open my eyes after my weird contemplation, I find Warrin staring at me with a big smile. Confused, I pull the fork from my mouth while trying my best to get all the chocolate off with my lips. It's not until I see him eagerly watching the motion that I realize what has his attention. I flip the utensil over and drag it over my tongue. He grunts, which breaks the spell enough to make me laugh.

Draven rolls his eyes at our antics while Anders looks at us with fondness. I'll focus more on the latter reaction than the former. I like knowing someone is fond enough of me to brighten up so much. He's like a sun compared to the darkness of the black bear.

After seeing them last night, I can't help but think of them as my bears, even Draven. My men. My shifters. My bears. All mine. My eyes look over at the man with long, dark hair scrubbing a nonexistent speck of dirt from the counter. All mine eventually. I'm not sure when the determination hit, but I will have Draven as well. Call me greedy. There's something about him that turns me on. I simply need to convince him.

Anders pulls the fork from my lax hands, scraping the icing off the plate and turning the tables. Watching his tongue reminds me of our time upstairs, and heat climbs within me. Okay. This is only fair when I'm the one doing it. By the grin he flashes at me, I can tell he knows exactly what he's doing to me. Can they smell that too?

"Get your boots and coat on," Warrin says beside me.

"What?"

"Hike. Let's go."

"The sky just dumped a foot of snow."

"Makes it more fun."

"I—"

Warrin lifts me from the stool. Giving in, I make my way over to grab my coat and boots. I'm surprised to find the air isn't as bitter as I expected. There's a definite chill, but it's windless. The sun gives the deception of warmth well enough that I don't feel like I'm freezing. Warrin engulfs my hand in his, which makes it feel even warmer. Careful not to fall, I put one foot in front of the other until I'm off the stairs. Draven brushes past without looking back.

Anders leans in close. "Let us know if you get too cold and need to be warmed up."

Gulping, I nod my understanding. He follows after Draven, and Warrin pulls me along. Everything has a layer of sparkly white over it. It's beautiful. Beauty like this doesn't visit the city often. If it snows, the whiteness turns into grayish-brown slush. I can see why they come out here every weekend, besides the bear thing.

Most of the trees are brown and dead, ugly if not for the snow that clings to them. Some are evergreen, full of prickly needles and some with pinecones still. A twig snaps to the left, and I turn to see a doe watching from behind some brush. I stop and stare, sure my mere presence will send her running. She only watches, ears twitching with the movement of the two ahead of us.

"Why doesn't she run?" I ask.

"She would if you moved too much. For the most part, she's more wary of us because we smell and move like predators."

When Draven trips and yells, the deer turns and hops over a fallen log. Soon, all I can see is the white of her tail as she flees. Although I was reluctant at first, I don't regret giving in. This is a part of the world I've never seen before. How can these men change my perspective so much in such a short time? Nature is—I refuse to say magical—stunning.

To think such life and peace exists outside the environment I grew up in. When we come to a frozen pond, I gasp in wonder. All cold ceases to exist in my state of constant wonder. The shimmer of the sun on the ice creates a winter wonderland. Trees surround the frozen water, some even growing out of it. I stop by a pine to crouch down and look out over the ice.

"Do you think it's frozen enough to stand on?" Warrin asks.

"I doubt it. It's cold but not that cold yet. Definitely not for us. Eddie possibly could, but it's not worth the risk," Anders answers.

"Why would you want—" My words stop when I notice all three men freeze and glance around, completely tense and alert.

I strain to see if I can sense what they do. None of them move, as if waiting for some silent signal. It isn't long before I hear a howl echoing in the frozen air. More pick up the eerie sound and repeat it. Warrin turns to grip my waist. I argue as he lifts me toward the lowest branch of the tree beside me.

"Don't fight me on your safety, Eddie. I won't risk losing you. The pain of losing a mate is too strong. It took Anders years and the promise of vengeance to pull through," Warrin says.

His words tell me the danger he faces, and I cling to the branch in fear. Anders and Draven are already in bear form. I'm holding him back, so I nod my understanding. "Be careful."

"Always."

As Warrin starts to change, he's hit by a gray blur, thrown right out onto the ice. His heavy body slides out toward the center, then the ice gives way. My polar bear falls beneath the frigid water. "Warrin!"

I turn to yell for the other two to help, but they're fighting off a small group of wolves. My fear causes me to look between the two close and the hole where Warrin disappeared. One wolf jumps at the branch holding me. I scream and climb higher. A large branch breaks off under my hands, and I almost fall. The wolf jumps for me again.

Anders tries to reach me, but two more are on him before he can take more than a single step. He's too occupied fending off the attacks to help. The sound of violent cracking and splashing drags my eyes to the lake. My gentle polar bear climbs onto shore, taking my hopeful attacker by surprise and snapping its spine with his strong jaws. Not gentle in the protection of me. I breathe a sigh of relief to see him safe and alive, feeling stupid for thinking a polar bear couldn't survive an icy dip.

The polar bear chases one of the attackers a little before grabbing its hips and paralyzing it. In my excitement to see him winning the fight, my hand slides on the branch. I wrap both arms and legs around it to keep from falling. While I hate being stuck up here with no way to help, I'm not delusional enough to think I'd stand a chance on the ground. I'd be overwhelmed by teeth in a matter of seconds.

Draven stumbles backward until he's under me. He roars as he tries to shake a wolf off his back. It stubbornly holds on with claws and teeth. I see wet glistening on the bear's black fur, and I'm not sure if it's wolf slobber or blood. I fear that wetness is the latter of those two options. Desperate, I look around, my eyes falling on the broken branch that almost threw me into the jaws of a wolf.

Standing, I grip the wooden weapon and tug on it until it breaks free, almost losing it and my footing when it snaps off so suddenly. Crawling back down while holding the branch isn't easy, but I manage to find my way back onto my belly. I ignore the sap that's probably soaking my coat and the stickiness it leaves on my hands. When the black bear rears in an effort to make the enemy slide from its back, I stab down with the pointy end. My hopes to hit my mark and not Draven are met. The wolf yelps, rolls off, then lands with a thud.

It's unfortunate that the movement makes me slide sideways because I find myself falling. I land on top of the injured animal. It snaps at me, making me scramble away before standing. I swing the branch like a club until the wolf stops moving. Draven growls at me and pushes me until I'm standing against the frozen lake. He positions himself between me and any possible attacker.

As soon as the wolves notice my feet are on the ground, some leave the others to keep Anders and Warrin busy while swarming Draven. His giant black paws swipe back and forth while his teeth score flesh. Two wolves fall. A third almost gets past him. A fourth does. I swing the branch, trying to keep the deadly animal back. Nothing connects, but it watches the weapon with wary eyes, looking for an opening.

I don't realize I'm backing up until ice under my feet throws me down. The ice breaks when I hit. Only my butt gets wet thanks to how shallow the lake is at this point. Damn, that's cold. A light gleams in the wolf's eyes when it sees me fall. I lift the pointy end of the branch when it launches at me. Splintered wood cuts into my would-be murderer's shoulder. It snarls and falls to the side, grabbing the branch with its mouth and tearing it from my hands. Pain registers, but my eyes are on the triumphant flash in my enemy's hungry gaze.

This time, when it lunges, I have no protection. Anders jumps between us, swatting the wolf's head hard enough to crack its skull. The animal falls onto the ice. Looking around shows me all the wolves are dead. I'm too tired to count, but there are a lot of dead wolves. Warrin walks over in human form, pulling me from the hole my rear end made in the ice. The hike's over, so we make our way back toward the cabin. Anders and Draven remain in bear form while a nude Warrin helps me walk shivering between them.

My gentle giant takes me inside. The other two follow behind after shifting back. At this moment, I don't even feel like ogling their nakedness. The men look over their injuries. Draven has some angry gashes on his back that Anders takes the time to stitch closed. Warrin dabs at a deep wound where his shoulder meets his neck. All three are covered with smaller scratches and bites.

"Were they shifters?" I ask. Anders nods. My mind races over the conversation I heard this morning. "You said earlier that wounds caused by shifters cause you more issues. Do we need to call for an emergency evacuation?"

Anders sighs. "No. The wounds won't kill us or make us sick. They won't heal like normal injuries though. It will be faster than humans but still longer than normal. There's also a chance of infections."

Warrin walks over. "Are you hurt?"

I shake my head. "Just a little unsettled. They seemed to make me a target."

"They know I'm mated to you. Killing you will weaken me for a time."

My eyes find him, realizing what loving me may cost him. "I'm sorry."

"It's not your fault. I don't regret what we have and never will. I'm going to take a shower to help clean this gash out.

The others will probably need to as well. Sit in front of the fire to get warm."

I watch him climb the stairs with my teeth digging into my lower lip. It's not my fault, but mating me gave them a weakness to exploit. If I die, he'll be an easier target. I need to convince Lex to move. Safety is important. It won't be easy. How will I make Lex understand?

A roar and banging behind me startles me. I jump and spin to see Draven standing over the liquor he threw off the shelves. The acrid scent of the liquid covering the floor makes me grimace. The fury in his eyes forces me to take a step back.

"Calm yourself," Anders says.

"How can I? The bastards invaded our private retreat!"

"I know. They'll pay for this intrusion. We have to be smart about how."

"I'm way past slow and steady, Anders. They came after what's mine."

The look Draven sends me makes me wonder if I'm included in what he considers his. Without sparing us another glance, he stomps toward the stairs. Anders tells me to let him go cool off. He follows the dark-haired man with a sigh. I look between the upstairs railing and the fireplace in thought. Only one thing will take this chill from my bones.

WARRIN

The hot water streams over my body in rivers. As a polar bear, I usually like cold showers, but the heat is needed to clean my stinging wounds. The one on my shoulder is the worst. It'll heal, and the pain is manageable. It takes more than that to knock down a polar bear.

If only the steam and water could wash away the pain of near failure. I should have been more alert, more watchful. Anders would tell me it's on all of us. It's not. She's my mate. Her safety should be the top priority for me. Yes, the other two aspire to make her theirs as well, but she's not yet. Eddie is mine to love and protect. We got too close to losing her today.

My fist hits the stone of the shower wall, opening old wounds and smearing blood for the water to wash away. I have to do better. I need to keep her safe. Not just because it would weaken me to lose her, but because it's my duty. We pulled her into our world. I fell in love and made her feel the same. I must do better. What would Mama think? She loves Eddie as well, even though she only had a short time to get to know her. How couldn't she? Eddie is very easy to love.

The door clicks open, and the scent of glacial freshness reaches me. I straighten and look toward the blurred reflection of my mate through the frosted glass. She closes the door and hesitates for a second. After a moment, I watch her form lift the shirt over her head and remove her bra. Her bottoms are next, leaving me with a stronger sense of her delicious smell. This woman deserves the world.

At the shower door, she hesitates. "Can I join you, Warrin?"

I slide the door open and watch her avid appreciation as she looks up and down my naked body. "You're always welcome anywhere I am."

She smiles, turning my heart to mush. How am I such a lucky polar bear? I have the most beautiful woman in the world. A woman willing to risk her life and freedom in the pursuit of helping others. A woman who gave me her heart without question. All mine.

I step back to let her in. Once the door is closed, she grabs the soap and begins to wash me, careful of my wounds but thorough. I should be doing this for her, but it's clear Eddie wants to do this. There's nothing in this world I'll deny her.

Eddie attempts to look up at me, getting hot water in her eyes in the process. Her giggles make my heart skip a beat. Lifting her, I ignore the pull of my injured muscles to kiss her. She returns it with hunger, and I'm soon dealing with a hard cock. Not that I wasn't interested before. I was trying to be respectful.

She looks down at my hard shaft with a grin. "Sit," she orders.

"Why?"

"You're injured, so this is the best way. Now sit down, Mr. Polar Bear."

Unable to argue with her command, I plant myself down, realizing that the shower is just big enough for whatever she has planned. Eddie straddles my lap. She moves forward until my tip pokes into the bottom of her stomach. The mere touch of her body knocks the air from my lungs. Small hands run over my chest and behind my neck. Eddie leans forward for a kiss.

Her mouth tastes sweet and spicy at the same time, a flavor I want to explore more and more. My fingers find her breasts, kneading gently. Thumbs graze both her taut nipples at the same time. The sensation of her gasping into my mouth starts a rumbling in my chest. As soon as her hand circles my shaft, I'm paralyzed.

This sweet woman slides her wet warmth down over my length. I bury my face in her neck and moan. Nothing can feel better than being embraced inside my mate. I pepper her neck with kisses, finding out how wrong that previous thought is when she starts moving up and down. The bear inside me roars into existence.

Eddie pulls her neck away from my straining lips to engulf my mouth with hers, all while continuing to move up and down to send hot sensations over me. The whimper that escapes her sets all my senses on edge. The taste of her. The smell of her. The exquisite feel of her. I will never have enough.

Her body clenches around my dick, and I thrust upward to make sure she gets her fill while grunting my release. When we both come down from our high, Eddie leans her forehead against mine.

She whispers, "I love you."

The words embed themselves into my heart, unable to shake loose; not that I would ever want to. "I love you too, my mate."

She kisses me softly, showing me love instead of desire this time. I give back in kind, relishing all that is the woman that I love.

CHAPTER TWENTY FIVE
CONFESSIONS

Heavy snoring greets me when I open my eyes. Judging by the dimness from the window, I'm going to guess it's either cloudy or still early. My mind whirls over everything that's happened this weekend. I've fully committed myself to all three men. Enjoyed the attention of two of them at once. Been attacked by wolves. Called his by Draven. At least, I believe that's what he meant. I'm not sure how to feel about all my tumultuous emotions right now.

My head jerks up and down with a particularly loud snore from my gentle giant. I revel in the feel of him under my head, remembering that I admitted love to him yesterday. It feels too soon to utter those words, but I feel them with all my heart. Warrin is the easiest man to love. Do I feel the same about the other two?

Anders is a rock. He's confident, knowledgeable, and commanding. Above all else, he thinks of those under him as assets that deserve the best treatment. From the start, he didn't look at me as an obstacle to conquer. No, I became a useful asset. Now, I'm so much more to him. Love is close, but I'm not quite there yet. That won't stop me from giving myself to him.

Draven is more complicated. Love? Not even close. Fondness and desire? Stupidly, yes. Something deep down inside pulls me to the infuriating bear of a man. That something feels like it can develop into something beautiful, given the chance, but we have to get there first. Draven keeps shutting me out while also holding me close. It makes me dizzy.

Sighing, I tell myself these swirling thoughts don't need to be addressed right now. There's time, as long as we can take care of this threat. And there it is; me thinking of this situation in a sense of we. There's no doubt in my mind that I'm committed. If only the cranky one would realize that.

At this point, I realize there's no more sleep waiting for me. I lift slowly from my polar bear, unwilling to wake him up. I look out the window to see both clouds and the sunrise behind it. No need to wake him yet. My shower is less fun than the one I used to get warm with yesterday. It felt good to take care of my polar bear.

Out of the shower, I wipe the fog off the mirror and check to make sure I don't need to bleach again yet. I know it's only been a week, but I hate my dark roots. They're a reminder of my greatest failure as a daughter. Pushing the thought away, I bite my lip. Every day, I wonder why I continue to let my mother live in my head. I can't seem to get her out.

With a shake of my head, I step away, get dressed, then head out. When I peek in, Warrin is still snoring. No one is downstairs, so I have the whole floor to myself. Walking over to the fridge, I open it to browse. The contents give me an idea and a smile. I need coffee first.

Watching them cook all those times ensures I know my way around this kitchen. I pull out a couple of skillets and place them on the stove while the black liquid gold percolates. As soon as it's done, I pour a cup and get to work. Cracking eggs isn't a talent of mine, so I spend as much time removing shells as I do cracking them. They go into the larger skillet when scrambled. Next, I put bacon in the other pan to snap, crackle, and pop away.

It's not long until I hear movement going on upstairs. Doors open and shut. Floorboards creak. No one comes down yet.

Once the eggs and bacon are cooked, I take some soft tortilla shells out and line them up on the counter. Bacon, eggs, and cheese go on each one before I roll them and slide the breakfast burritos into the oven. I make toast until the stack is taller than me. By the time I remove the main course from the oven, Anders is walking up behind me.

Strong hands grasp my hips as he looks over my shoulders. My heart skips a beat. Anders breathes deep. "I thought I told you this weekend was for you to be spoiled."

The feeling of his breath tickling my neck causes a lump to form to keep me from answering. I swallow and clear my throat, finding myself leaning back into him without conscious thought. His hands rub down my thighs and back up to my hips. Anders plants a kiss on the side of my neck before stepping back and taking his warmth with him.

I take a deep breath to calm the raging heat that threatens to consume me. "I was up early because I couldn't sleep. It feels good to take care of my bears for once. Sit."

As I pour each man a mug of coffee and a glass of orange juice, the other two join us. Warrin touches his lips to my cheek before sitting. Draven watches me with one eyebrow raised. I give him a challenging look, daring him to make a smartass remark. He only throws a sarcastic smile my way before taking a sip of juice.

I settle on the empty stool between Anders and Warrin. After we finish eating, I'm happy to see that I made enough to make them happy. My polar bear wraps an arm around my hips. "We already packed up. I wasn't sure how you wanted to pack everything, so I didn't take that liberty. You go do that while we clean up. Leave the bags; I can get them when you're done. No need for you to lug them down the stairs."

Nodding my agreement while promising myself to carry my own bag, I finish the last of my liquid energy and slide from my stool. It takes me longer than should be necessary to gather my scattered clothing. I make my way to the bathroom to gather and dry my bath stuff. On the way back, I look out over the railing to see the three men chatting out on the deck. The sky remains cloudy, threatening snow but not promising it yet.

This is my chance to get my bag downstairs myself without sending Warrin into a panic attack, so I hurry back to the room and stuff my bathroom things into the bag. At the bottom of the stairs, I stop and look around. No one is visible outside the door any longer, and the bottom floor is empty. I drop my bag by the door, slipping my boots and coat on.

Outside, Draven relaxes in the hot tub, but the other two are nowhere to be seen. "Where are Anders and Warrin?"

"Patrolling the woods for any sign of wolves. I was left behind to babysit the mutt."

"I don't need a bodyguard, Draven."

"You did yesterday."

I bite back a haughty retort and instead say, "Well, a bear protects what's his."

Draven stretches his arms over the edge of the hot tub behind him. His lithe muscles flex and twitch with the movement. "When I said that to Anders, I meant our land."

"Sure you did."

He smirks, and I find irritation growing within me. It's clear he's preening in front of me as he flexes his shoulders. If he wants, two can play this game. I walk into the cabin, dig through my bags for the bikini I brought—learning my lesson for not having a bathing suit last time. Slipping into the downstairs bathroom, I ready myself.

Cold air blasts my half-naked skin when I return to the deck. Draven's eyes are on me, so I do my best to ignore the cold. His eyes drag down my body, then back up, stopping on what I'm sure are hard nipples due to this cold. Even though I want to hurry into the heat, I force myself to walk over slowly and slip one foot at a time into the water. I can't stop the sigh when I submerge myself in the warmth.

"Was the show worth the torture of freezing temperatures?" Draven asks.

I watch his body move with a smile. "By the way you're shifting your lower half, I think my walk over here was just as uncomfortable for you. What are you hiding under the water, Draven?"

He stands, showing me that he's completely naked. His shaft stands at attention. "I'm not hiding anything, Mutt."

I gulp. "You're naked."

"Very observant of you. I didn't feel I needed to hide. After all, you already enjoyed the show Friday night. Like what you see?"

"As much as you do when you look at me."

Draven's dark eyes flash. "How do you know what I feel?"

My eyes fall on his hard cock, one eyebrow raising to say it's obvious without voicing the reply. Draven moves to stand in profile, as if providing a better look. It shouldn't turn me on this much, but it does. His cocky attitude is both infuriating and wet panty inducing.

He leans down in front of me, closing the distance until his lips brush my ear. I can feel his cock press into my thigh. "Is this what you want? Yes, I find you attractive. Yes, I'd love to feel you on my dick. But here's the thing: I have greater self-control than my newfound brothers. I don't fall so easily, particularly not for a human. I've seen their worst side."

My body yearns for him to stay, but my mind wins out and pushes him back. "You work with humans."

"Out of necessity."

"What did we do to you that makes you hate us so much?"

Draven's teeth clench. "Your people killed my entire family."

My mouth goes dry at his words. He settles back into his seat. All the warmth of the jets swirling water around me can't touch the chill his confession brings. It's as if my veins turned to ice. "What happened?"

"What makes you think that's something that I'm willing to talk to you about?"

"You don't have to be an ass about it."

"Lose your entire family, then come to me and say that again."

"I'd have to have a family that cares about me before I could relate."

Draven is silent for a few seconds before speaking again. "Family is family. You should always treasure them because you don't know what you'll miss until they're gone."

I scowl at him. "Real original. I've never had people tell me that before. Funny thing is, they never told my mother that. I was nothing but a source of shame, the reason her life was miserable. Until you have toxic parents, you have no right to say anything to me about my feelings. Learn what it's like to be hated by your family, then come back to me and say that again."

His chin rises into the air. "Why does she hate you?"

"You think I had to do something to deserve it? I existed. That's all the reason she needed." I'll admit this isn't the first time I've heard that question. It's usually asked with a condescending tone, as if it has to be my fault; I had to do something wrong. How does being born make it my fault?

The black bear in human skin watches me for a few moments. I can see the wheels turning in his head but have no idea what he's thinking. I wait for the inevitable blame shifting; the shame thrown at me simply for not taking my mother's abuse anymore. No one ever understands. Lex is the only one who saw it. She was the perfect mother in public.

"My family and I were out in the forest outside the city one evening. It was still light out, but dusk was quickly approaching," Draven says.

I jerk in shock. No ridicule. No shame. No blame. Instead, he's talking about himself.

"We were enjoying the last bit of warmth before snow brought the cold in," he continues. "I was only ten at the time, but I was fiercely protective of my little sister. She ran off ahead, and I warned her to be careful. Mom and Dad were hanging back, sniffing at some berry bush they found. That's when I heard a human scream.

"The crack of gunfire echoed through the air, slicing into me as if the bullet hit me. I ran forward, but my mother was faster. We had to get to my sister. The only thing I can think that happened is she came upon the camper by accident. She was always a curious cub. She probably saw the human children and wanted to play with them. My sister loved making new friends. The mother saw her, screamed, and the father came out with his shotgun."

His voice breaks up. I want to reach out to him, but I'm not sure if he'd appreciate the action, so I hold back. Silence stretches between us. I wait for him to be ready to continue.

"She was lying in the dirt in front of their camper, twitching and bleeding out. The wound was too great for her body to heal. My mother went into a rage. They don't use 'mama bear' as a term to mean the protectiveness of a mother without reason. She rampaged. The shotgun blasted again. Dad came from beside, swatted the gun out of the man's hand, and sunk his teeth into his neck. The man died, but it was too late. Mother was already gone.

"The woman in the camper was calling rangers, so we couldn't even stay to collect the bodies. Unlike movies and books, shifters' bodies don't return to their human state. We couldn't shift in front of them. We couldn't drag the bodies out of there. There was nothing we could do but run from the sounds of jeeps driving our way."

"I'm sorry," I whisper, but he doesn't hear.

"My father lived a few more years, but he died of a broken heart in the end. Some shifters never recover from losing their mate. Anders did because he focused on revenge. My father wallowed until his grief killed him, leaving me alone and in foster care at the age of thirteen. I was lucky enough to catch the notice of a bear family when I was sixteen and was taken from the human facilities. My father always wanted me to make something of myself, and I swore I would."

I look down at the churning water. When I look back up, I see a challenge in his eyes. Is this his way of making me want to tell my story? Looking around, I see no sign of the men that told me Draven has a reason to be who he is. I believe them now. He lived through so much. It couldn't have been easy for him to open up. The least I can do is reciprocate.

I sigh. "My mother was married to a wealthy man. Both had blonde hair and blue eyes, the perfect family for portraits. When Mom got pregnant with me, they were ecstatic. The man she was married to spoiled her and had plans of spoiling me. Unfortunately, when I came out with dark hair, the man who thought he was my father became suspicious. My mother convinced him I was some sort of throwback, and he bought it; probably only because he wanted to.

"As I grew, it became apparent that I looked nothing like him, so he demanded a paternity test. By that time, I was thoroughly invested in him as my father. I called him Daddy and followed him everywhere because he was warmer than my mother. The test proved I wasn't his. He kicked both of us to the curb, his prenup agreement leaving nothing thanks to my mother cheating."

Tears form at the corners of my eyes, but I blink to keep them in place. "I lost the man I thought was my father. He cut off all contact and showed me how little I really meant to him. I met my real dad once when he came to bitch out my mother for not being able to keep up the ruse. You see, he was blackmailing my mom. He wouldn't spill the secret if she kept giving him money. The man I called Daddy was loaded.

“I look a lot like my real dad, which was my biggest failing to both of them. I ruined a good thing by not coming out with blonde hair and blue eyes. My mom did the bare minimum required to keep her out of jail. My real father walked away. I was reminded multiple times a day how much I ruined my mom's life. At eighteen, I left and never went back."

"Oh, Eddie." Jerking my head up, I see Anders and Warrin watching me with pity I don't need. Their footsteps were covered by my words. I didn't hear them approach.

I wipe my eyes. "Hey, guys. Any sign of wolves?" When Warrin opens his mouth, I shake my head. "Don't, please. I don't want to talk about it anymore. Maybe later. Not right now."

Instead of pressing the matter, the men all usher me into the house, Draven swinging in the wind in front of me. Even that isn't enough to dispel the terrible thoughts of my inability to be good enough. Feeling helpless, I stand in the middle of the room and look around.

Warrin wraps a towel around me before guiding me to the leather couch and pulling me into his lap. I inhale his musky scent. This is right. This is where I belong. To Warrin, I'm perfect, and there's no way I'll ever make him believe otherwise.

DRAVEN

Eddie leans against Warrin with her fingers twined with his. The choppy blades whir and thunder around us. I can still hear, but no one speaks. I'm not sure what triggered me to bare my past to this woman. I never expected to learn what I did. She's not just some spoiled brat stealing what isn't hers because she doesn't have it. If I have to admit it, I'd say she fits perfectly in our band of misfits. Not that I'll ever tell her that.

I grit my teeth and look away when her brown eyes fall on me. It's clear that retelling her past has had an unfavorable effect on her. Not that I can blame her because I, of all people, know the pain of talking about the past.

Much of it makes sense now. Her stealing from the rich stems from her original father taking everything from her because she wasn't his, destroying the life of the child that looked up to him. Her bleached hair to hide the dark locks that made her mother and real father hate her. Add in her unwillingness to take shit from me. Why should she when she's been taking it all her life?

And, as much as I hate to admit it, I desired her more than anything when I saw her in that bikini. If it weren't for my inhibitions, I would have taken her right then and there. Eddie isn't good at hiding the fact that she feels I should add myself to her little harem. My body wants to follow her wishes, but my mind still holds back.

Glancing back at her snuggling Warrin reminds me that she has made her choice. This isn't some fling that will leave him in agony, suffering from loss. She's committed enough to mate with him, even if that means being his for all time. Anders has even had a taste of her desirable body. The thought of her legs wrapped around my hips is far from comfortable. I shift around until I'm sure I'm not making a tent, which seems to happen way too easily around her.

Jealousy swarms like angry hornets in my stomach. It's not a malicious envy. I'm glad Warrin is happy and has the mate he desired. I'm also glad Anders is finally putting his heart back out there. I was worried he'd go the way of my father once our vengeance is through.

What do I want? I want her as mine as well, but I can't break through the stubborn block of hatred toward humans. Someday, she will be mine.

CHAPTER TWENTY SIX
THANKS TO BETSY

I notice Draven watching me, so I snuggle closer to Warrin. All three men have been so understanding, even the aloof black bear shifter. I wasn't expecting to bare my heart to him, and part of me screams that I was an idiot. The rest of me understands the importance of my confession. Nothing hides between the three of us anymore.

Through my own pain, my heart aches for the man staring at me with dark eyes. I bite my lip, noticing his gaze falls to the movement. Looking away, I bury my face in Warrin's shoulder. I hate being vulnerable. Vulnerability leads to weakness. Weakness leads to mistakes. Mistakes lead to danger, possibly fatal in the context I've been thrown into.

Still, we all know why each other is where we are today, what it took to become who we are. I don't regret it. That doesn't mean I'm happy to relive it. The smacks for asking for extra food when I'm the one that made us poor. The laughter when I mentioned a crush because I pushed her husband away. My long brown hair being pulled at every opportunity to remind me of my faults. Being unable to look my mother in the face without a sneer and a reminder that I look like my biological father, who she considered ugly now that he was done with her.

Lex was my one saving grace. His life wasn't perfect, but he did what he could to shield me as much as possible. He made me laugh when I was on the verge of tears. He told my mom off on multiple occasions. Everyone thought we'd end up together, but neither of us looks at the other that way.

We're found family. Brother and sister that don't share DNA. There for each other through everything, even if we feel what the other is doing is stupid. I'd give my life to keep him safe, so how do I talk him into the fact that we need to move in with my men? I hate lying to him.

This is all such a big mess.

Once back on the ground, Warrin drives me home while the other two head back to their building. He reaches over and grabs my hand. "Are you okay?"

I nod, continuing to watch the lights go by. It's dark, so all the streetlights that work are bright, which fizzle out as we get closer to home. What would it be like to live somewhere I don't have a need for Lex's self-defense moves?

"I'm fine," I say with a sigh. "Now you know why you can't meet my mother."

"I'm sorry I pressured you that day."

I shake my head. "It wasn't you. How could you know when I didn't tell you? There was one time when my mom was drunk. She came screaming into my bedroom while I was doing homework with an electric razor. Do you know how cruel twelve-year-olds are when you show up to school bald? Lex used his birthday money to help me buy a bleaching kit when my hair started to grow back in. I've hidden the shameful darkness on top of my head ever since."

My building comes into view, and he pulls up in front of it. When I try to climb out, he squeezes my fingers tight. "Look at me, Eddie." I'm scared to see the condemnation that might be in his eyes, but I force myself to look. He places a gentle hand on my cheek. "None of what happened was your fault. You didn't deserve any of it. Your mother paid for her own mistakes, and you were caught in the unfortunate crossfire. Blonde or brown hair doesn't matter. You're beautiful no matter what. Her actions speak of who she is, not who you are. You're perfect."

Tears roll down my cheeks, and I sniffle. I wish I could believe those words. Even if I can't, I still need to hear them. Leaning over, I brush my lips over his. There is no greed or hunger in the kiss, only the need to feel loved and cared for. Something I never got from the one person who should have given it to me. If my own mother can't love me, what does that say?

"You're perfect too," I whisper.

"Let me walk you to your door."

I shake my head. "It's been a long day. All I want is a bubble bath, warm PJs, and my bed. You have your own unpacking to do. I can make it home."

"It's no trouble."

“No, really. Let me do this myself."

"If that's what you really want..."

This man can't be any more loving than he is. It's all about my wants and needs. Something else I need to get used to. "It is. I'll text you before I turn in."

"Okay."

One last kiss, I'm out the door with my bag hanging from my shoulder. I barely notice Warrin drive away or the ride up the elevator. Real life doesn't come back to me until I notice Mrs. Barlow sticking her head out of the door and shaking it. I shove the keys I was removing back into my pocket. My feet pause. Looking down the hall, I see our apartment door partially open.

The bag drops silently off my shoulder and onto the dirty carpet. I motion for Mrs. Barlow to return to her apartment. Lex must have left the door open, but I tiptoe closer, just in case. Crashing reaches me from the open apartment. It silences when I get close enough to look into my violated home. Our furniture is thrown all over the floor, shredded and trashed beyond recognition.

When the door swings open, I yelp and jump back before making a run for it. I make it as far as the entrance to Mrs. Barlow's apartment. Something grabs my coat, which is sticky with sap from hugging the tree Saturday, and I'm slams into the wall. The man pinning me against the hard surface snarls at me, showing teeth that are starting to elongate. I try to bring my knee up, but he blocks the move and pushes against me so hard I can barely breathe.

His breath is horrid. "You little ursa whore. Too stupid to listen to warnings."

"I'm smart enough to talk in full sentences."

He slams my head against the wall, making me gasp as the world spins around me. Movement behind him catches my attention. I try to signal Mrs. Barlow to close the door without my attacker noticing. I'm relieved when the door behind him closes. I don't need her death on my conscience, and no one needs to see this. Not that it will matter much. There's no doubt in my mind I'm dead. Whether he does it right here or drags me back to my apartment is up for debate.

"You should have left well enough alone, bitch. Now, you have to pay for your meddling. The stupid polar bear will be next."

Warrin. I can't let him kill me. My mate won't suffer my loss well. I have no doubt he'll end up like Draven's father and not like Anders. He's too in it, too in love and connected, soft-hearted.

When I realize that he's not only going to kill me in the dirty hall but use his fangs to do it, I start struggling harder. It's no use. I'm too smooshed. I have one chance, and I don't relish doing it. I've never been able to do this move without incapacitating myself as well. I don't have a choice.

My head shoots forward, slamming into his face hard enough that I feel a fang skid over my forehead before breaking off. Stars flash in my vision as he pulls away. Next, I slam my knee up. He folds over but doesn't let go. Why can't these wolves get the hint? Leave me alone.

The door behind him opens again. I'm about to shout for her to stay inside when a ball of fur flies through the air with a yowl. The door clicks shut again. The furball latches onto the back of my attacker's shirt. He spins in an effort to get it off, giving me the freedom to move and a full view.

"Thank you, Betsy," I mutter as I take off down the hallway. I skip the elevator in hopes of putting more distance between me and the wolf hell bent on murdering me in public. Who knows how long I'd need to wait. As the stairwell door closes, I hear barking join the fray. If anything, the poodle should buy me more time.

I only run down half of each set of steps, jumping to land on the platform between each flight. This helps me reach the bottom faster than I ever have before. People shout as I push past them and out the front door. Outside, I take a deep breath and decide on a course of action. My tired legs turn toward the parking garage.

Ducking down an alley seems like a good idea until I find myself slipping on trash. At the next building, I head back to the road. Strong arms wrap around me upon my exit. I kick my feet up, but they keep their grip on me. The smell of unwashed flesh assaults my nose.

I look at my attacker. "Myrl?"

"I'm sorry, sweet angel. I really like all your gifts, but I must give you to the demons that roam the night. If I don't, they said they'll drag me to hell."

"They're not demons. Please, let me go."

"You can't trick me. I have to do this."

"Don't make me, Myrl."

"They'll be here shortly."

Biting my tongue to keep from pleading with him again, I let myself realize that it has to be this way. I slam the heel of my foot down, and the old homeless man stumbles back. He doesn't let go, so I grab his hand, bend it back, and flip him onto the ground. I'm both cursing Lex and thanking him for making me into a dull weapon. Myrl doesn't deserve this. He isn't right in the head. It's either this or the wolves.

My feet hit the concrete of the sidewalk again. At the parking garage, I once again take the stairs. Anything to keep my lead on the wolf. Waiting for the elevator will make me a sitting duck.

I burst through the door to my level, running toward my car while digging the keys out of my pocket. My bag is still in the hall by my apartment, but I'm happy I kept my keys on me.

The sound of paws and nails clicking on concrete increases my heart rate. I swear I can feel it in my throat. Through all my risky jobs, I've never been this terrified. Not once did my life hang in the balance like this. Humans, I can take. Wolves, not so much.

As I twist the key in the door, I hear a growl much too close. Time slows, and my breathing stops. I wrench the driver's side open, practically diving inside. I sit up and bang the door shut. An angry wolf slams into the window so hard the glass cracks. I scream.

My fingers drop the keys, and I bend down to feel around. When my phone falls from my pocket, the picture of me with my best friend lights up. Lex. I grab my phone and pull up our messages.

Me: Do NOT come home!!!!! Get to the office. For the love of God, don't fight me on this.

The window cracks a little more with the next hit. I thrust my keys in the ignition and turn. When the wolf hears my engine, he scrambles onto my hood, bouncing his paws off my windshield. Hitting the gas, I burn rubber while backing up. The wolf falls and rolls.

With a growl, I throw the car into drive and floor it. My front tires thump over the animal, followed by my back. The entire car hops over the living speed bump. Knowing the resilience of shifters, I'm not stupid enough to think that it's dead, so I don't look back as I squeal tire around the first curve.

By the time I make it to the street, I'm grateful I didn't meet anyone coming in. There's no way I would've avoided a collision, which would've put me right where the wolf wanted. I doubt he'd worry about killing a witness if it meant erasing me from the equation.

My phone chimes, but I'm too shaky to check it while driving. Limbs tremble with fright, the adrenaline coming down and making me feel exhausted. I pull into the parking lot and let my forehead hit the steering wheel. Only after a few breaths do I pick up my phone.

Lex: What?! Why?!

Me: Someone broke in and trashed the place before attacking me.

Lex: I'm tired of these men dragging us into their trouble. Maybe I'll just stay with Jared.

Me: Please. I'll feel safer with you here behind security guards. If either of us would've been home, I don't think we'd be breathing right now.

Lex: Fine, but only because it's you. Be there in 20.

My legs wobble when I step out of the car, but I don't hesitate. A wobbly run is better than an attack in a dark parking lot. The security guard jumps up from the desk when I run up to the glass door and pound on it.

He lets me in. "Ms. Hart? What are you doing?"

"I need to speak to the bosses. It's urgent."

The guard looks about to argue, but he thinks better of it in the end. I don't know if it's my torn clothing, the blood running from the gash on my forehead, or my terrified expression. Whatever it is, I'm thankful to see all three run from the opening metal doors. For the first time since I walked off the elevator in my apartment building, I feel safe enough to let myself fall to my knees. The men are on me in seconds.

CHAPTER TWENTY SEVEN
DISTRACTED

"Thank you, officer."

The cop tips his hat my way. "Of course. Don't hesitate to contact us if you remember anything else."

I close the door and turn to lean on it. They showed up this morning, searching for me to make sure I am okay. Mr. Elsher called to report the break in and destruction of my apartment, which is an unadvisable move in our neighborhood. My place of employment was the first place they thought to look for me. I had to explain being attacked in the hall and my shattered window, since I haven't moved my car into the parking garage yet, without mentioning werewolves. It wasn't easy.

"I can't believe I have to be here."

My eyes open to reveal Lex glaring at me from the door leading to his room. "It's not like I planned for this to happen."

The suite is enormous, with enough space for both of us. Lex is mad at me and utilizing that space as much as possible. I don't blame him for being upset, but it still hurts. He's my best friend. How much more strain can our relationship take?

"You got in bed with the enemy, literally," he argues.

"I was keeping us out of jail. What was I supposed to do? Turn down his offer and let the cops place cuffs on me? Or let Draven do away with me? I didn't have many options when they caught me. Besides, we both know what kind of good the money they offer can do."

"For once, put yourself before the less fortunate. Keep yourself, and me, alive."

I sigh and rub my eyes, wincing at the soreness of my forehead. The gash from the broken tooth and the bruise from the headbutt aren't pretty. It's been a long night. First, explaining to the guys what happened took a while. All three were angry and ready to take the fight to the door of Lunar Financial. Yes, I finally found out what they named their business. Yes, it's predictable for a pack of wolves. Next, Lex showed up for the encore of my explanation. Then we had to settle in.

To stay in or leave to supervise the contractors coming in soon. That's the current dilemma I'm dealing with. I can either stay in and be scowled at all day, or I can drag my ass down to the safety deposit boxes and watch the installation of the new ones.

They're confiscating two unused offices to make a new room, then converting the old one into an extra security guard station once everything is moved over. Warrin wants me to help him direct the workers. While annoying, it's preferable to the icy emotions permeating through the air of our new home.

Well, I guess I don't need to find a reason to get him to move. We're already here.

My lack of response must drive Lex crazy. "And another thing, do you know how hard I worked to acquire all that equipment?"

"I'll talk to Warrin about the loss. I'm sure they'd be willing to cover it."

"I only hope the cops don't confiscate things," he continues, as if I said nothing. "Not only is my very expensive equipment smashed to pieces, but there is incriminating evidence on it."

"Why would they snoop? We're the victims."

Again, I'm ignored. "I can't even go in to pick the stuff up because it's a crime scene and off limits. This could be disastrous."

At this point, I find myself wishing Lex would stop talking, go back to his surly silence. I love my best friend like the brother I never had, but I can't take this right now. There's too much crazy in my head. I don't need this. My decision is made by the continued rant I no longer listen to. What's the point of listening when I can't get a word in?

Without saying anything, I walk out the door. At this moment, I don't even have a change of clothes. Lex has a little because he brought what he took with him to Jared's. My weekend supplies are who knows where after I left them in the hall. Someone probably took them to sell. As soon as the door closes, silence fills the space around me. I sigh and push the button for the elevator. This floor also holds a small laundry room, which would be handy if I had clothes.

Warrin already speaks to the contractor when I step up to him. He offers me a quick smile without stopping whatever he's saying. They won't be able to start installing boxes for another month, so I'm not really useful right now. As they walk down the hall to look at the space they have to work with, I chew my lip, trying to decide what to do with my day.

My polar bear takes my hand. "You still look rattled. Maybe you should rest a bit more."

Always thinking of my needs before I do. I shake my head. "I can't take Lex right now. He's angry at me for putting him in this situation and having all his equipment destroyed."

"I've already talked to Anders. We plan on reimbursing you for everything lost, plus extra. I'm sorry he's upset. I'm sure it'll blow over because you two are pretty close."

"I can only hope so. I've never lied to Lex in my life, Warrin. Now I'm keeping secrets left and right while putting him in danger. I know it's needed, but I feel like our relationship is straining. Everyone has a breaking point. I can't help but wonder how close Lex is to it."

The giant of a man pulls me into his arms. "Why don't you go take a nice bubble bath in my suite, then rest? After work, one of us will take you and Lex out to buy new clothes and whatever you need to make your place more comfortable. Lex can also show us what kind of electronics he needs to set up while here. He can then either take it with him or stay here, although here is safer, so I hope that's his choice."

"Me too. Alright. I'll take you up on your offer. What is my landlords' pet policy?"

"Are you talking about your cat?"

"Yeah. The police told us Mrs. Barlow took in Clancy."

"I'll go myself to pick him up later." Warrin reaches into his pocket and hands me the key to the elevator that has access to his room with the promise to get me a key made. "Stop on the fifth floor on your way. Anders said he wanted to speak to you when you were ready."

Nodding, I turn and make my way back to the elevator. Warrin lets me go without any further fawning, which I'm thankful for. Rest while surrounded by his musky scent sounds perfect. I send a text to Lex to let him know the shopping plans and receive a "whatever" reply. I sigh, hoping Warrin is right. Losing my best friend is the last thing I want to do, but I can't leave my mate. I'm too tired to figure this out right now.

The elevator dings to indicate I've reached the fifth floor. I've been here before, once when I was evaluating the security. Today, a secretary looks up at me, scans me from head to toe, and grimaces like I'm found wanting.

Before I can walk past and head for Anders's office, she says, "Excuse me. Are you sure you're in the right place?"

Her tone raises my invisible hackles. "Seeing how Anders Hayes asked for me to stop in, I would think so."

"He's busy."

"Then why did he call me up?"

She shrugs. "You probably got bad information."

"Since Warrin Carter is the one who told me, I'm going to say it's a pretty solid source." I feel like I'm talking to a child.

"So you say. You don't look like a client."

"I'm not. I'm the security consultant that Anders calls *Darlin*."

With that, her mouth drops. Taking advantage of her shock, I slip by. She tries to chase me down, but I make it to his door before she can and swing it open. Anders sits back in his chair, squeezing a stress ball that looks like it's seen better days. His brown eyes light up at the sight of me.

The woman behind me pants. "I'm sorry, sir. She said you were expecting her and wouldn't listen when I tried to tell her you're busy."

He looks between me and the stress ball. "I didn't realize I was too busy to receive someone I asked to come to me."

I have the pleasure of watching her jaw drop to the floor. "Told you. I'd suggest working a bit on your cardio. You didn't run far enough to be having trouble breathing."

Her jaw closes as her cheeks tinge with pink. I wiggle my fingers in a wave and close the door on her. I'm half expecting her to barge through, but she doesn't. Probably returning to her desk to mope.

"Your secretary really needs to work on her customer service skills," I say.

Anders chuckles. "Don't mind her. I've had to tell her multiple times to stop gatekeeping my guests. Another reprimand is in order."

"Are all the guests held back women?"

"Seem to be. Why?"

"Think she might be jealous."

He laughs but stops when I don't join him. "You're serious?"

"You're a sexy man, Anders. I gathered from her tone that she simply wanted to hold me back. It's obvious you aren't actually too busy for her to call back."

His soft lips press into a hard line. "I'll make sure to speak with her. So, you think I'm sexy?"

The way his face softens with the question makes me laugh. "Can you possibly doubt that?"

"Well, I've apparently completely missed my secretary's interest."

"True. You seem to be a bit blind." I walk over and lean back against his desk.

He reaches to squeeze my hips and pulls me until I'm standing right in front of him. "Not so blind that I'm not affected with a strong desire just by looking at you."

"Is this why you called me to your office?"

Anders chuckles. "I was going to ask you if you're doing alright, but I got distracted by your beauty."

"Smooth. As far as your question, I'm as fine as I can be. Warrin said someone will take us out to get what we need while he goes and picks up my cat."

"I forgot you have a cat."

"Will his presence be a problem?"

"Not at all. Pick up what he needs while you're out too. Anything to make you happy."

My heart warms. I lean over to brush my lips on his. "I know you said about doing plenty of other things, but what would you say if I tell you I want to be mated by more than one bear?"

Anders pulls away to look into my eyes. "Are you sure that's what you want?"

"Well, I already have a polar bear that's mine. A grizzly seems like an excellent addition to my collection."

To emphasize my words, I strip until nothing stands between my body and his eyes. With a growl, he pulls me onto his lap. I unbutton his shirt, glad that his suit jacket is already off. As soon as his muscular chest is out in the open, I lean down to run my tongue over it. He sucks in a breath before bringing my lips up with commanding hands to meet his.

Strong hands move to my breasts. I moan into his mouth, enjoying his fingers pinching both my taught nipples. The ache in me grows quickly, ready to feel the man inside me after all the pleasure he gave me at the cabin. I lift from his lap enough to undo his pants, which he helps by cupping my ass for support. His length pops out with little effort.

Anders moves his warm mouth to my neck, and I find I can't wait anymore. I settle onto him, taking all of him into me on his desk chair. He bites down with a groan that sounds like a mixture of agony and ecstasy. I can't say I'm quiet without lying. Do all bears feel this good?

I ride him, moving up and down while also rocking my hips. His fingers dig into my skin, urging me to move faster and stronger. I oblige, enjoying the feeling of his large cock moving in and out of me. The burning becomes so intense that sweat breaks out on my forehead.

Pressure builds until I feel like I'm ready to explode. Anders continues to guide my movements and speed with his strong grip. My fingers squeeze his shoulders in response to his touch.

All my muscles tense, ready for release. Anders whispers, "I'm not sure I can hold out much longer."

That's the permission I need to give into the release my body desires. I shudder and clench, feeling him bite down into my neck. He jerks inside me, gushing his desire deep. He presses down on my hips to make sure he reaches as far as possible inside me. I welcome it all.

When we both finish, I pull myself off of him and start dressing. "I'll let you get back to being busy, Mr. Grizzly Bear."

"I wish you could stay all day, but I do have some clients to handle. Otherwise, we'd do that again and take our time. Your body deserves a proper worship."

Shivers run up my spine, and I make a note for later demands. "I'm not far. For now, I'm going to head to Warrin's room to take a hot bath and rest without worrying about Lex's disapproval and scowls."

"That bad?"

I sigh. "I hope it'll blow over soon, but I did kind of destroy everything in our lives by bringing the wolves after us."

"That's more my fault than yours."

"What's done is done. While I miss happy Lex, I wouldn't trade the three of you for anything."

"All three of us?"

"Yeah. Draven just hasn't earned it yet."

I'm falling in love with the sound of his chuckles. "He'll come around. He told us that he told his story, so he's getting there."

"I can be patient. I have two hot bears to keep me busy for now."

"And we are happy to provide distractions."

I give him one more kiss before heading to the door. As I pass the secretary's desk on the way to the elevator, I give her a smile and a wink. Her scowl as the doors close makes me grin. She and everyone else will know that these men are mine.

CHAPTER TWENTY EIGHT
LINGERIE

Lex wanders the aisles, grumbling about how these clothes are too rich for him. The price tags are a bit much, but it's where Draven brought us. When I see the price of the bra and panty set I hold, my jaw drops. No more bargain bin undergarments for me. These men are going to spoil me, and nothing I say will deter them. My cranky best friend gets to come along for the ride.

"Oh, finally. I found some jeans. Who the hell pays this much for denim?" Lex exclaims so loudly that I can't help but look around at the annoyed faces. Draven scowls at him.

Dark eyes find me, and for once, the annoyance in them disappears. Draven has been a lot kinder to me since our emotional dip. He was as angry and worried for me as the other two when I showed up battered and panicked last night. The closed off black bear cares.

To tease him and remind him what he's missing out on, I hold the set of undergarments up to my chest. His dark eyes heat as he pictures me in them. That's one thing I love about Draven. The man is an observer and a thinker. You can see when he's picturing something or trying to figure something out. Of course, I can only guess about his thoughts, but I'd bet my life on my assumption.

Acting as innocent as possible, I bend over to look at another, holding the two up to him like I'm asking for his opinion. Draven leans back against the wall, eyebrow raised. He can act as nonchalant as he wants; I can see the growing bulge in his pants. My brain tells me that antagonizing the man may not be the best idea, but I'm hoping he breaks and gives me consequences.

Once my basket is full, I make my way to the changing rooms. There is only enough here to give me changes for the week. While they wish to spoil me, I'm not comfortable with these prices, so I don't find more than I need. I did pick up another dress, this one red. You know; just in case the guys want to take me out on a date. When I reach that, I step into it and pull it up. As usual, there's a zipper to contend with. I can't know if it fits for sure unless I zip it, and I am not wasting this kind of money by picking something that doesn't fit.

I growl. Draven's voice comes through the door. "Everything alright, Mutt?"

"I need zipper assistance. Can you get Lex for me? I'll unlock the door."

As soon as the latch is no longer barring entry, the door opens to reveal the man I didn't ask for with something bunched on a hanger in his hand. "Lex is busy running up my credit card limit. I didn't want to let you out of my sight, so I gave him my card."

"But you're fine letting *him* out of your sight?"

The empty hand turns me to pull the zipper up. "We're in an expensive store with numerous cameras and alarms everywhere. He isn't going anywhere. You're more fun to watch."

His hand pulls me back against him, so he can press his hardness into my back. The sensation makes me let out a quiet gasp. Draven's head appears over my shoulder, scanning me from head to toe with hungry eyes. A shiver runs up my spine.

"This dress is definitely perfect, but I want to see this on you as restitution for the naughty teasing you did out there."

He hands me the lacy garment he's been hiding. I lift the hanger to let the fabric attached to it fall. My eyes go wide. "This?"

Draven pulls me back again, his hand running down my side, over my hip, and around to the inside of the top of my thigh. I almost drop the sexy lingerie he brought in. "If you want to offer me the chance to see you in your underwear, I want a show. Put it on. I'll be waiting outside."

Draven walks through the door to my dressing room after pulling my zipper down. When I first entered, I thought it was quite large for a dressing room. Not with Draven in it. This room could fit four people, but Draven's lithe presence is full.

Gulping, I lift the lingerie he gave me. How can something that stretches from the breasts to the hips look so skimpy? I shimmy out of my dress, debating on whether I'll follow his command or not. This is what I wanted, isn't it?

Just the thought of his eyes on me in this thing sends a pleasant shudder over my body. That decides it. Careful not to tear the lace—he is not buying this—I pull it over my head, marveling at the fact he got my size right simply by looking. When I pull the panties on, one small detail makes me gurgle some kind of whimper.

Draven takes the sound as a cue to return. His eyes rake over my body, leaving hot trails in their wake. I swallow, feeling the familiar ache build between my thighs. I need to stop, or I'll make this unable to be returned because the panties are damp.

"Mmmm," Draven says.

A shiver runs over me. "Draven, these are crotchless panties."

"Better for what's about to happen."

"If we do something, we won't be able to put this back on the shelf."

"Who says anything about putting it back, Mutt? Now that I see this on you, I'm definitely buying it."

He spins me to make sure I can see myself. His breath fans my ear. "You're going to pay for the reaction you egged out of me earlier. You were a bad girl."

Okay. The whole bad girl talk has never been a turn on for me. What does it say about me that Draven saying them makes me melt? These panties are not going back on the shelf. They're soaked through.

"You smell delicious," he growls before taking the lobe of my ear between his teeth.

Trying to hold in my moan, I let a soft grunt free. Draven's hands grab both breasts and give them a harsh squeeze. There is a little pain, but it hardens my nipples instead of turning me off. He's careful to squeeze just hard enough to get a reaction without too much pain.

Draven backs us up, keeping me facing the mirror, then drops onto the bench. He pulls me down to perch between his legs before whispering in my ear. "Watch yourself. I want you to see what you look like when you unravel under my touch."

I open my mouth to argue, but his fingers moving from my breast, down my stomach, and between my legs makes all words impossible. He finds the slit of the panties, using the mirror to guide himself, then he delves deep.

I shove the side of my hand into my mouth to bite it. Moaning in the store isn't exactly on my to-do list right now. I've never done anything like this in such a public place. Draven's fingers exit, moving in lazy circles up to my clit. My entire body tenses.

"Don't let go yet," he tells me. "I want to watch for a little longer."

Not like I was going to, but I nod my head. Anything to keep him doing this. I push the rising tide of pleasure down, holding on as much as I can.

"Good girl," he murmurs into my ear.

Fingers are replaced by a thumb, so they can explore my wet heat once again. My hand slaps down on his leg, squeezing to help me keep control over my body. In the mirror, I can see the light glistening on the sweat of my exertion. His entire hand consumes the area between my thighs. A moan escapes.

I slap a hand over my mouth, but it's too late. Someone had to have heard it. Leaving the dressing room is going to make me blush. Right now, in this moment, I let my later humiliation fly away. Nothing will stop me from enjoying this.

The ache spreads from my core to cover my entire body. It burns in a way that has me wanting more. I try to throw my head back, but Draven uses his free hand to keep me looking at the mirror. I can't hold on much longer.

"Let go," he says.

As if my entire body has been waiting for his command, I feel myself swept away by the pleasure. I see my hips move, riding his hand as if it's my only lifeline. Both hands cover my mouth because nothing can stop the bestial sound that bursts from me. I shudder and clench, unable to hold any of it back. My pleasure gushes through and out of me until I find myself sitting boneless between his legs.

Draven kisses the back of my neck. Before he can protest, I spin and drop to my knees. His cock is out in a flash, in my mouth even quicker. My tongue moves around his head, flicking over it a few times before my lips move down his shaft. I bob my head, listening to him hiss.

It's my turn to have him at my mercy. Long fingers tangle in my hair to guide speed and depth. With each bob, I run my tongue along his shaft. When his fingers tighten, he tenses and spurts. I take it all until he's done, then step away.

With a smirk, I strip right in front of him to redress in my old clothes. He watches with his dark eyes and a smirk on his face. Draven helps me put everything back into my basket. When we step out, Lex glares at me from his seat not far from my dressing room. There is no way he didn't hear any of that.

Lex ignores me, immediately walking from the front door to his bedroom. I sigh and drop my keys in the little bowl by the door. He was more adamant about the electronic store. There, he didn't complain about price, going for the most expensive pieces. I don't blame him for getting what he wants out of this situation. It's us who brought the danger to him. He didn't want to be a part of any of this.

Dropping onto my cushy couch, I pull out my phone, lift my legs, and use the coffee table as a footstool. My eyes stare at my game without seeing it. Instead, my mind goes over everything Draven did and said. I never expected having the black bear would be like that. He was gentle yet rough. His fingers were magic, and he tasted perfect.

Lex didn't speak at all after hearing what happened in there, which doesn't surprise me. My best friend makes his feelings about my relationship choices very clear. He doesn't even know the half of it. It doesn't matter. I never push about his strange friendship with Jared, so he has no right to deny me my happiness with three doting men. I deserve this.

We just have to end the threat first. I close out the game and open my browser. Within moments, I'm on the website for Lunar Financial. Seeing Eclipse Security boasted as their choice security experts, I put away any thoughts of sneaking in for a look. They're the top security in the country. Expensive, but the best. I turn down any job where I have to deal with them.

Scrolling shows me a fundraiser ball happening tomorrow night. I grimace at the price of admission. People who can pay an entire month's salary for a middle-class worker to attend this thing can't be all that generous. It's probably a way to get their names in all the papers. It sickens me how they use charity for tax breaks and PR. They don't care about those deemed less than them. All they care about is their image, so they can make more money.

I return to the search bar and type in the name of their CEO. Steven Hodge. What an ordinary name for a psycho wolf. A little digging shows me that he lives at the edge of the suburbs outside the city. Probably so he can run as a wolf whenever.

None of this is useful at all. Sighing, I stand and stretch. Tomorrow is another long day of dealing with Lex's disapproval. Better get my rest. An orange and white ball of fur greets me on my bed.

"Clancy, you lazy furball," I say. "Can't even come out to greet me?"

He looks up and purrs with my touch. I'm happy to know he's safe, but I wonder about Betsy. I hope Mrs. Barlow didn't sacrifice her favorite yowling assassin for me. I take the time to set up the litter box, food and water bowls, and the luxurious cat bed that will probably be Clancy's favorite. The cat tree can wait until tomorrow. Not that I think he'll use it much. Clancy is allergic to exercise.

Once done, I return to my bed, the cat in the exact same spot. I move to the opposite side of the bed to find a place under the covers. It's amazing how much space such a small animal takes up. I let slumber take me, determined to leave my troubled thoughts to be handled when I wake up.

CHAPTER TWENTY NINE
ASSESSING ONE'S SELF

The phone ringing breaks me from dreams of three sexy bears during some three on one time. I groan, throwing my hand out to reach for the phone on my nightstand. When I feel the edge of the foolproof case Lex suggested after my last one failed at its job, I grasp at it. It moves across the table until I hear the thump of it hitting the floor. As if the annoying Waker of Eddie gives up, the ringing stops.

I lift my head high enough to see that the curtains are starting to lighten up in a sign of sunrise. Forget this. My face hits my pillow with a groan. Whoever it is can wait until the time is fitting. I am not getting up.

My door slamming open makes me scream and sit up with a start. I look over at the sudden intruder. "What the hell, Lex?!"

We've apparently gone from not speaking to bursting in at the butt crack of dawn. At this point, I'd rather he go back to not talking to me. There are sexy dreams to be had and burning of eyes to dispel.

"Why didn't you answer your phone when Anders called?" he asks.

"That was Anders trying to rudely wake me? The sun isn't even up, Lex."

"Eddie! Stop focusing on the time. We have a problem."

That almost does it. "What kind of problem?"

"There's been a security breach."

And that definitely does it. Swearing, I jump out of bed while Lex goes to change out of his video game pajamas. I rush over to my drawers and pick out the first pair of jeans and the first shirt. It doesn't matter what I look at right now.

We reach the elevator at the same time and ride it down to security. A programmer sits at the computer with the three men hovering close. Lex pushes past them and shoves the guy at the keyboard. "Move."

The man glares at him but moves when the guys tell him to. Anders says, "They seem to be stealing all our client information and deleting it from our servers. Rick here can't stop them."

"Give me a couple of minutes." Lex's fingers fly across the keyboard. Anders and Warrin flank me as if I need protection from the hackers. I watch as Lex types furiously, biting my lip in hopes he can stock the attack. "Shit!"

"What?" I ask.

"That file I found the first day; It wasn't some harmless file. I missed it! It was planted as a backdoor to all your systems. They tricked me! It was so cleverly done that I couldn't see the path in from outside."

"Can you stop it?" Anders asks. "It was obviously a clever trick if you missed it. There's no sense in beating yourself up over it. The big question is if it can be fixed."

"Already done. Their connection is cut off, but there are still paths I need to close."

"Did we lose all our data for good?"

"No. One of the first things I did was set the system to back up to another server designed to keep data safe. It's there."

"What about our clients?" Draven asks. "If their information is leaked, we can be dealing with losing our entire business. There will be investigations and lost trust."

Lex scowls back at Draven. "I'm not an amateur. I set the information to self-destruct if taken from our servers without my permission."

"You can do that?" Warrin asks, his blue eyes wide.

"You hired the best of the best. Well, I thought I was. They still got around me."

I rest a hand on his shoulder. "It was a clever decoy."

"It was still a decoy I missed. Give me some time, and I'll figure out who installed it onto your system. I can at least do that much."

"You can do a lot more than that," Anders says in an attempt to console Lex's battered ego. "I've sent out emails and texts to the employees to give them the day off. Security will still be working, but the building will be empty. Do whatever you feel like you need to do."

Lex replies with a nod, fingers moving and mouse pointer gliding. He will work hard to make sure every trace of the wolves is out of the system. They will not get back in. If anything, Lex does not like to lose and will do anything to beat the enemy. The wolves have been threatening me for getting in the way; little do they know, I'm not the true threat.

Satisfied my best friend has this, I walk out and take a few deep breaths. Warrin wraps an arm around me. "Are you alright?"

I laugh. "You ask me that when it was your business that was just attacked?"

"You seem shaken."

"It's just..." I say. "What would have happened if we didn't come along when we did? Like what would have happened if I chose to wait a week to decide to try to rob you? Lex only got the systems updated last week. When I was attacked in the laundry room, the wolf said that they were almost ready to make a move. We should have been more thorough and ready."

"You did the best you could. Maybe you being caught by us was fate," Anders reasons.

"Fated to be mated?" I say with a smirk.

Draven laughs. "It seems to have gone that way, Mutt."

"What do you need to do to unwind?" Warrin asks.

I look around at all three pairs of eyes. One thoughtful. One hopeful. One curious. "I still have some extra money from last week's pay since none of you will let me spend it. I'll need to go out for a while."

"I'll go with you," Draven says.

"Your business was attacked."

"And there are two other people to keep an eye on things. If I sit and stew, I'm going to go crazy."

I shrug. "Fine, but we're walking. I like to walk from time to time instead of being chauffeured everywhere."

After grabbing some cash and my checkbook, we head out. December is in full bloom. Small snowflakes that won't cause any significant accumulation float in the air. My breath mists in front of my face. Draven walks close but without touching. It's a companionable silence.

Well, until it's not. "You should let your hair grow out. Bleaching constantly can't be good for it."

"I think I liked you better when you weren't talking," I mutter.

"Tough luck. I speak my mind. You should know this by now."

"My previous statement still stands."

"Well," he says, blatantly ignoring the hint for him to shut up, "I get why you do it after what you told me in the hot tub."

"Something I'm really regretting right now."

Draven chuckles but keeps plowing on. "You aren't who your mother made you believe you are. You don't have to be blonde to be accepted. As far as the miserable trash that gave birth to you, she won't admit that it wasn't your fault because she'd have to admit she did something wrong. She chose to cheat on the man you thought to be your father.

"That man was garbage for just throwing you out of his life like you meant nothing. You weren't his child by blood, but you made him your father regardless. It was cruel to treat you like you were nothing. As for your biological father, I won't even talk about that piece of filth."

I bite my lip to hold the tears at bay. He spouts these words like he understands. How can he when he had the perfect family? His disdain for the adults I grew up around is noted, but there is no way I can just forget everything and be normal. Instead of replying, I keep silent. I'm pretty sure I'll start crying if I try to speak.

"I know you think I don't understand."

I look at Draven with wide eyes. "Have you become a mind reader?"

"It doesn't take a mind reader to know what you're thinking. One just needs to be observant."

"Well, you can stop observing me anytime."

"I'd rather not. Now, see, just because I had a happy childhood doesn't mean I can't understand where you're coming from. Your mother made the fact that you have dark hair into something shameful. It's not. You're beautiful as you are. No amount of bleach can improve on what's already gorgeous."

"You admit I'm beautiful?"

He sighs. "We've already established that, unless you are not as observant as you should be. Anyway, stop trying to derail the conversation. We are having it."

Stopping, I fold my arms over my chest and glare at him. Who does he think he is? He can't tell me what conversations I have to have.

"Don't look at me like that," he says. "Your past is causing you pain. It's best to confront that. Am I right to assume that you're a thief stealing from the rich because of the man that abandoned you?"

"Drop it, Draven." I don't like how close to home this conversation feels.

"Answer this one question, then I'll let you be."

Angry, I stomp away. "I don't have to answer anything, Draven. I'm fine just as I am."

"Then why does thinking about it bring tears to your eyes?"

"As opposed to having no emotions?"

"I have emotions."

"Besides anger and frustration?"

A pensive look crosses his face, and I welcome the silence that comes with it. I'm not having this conversation with him. I'm not stuck in the past. I do what I do to help others. There's no other reason.

"I have plenty of emotion," he says after a while. "When I lost every member of my family, I became an angry youth, which seems to have stuck. That doesn't mean I don't have other feelings. Many therapists told me so."

My feet pause again. "Therapists?"

Draven laughs. "The big bad bear can't talk to professionals?"

"You didn't seem the type."

"You're obviously wrong. Anger and hatred toward the humans that killed my family festered until I took it out on all humans. I still do. That's why I am who I am. The only way to grow is to learn why you are the way you are. Is this where we're going?"

Startled by the abrupt change of subject, I turn my head to see my hand reaching to the knob leading to the bookstore. I glance back at him, nod, then enter without verbally answering him. The truths he speaks of are unsettling.

"You seem so closed off," I say, heading to the children's section. "I never thought you'd speak to others like that."

"It was forced at first. The humans that fostered me couldn't handle my hatred. I was eventually forced into therapy. Opening up wasn't easy, and I resisted for a long time, but I felt better once I did. I had a greater understanding of myself, even though I couldn't tell them the real reason for my anger."

"Hold these," I say, laying stacks of books in his waiting hand while he looks at me in question. He'll find out why soon enough.

"Which is why I asked the question you refuse to answer," he continues.

I grimace at the fact that he keeps coming back to this. "Fine. I know exactly who I am. I take from the rich and give to people who would greater benefit because they won't."

"Like your almost father and you."

"Well, as soon as he found out I didn't carry his DNA, then I was expendable. I didn't belong to him, so I didn't matter. So yeah. Most people of your means don't care about the little people, just like him. They take without giving anything back. I make sure they do."

At the register, our conversation stops. Draven lets it go as we walk down the sidewalk again. I'm not sure what he wants me to see. I know who I am. I know why I do what I do. It's no secret.

"Before you met us, did you ever stop and think that not all people with money are the evil you think they are?" Draven asks.

I groan. "Can we drop this? No. You aren't like them. I get it. The fact is most of your type are. Did you ever stop and think that all humans aren't worthy of your hate? Or did you think that while what happened was horrible, it came from a place of fear? They weren't maliciously trying to kill your family, Draven. The man was trying to protect his own. And before your scowl burns a hole in me, I'm not trying to justify anything. It should never have happened."

He sighs and looks away. The scowl disappears into a look of deep introspection. At least the focus of the conversation is no longer on my shortcomings. He can think of his own instead.

When I turn toward a building that gives children a safe place to go when they have no other, I hear him mutter, "So you use your extra money to take care of others, like you wished someone would do for you."

It's my turn to scowl, but I try to force it away before stepping inside. No need to frighten children into thinking of here to smite them for something not their fault. I'm sure there are plenty that receive that at home. I move toward donations.

"Merigold would have loved this," Draven says. "So many new friends to be had."

From what he said before, I'm going to assume Merigold is his sister. My anger softens as I look back to see him staring into a room where a bunch of kids run around. For the first time today, I break into a smile and make my way to the counter.

DRAVEN

"Pleeeeease, Draven. I'm bored."

I pull my eyes off the drawing my fingers cover the page with. My mind stops transferring what I see to paper. Merigold has been dancing outside for the last twenty minutes while I immortalize the view with pencil.

"I don't dance, Merigold. You know that," I say.

"That's because you've never tried it with me. You'll do wonderful."

"I'm busy. Play with one of your hundred friends."

Her lower lip comes out, and her dark eyes sparkle. "They're all in human school. I only get to see them on weekends."

"Because bears don't mix with humans."

"I wouldn't have to if my big brother would dance with me."

I scowl and shake my head. Dancing is silly when there are bigger things to deal with. Nothing she says will get me to dance with her. I'll keep her safe, but I won't do that.

And two days later, she was gone. I press my lips together, watching the children play on the indoor playground in the center of the room. For a bit, I can picture my little sister dancing through the crowded space, picking up any child that will let her. They'd all be dancing in no time.

The lady at the desk thanks Eddie for the books. The golden-haired woman writes out almost all her salary from last week on the check. My eyes find the children screaming and giggling, just like Merigold used to. I take a deep breath and hold it for a few seconds before blowing it out again.

Eddie is right. Not all humans are responsible for the murder of my family. These children are young and innocent. They haven't hurt anyone. Maybe if I show them kindness and generosity, they'll learn it in return. Merigold would approve.

The last thought decides for me. I trot over to the counter. "Do you take credit cards?"

I'm happy to hear they do. The amount I fill out for her to charge widens even Eddie's eyes. What better way to help than to allow children to play in a safe place, away from grouchy brothers and men with shotguns.

CHAPTER THIRTY
PROTECTING THE BEARS

When we return, Draven hurries ahead. He received a call on the way that the other two started a security meeting and to join when he got back. The lobby is empty of all but a single guard. It feels weird. This is how I came into their lives. I can only hope it isn't a sign of me leaving them. The thought sends a shudder over me. Such negative thoughts aren't needed. I'm here to stay.

I watch the dark-haired man enter the elevator while biting my lip. He surprised me with his donation. After all, it was for human children. Something in his eyes kept me from asking. Unlike him, I know when to shut my mouth—most of the time.

Shaking my head, I wave to the guard and go looking for Lex. As expected, he's still in front of the computer in security. I can hear murmurs down the hall, ones I'd know anywhere. "Any luck?"

Lex sighs. "It took a long time to weed out the intruders. They had paths everywhere. They must have been working on it for a long time, but I destroyed all remnants of control that file had. I'm having issues figuring out who planted it. The sign-in logs have been erased."

"There's no way?"

He removes his glasses, rubs his eyes, then gives me a grin that reminds me of the old Lex. "Have you ever known me not to get the information I need?"

"Never. But how?"

"The file was either planted by a pro, or someone less knowledgeable with instructions. Small mistakes I saw while digging around tell me it's the latter. I'm digging deeper, seeing if there's some sort of imprint or carbon copy they missed. These systems are always full of—son of a bitch!"

"What?!"

Without answering, Lex jumps up from his seat. I follow him as he runs down the hall and bursts into the security meeting. All four men, my three and Jeff, hop out of their chairs. I see Anders hide his fangs at the last second. Do not startle a bear shifter. Noted.

"Stop the meeting," Lex yells.

"What is the meaning of this?" Jeff asks. "You are rude and not authorized in this meeting. All you've done since you got here is order us all around like you know everything. I advised them against bringing you in."

"I'm sure you did," Lex says with a flat look.

What could that possibly mean? Why would Lex answer that way? Then it hits me. My hand covers my mouth.

Anders is calm once again. "Care to explain the intrusion, Lex?"

"He's not welcome here," Jeff butts in. "He does not have the clearance—"

When Anders holds up a hand to silence the security chief, he snaps his mouth shut. Jeff pulls a handkerchief out of his pocket and mops the sweat glistening on his baldness. I stare at him in disbelief.

"Well," Lex begins. "The logs were wiped for the day of the file implantation, so I had to look at it from a different perspective. First, I checked the schedule for that day, and looked to see who was on duty. I then compared work done on the computer with the time the file was uploaded because someone missed clearing the needed information there. What I found had Jeff's signature in the file details."

"That just means someone might have hacked in with my information. That doesn't prove anything."

This is true, but his trembling and increased sweating does provide proof. Draven sniffs the air, his eyes growing darker. Anders looks at him. "Take care of this traitor."

Draven nods before dragging Jeff to the elevator. Lex will assume it's to have him kicked from the building, so he offers to change his authorization. Warrin tells him to change all until they can question everyone thoroughly to look for other compromised guards.

As soon as Lex leaves, I ask, "Did Draven smell something on him?"

"We all did when we knew what to look for," Anders says. "There is a faint wolf smell mixed beneath his increasing body odor. His heart rate also changed into something we're used to hearing in a cornered animal."

"He's a wolf? You can hear hearts?"

Warrin shakes his head. "Not a wolf, but he's been around them. It's faint, so we only caught it by paying attention. He's always been loyal. We don't make a habit of sniffing our employees. And yes, we can hear hearts beating if we focus. He gave off all the alarms that said he was lying."

"Will I ever learn all I need to know about you guys?"

Warrin looks embarrassed, but Anders only looks apologetic. The latter speaks. "We aren't hiding from you, Darlin. All we have is yours. It might just take time for you to learn everything."

That makes sense. They've been bears their whole lives. They don't know what it's like to be human. It will take time for me to learn and for them to show me everything. I look forward to learning it all.

"Draven wasn't escorting him outside?" I ask.

"No. Draven took him to the cell beneath the building. He will be questioned and disposed of. While I don't agree with Draven's dark friends often, they're needed at this point."

"So Draven won't do it?"

Anders shakes his head. "He can't live because of what he knows. I'm not sure how much our enemies have told him, but we can't take chances. He's as much a liability as that file was, maybe more. That doesn't mean any of us want to do it. Draven is gruff. He's threatening at times. Inside, he's just a giant teddy bear. We all are. That doesn't mean he hasn't made darker connections to help him, now us, with ways to do what is needed."

I nod. Somehow, it not being Draven's hands makes what's happening below the building better. Will he be tortured there or taken elsewhere? I don't have it in me to ask. I'm not a squeamish person, but the thought of breaking bones and blood under where I sleep makes me nervous. It's better to imagine whatever is happening will happen elsewhere, whether it's true or not.

Both give me a passionate kiss before leaving the room to speak more with Lex. I take a few deep breaths, but they don't calm my racing heart. This is only one attack. Me and my best friend are prisoners in this building; not from the people inside, but those outside that wish us harm. They'd take any of the four people I care about from me. They'd snuff out my life without thought. They must be stopped.

My mind travels over all the knowledge I have and my options. None will understand my need to protect them because they all try to protect me. They will all put their lives above mine, even an angry Lex. This time, I need to be the one to save them. I know just what to do.

I'm careful to avoid rushing. The last thing I need is for them to ask me what I'm up to. All of them would do their best to stop me in a heartbeat. At the elevator, I use my key. Now, I rush. Black leggings and turtleneck first. The hat goes into my bag in case I'm stopped. My lock picks are never far.

As I exit my room, I freeze. Lex is midway between the door and his new computer set up across the room. He takes in my apparel. "Eddie, what are you doing?"

"I was going to go for a walk."

"No, you're not. Where are you burgling?"

"I don't know what you're talking about."

"Eddie, haven't we established I'm not stupid? Tell me, or you'll have to fight me to get to the door."

I grunt and rub my eyes. "Lex, we have to stop them."

"No! They have the best security in the country."

"I know. I already researched them yesterday. They're fortified better than Fort Knox. The CEO's home most likely isn't."

"You can't."

"I can, and I will. You can't stop me, Lex. Finding out some way to take them down is the only way our lives can go back to normal. It's the only way to ensure we aren't stalked and killed. I need to go."

Lex rushes over to his computer. "Give me time to break into their systems. Take this and get me into their computer. All you have to do is insert it, then hit enter when asked. It'll copy the entire hard drive."

I take the tiny USB drive and slide it into my pocket. "You don't have to do this."

"I know, but I'm not letting you commit suicide. Call me when you get there. Give me time."

"You have until I arrive. There's a charity ball going on tonight. I have a short window."

While my hacker swears and falls into his chair, I rush out of the suite. I use my key to get to the private garage. Once there, I open the driver's door with the new window the men insisted on repairing by unknown means. I'm out before anyone but Lex can guess that I'm missing.

I stand behind a tree, wishing I had bushes to hide behind. Even with a thick trunk, I feel exposed. This is the first time I've done a job where I didn't have a chance to case the location in advance. All I know is what the internet and the "Protected by" security sign tell me. At least it isn't the same as their office, which surprises me.

I dial Lex, listening to the phone ring in my ear. He better not forget again. We need to do this, and there's no Jared to distract him. That's another fact that seems to make him irritable.

"You there?" Lex says.

"I wouldn't call you unless I was."

"Can we forget our usual pre-job banter? I'm not feeling up to it. This isn't a normal job."

"All the more reason to treat it as normal as possible."

I can hear his groan. "Eddie, we haven't done any proper reconnaissance. All we have is what the website says."

"I know there's a wall and a security company. That's something. I think I see a guard in the booth at the gate."

"They wouldn't have an unmanned booth. I'm almost through to their cameras. There they are. Looks like two patrolling outside. There's a tree closer to the wall in the back. That's where I'd go if I were you. I don't see any sign of electronic locks. Upstairs windows are a weak spot for the security company. That's all I have for you."

"It will have to do," I say with a deep breath.

"I need to ask your boyfriends for a drone. This would be so much easier. Think they'd give me one?"

"Probably. We'll talk to them together when I'm back. Here I go."

I pad across the grass, careful to keep to the shadows. I pause at the side, watching to make sure no neighbors can see me dashing around to the back. It takes a few seconds to locate the tree. Lex didn't say it was on the inside of the wall.

"I didn't bring rope, but it looks like the wall is rough," I say.

"Be careful, Eddie. I have a bad feeling about this."

"It's only a wall."

"That's not what I meant."

"I know, Lex."

"Come home."

"Promise."

What I don't tell my friend is that I have a bad feeling too. If this was any other job, I would have backed out by now. My senses are screaming at me that I need to leave. I can't. I need to protect my bears. Forewarned is forearmed and all that.

Right?

Swallowing, I throw myself at the wall to grab a particularly rough spot. I'm not telling Lex about my current misgivings. If he knew what my intuition is telling me, he'd put away his inhibition about my men and run to them to try to stop me. I can't let that happen. I just need to be extra careful.

I get to the top, navigate the spikes, then grab the branch of the tree. Lex tells me to duck, and I almost fall off the wall in compliance. When it's clear, I hurry over and follow Lex's instructions to a covered gazebo.

My eyes search the back of the house, looking for lattice I've never been lucky enough to come across. You see it all the time in movies and TV shows. Very few people seem to actually like flowering vines crawling up their house. Mr. Hodge apparently doesn't like them either.

"Top left. Second from the corner," Lex whispers into my ear as if someone can hear him.

"Is that his room?"

"No idea, but the window is open. You just need to get there."

He's right. I stare at the open window above a sheer drop. "Time between patrols?"

"About five minutes. You have two before the next."

Nodding, I dash to an overhang I see. It seems to be some sort of balcony, so I jump up to grab the framework and shimmy up to hide on one of the crossbeams. Lex mutters that I need to remain unseen, which causes me to remain as still and small as possible, then gives me the clear to hurry.

I shimmy over to the side closest to the open window, loving the fact I realized the need for upper body strength when we first started doing this. Swinging back and forth, I fling myself to the next window, almost missing the small ledge on it. Moving to the edge is precarious, but I do another swing jump.

My hands grasp the next ledge, one gripping the easier place where the window is open. My right hand misses the ledge on the outside of the open space. My body swings, and my left arm strains to hold my weight. This would be an awesome day to be left-handed.

"Shit," I mumble as I dangle with one hand.

"Are you alright? You're in a blind spot."

"Yeah. Just in a difficult predicament."

"Well, you need to drag yourself out of the predicament in the next forty-five seconds. Patrol coming."

"Double shit."

I can do this. Using my legs for leverage, I pray my arm holds me for this. I'll be lucky to get out of this with a broken ankle otherwise. I push off with my right foot, sending my body twisting back around. My left hand starts to lose its grip, but the right grabs the windowsill before I can fall. Without thought for what might be in this room, I scramble in and sit on the floor, my chest heaving with each breath.

"Patrol didn't stop, so I assume you made it?" Lex asks.

I take a deep breath and look at my hand. It's scraped, but there's no blood. "With time to spare, like maybe half a second. It looks like I'm in some kind of library, but it's dark. All books. No desks."

"I'm going to guess his home office will be the best bet. I can't tell you where that is. The only camera I have access to is in the hall. You'll have to take your chances while searching."

"Great."

After a few more deep breaths, I stand and walk over to the door. Lex tells me it's clear, so I step out, instantly nervous. There is absolutely nowhere to hide in the brightly lit hallway. Not even an inadequate fake plant.

Each door I check gives me pause and causes me to send out a silent prayer. I'm thankful that the ball is tonight. The house is empty. Two bedrooms. A very large bathroom.

"Got it," I say, slipping into the office I find on the other side of the latest door.

"Great. Find his computer, plug the drive in. Don't worry about a password. This is my own program. Just hit enter."

I find a laptop on the desk. Sliding the tiny drive in, I watch a prompt light up and hit enter. A small bar appears on the screen, agonizingly slow. I move through the drawers to find a file about business partners and shifty requests that looks promising. By this time, whatever is happening with the laptop is done. I remove the drive and close the computer. When I go to place the drive back in my pocket, something tells me I need a better hiding place, so I slip it into the underside of my bra. Uncomfortable, but safe.

"Eddie, I lost camera feed. Get out of there."

Rushing to the door, I swing it open to be met with a fist to my face. Blinding light flashes. I feel myself fall. Lex screams my name in a way that seems familiar, but I can't quite place it right now. The last thing I hear is a growl. The last thing I think of is wondering if the empty lobby really was a sign I'll be leaving everyone alone. Darkness takes over.

WARRIN

After speaking to Lex, the three of us sequestered ourselves in the conference room to discuss our next step. Lex already retrieved what we lost, so our clients are safe, and we trusted him when he told us he placed a failsafe on our data.

What we needed to discuss was what retaliation would be taken. Draven was all for storming the fortress, but as usual, Anders used his cool head to calm his heated one. We decided to wait to see what happens next before making a full decision.

Anders is right; we need to do this in a way that won't blow back on us. Heated reactions will endanger us and play right into the wolf shifters' paws. We need to be smart, not emotional.

Those thoughts run through my head as I look in to see if my mate and her friend are still in the security room. It's empty. I know Eddie was shaken up about the turn of events, so I need to make sure she's okay. I hate that I couldn't escort her earlier, but I'm sure Draven will always do whatever he needs to keep her safe. That's all that really matters. She needs to be safe and happy.

I need to make sure she knows that and feels better now. If she's not here, Eddie will be in her room. My key works for her floor. At her door, I knock to be polite. I would never invade her privacy, so I wait. When she doesn't answer, I try again. Worry begins to nag at me.

Fear takes over the need for privacy, so I use the master key we all have. Anders is having one made for Eddie, and she knows we have one, so this won't be a betrayal. At least, I hope it's not. That thought makes me hesitate, but my concern is too strong to make me hold off for too long. Entering shows me that the apartment is empty. My mate's scent is here. It's faded. Maybe a couple of hours ago.

Lex's chair is knocked over behind his desk, so I walk over to right it. My hip bumps the desk harder than I like. It seems my body is just too big. The screens light up, and the chair falls from my hands. Lunar Financial's website is on one screen. The address for the CEO on the other. Panicked, I run for the elevator while dialing Anders.

"Warrin?"

"We need to check the security cameras. I can't find Eddie, and I think she did something dangerous."

"What do you think she did?"

I press the button and the doors close. "Lex's chair is knocked over. His computer shows information on the wolves. I think she was so worried that she went to the alpha's house."

"Get to security. I'll call Draven on my way."

When I get to the room, Draven is already in the chair accessing the feed. Anders joins us as he finds her running to her vehicle. Eddie speeds away so fast that it's clear she's in a hurry. An hour later, we find Lex running onto the elevator. His mouth is moving.

"We need to get cameras with sound," I say.

"Whatever he's saying, he's in a panic. Something happened," Anders says. "It's safe to say if she did what we think she did, he helped."

"It's clear the mutt did something stupid," Draven mutters. "She was wearing her thief clothes."

We follow Lex's path outside. He hails a cab but doesn't catch it in time. A black SUV pulls up. When he tries to turn and run, they knock him out, tie his hands, throw him in the back, then speed away. It's as if they were waiting for him.

All three of us are running for the elevator at the same time. "If they've done something to her," Draven growls.

"We'd know if they did, Draven," Anders says. "Two of us are mated to her. We'd feel her die. She's alive, and the two of us can track her. We know she went to the den of the enemy. We just need to pick up the scent."

"It doesn't matter," Draven argues. "I'm going to rip them apart limb from limb."

Not if I get to them first. I won't fail her.

CHAPTER THIRTY ONE
THE HUNT IS ON

My body bouncing on a hard surface shocks me back to consciousness. Blinking does nothing to dispel the fog from my vision or my head. When I try to move, I realize my hands are bound—duct tape I'd guess by the fact stickiness pulls the little hairs on my wrists. Another piece covers my mouth, which muffles my groan at the increase of my headache with the next bounce.

As my vision slowly clears, what happened comes back one piece at a time. The blurriness dissolves into what looks like the back of a huge SUV. I'm not allowed to talk or move, but I can see. That means they don't care if I know where we are because they don't expect it to matter. Not that I expect a simple slap on the wrist from a group of wolves who have been threatening my life for the last few weeks. I need to get out of here.

Pushing my feet out to test the hatch, I realize my ankles are bound as well. Come on. A little overkill? Okay, maybe not. A little unfair? Yes. How am I going to break free like this? Give a girl a chance.

The vehicle slams to a stop, making me roll into the back seat and smash my nose on something hard. If I could hiss through duct tape, I would be doing that. Let's just keep adding to my discomfort. I know being uncomfortable isn't something I should focus on right now, but I would rather not address the deadly elephant in the room, or trunk in this case.

Cold air hits my back when the hatch is flung open, reminding me that I don't wear warm clothes while slithering around in the darkness. I'm dragged out of the vehicle and thrown to the ground. When I curl to protect anything easily damaged, I feel something hard stab under my boob. Well, that thumb drive is in for the long haul it seems. Not that it's going to be doing me any good from here.

The man from the laundry room is leering at me from above. "Fancy meeting you here," I try to mumble through my tape.

Either he chooses not to answer, or he can't hear me. I'm going to go with the latter because even I can barely hear me. I'm hoisted and tossed over his shoulder, carried to a place in front of the headlights. That's when I realize there are two more vehicles because their lights are extra bright when combined. I land on the dirt and look to my right. My eyes go wide because I would recognize that blurred form in any condition.

"Lex!" At least, I try to say my friend's name. Who knew a three-letter word could sound so garbled?

A figure steps in front of us. It's hard to make out his features through the spots still swimming through my eyes from looking into the headlights. I can tell he's wearing sunglasses. Only idiots look into bright light without eye protection. Note for later if I can get out of this.

The dancing circles disappear, bringing the man in front of me into focus. When he notices my shock, he asks, "Recognize me?"

No way am I falling for that. I hate sounding like an idiot who thinks someone can hear her through a layer of duct tape. I've done that enough tonight. He cocks his head to the side, finally realizing the reason for my hesitance. Mr. Evil Wolf crouches down and removes the tape, making me cry out. Instant lip wax. Lex's yell tells me someone else freed his mouth.

I grimace my way to a grin. "Mr. Hodge. What a pleasant surprise. Very nice of you to invite me to your party in the woods."

Why would I be polite when I'm sure I'm about to die? The bastard won't see me beg. I sure want to. Sassy Eddie is what he gets, not scared Edith.

"Well, it's not like you were invited," he says in that cool tone only evil villains can accomplish. "You have a habit of being where you aren't welcomed. I caught the great thief that sneaks in like a slithering snake."

"I'm more like a cat. I'm not much for scales."

"Whatever you call it, you're a pest. One I'll be happy to be rid of. Did you really think my people wouldn't be watching for signs of your presence?"

I glance at my best friend. "This was all my fault. Let him go."

The CEO of Lunar Financial laughs. "He knows who we are. That won't be smart. Don't you think I know who the cyborg of the two of you is? The one that foiled my attempt this morning? I'm not as stupid as you give me credit for, which is why I made sure to have my men watch for you. I was notified the second they smelled you outside. So predictable. For instance, this wouldn't have done you much good."

Steve holds up the folder I was carrying when knocked out. He lights it on fire in front of me, going on and on about how it wasn't even good information. He planted it to lure me.

Prick.

"So, Ms. Kitty Cat. Want to see what wolves do to thieves of the feline variety?"

Without answering, I lift my chin. My heart thumps so hard against my chest my breastbone throbs, but I won't show fear in the face of death. They can probably hear it if they're like my bears. That doesn't mean I'm willing to show it. They can do their worst, which will probably be a lot since being torn apart by wolves can't be pleasant. I won't show fear. I only hope I can hold out.

Lex gasps as the two men behind the smug businessman change into wolves. If there was any hope they'd let us go—there wasn't—it's gone now. The wolf still in human form smiles at me. "What do you think will happen to your mates when you die screaming in agony? I can only smell two of them on you, but the other will still mourn. Anders won't survive the death of another mate. Warrin is too soft-hearted. Draven isn't as untouchable as he thinks."

"Mates? What?" Lex says, and my heart falls because between the wolves and mates, I have some explaining to do. If we make it out of here, he's not going to be happy with me.

"She didn't tell you. It seems like you two have something to talk about."

A knife flashes, and I wonder if we're going to be tortured for information before being turned into dog chow. Our hands and ankles are freed. I watch, wary of what's to come. I don't have to wait long.

"My associates here are hungry for fresh meat," he says, turning and motioning toward the wolves. "But, you see, wolves like the hunt. You two have three minutes. Use them wisely."

My heart stops as the meaning of his words hits me. We jump to our feet at the same time, taking off into the trees. Lex pants beside me. "Care to explain?"

"Now is definitely not the time, Lex."

Howls echo behind us, and I wonder if it's been three minutes. I drag my friend to a halt and point at the nearest tree. "Right. Wolves can't climb," he mumbles.

He scrambles up to the lowest branch, then another higher. I jump at the tree beside him instead of waiting for clear climbing space. A wolf lunges at my dangling feet, but it misses by less than an inch. Great. Another tree.

And like before, a wolf circling and growling. What's different? No bears to take the wolves out. My situation is hopeless. I can't get down without being torn to shreds. There's no way I can fight a mouthful of razor-sharp teeth. What's worse is I brought my best friend down with me. Can this get any worse?

"Can we talk now?"

My eyes find my best friend. I guess it can get worse. The accusation under the panic in Lex's eyes hurts. I'm going to die with my best friend hating me. It's what I deserve for getting him to the point of being stuck in a tree like a cat avoiding the predators below. No firemen will come rescue us though, so not completely the same.

"You knew," Lex says before I can answer. "I see it on your face. You're absolutely terrified, but you're not shocked. You knew these were werewolves. You knew and didn't tell me. What have you done?!"

His tone went from accusatory to hysterical in a short time. "Would you have listened to me if I came to tell you I know people who shift into animals are real? Or would you have worried about my sanity and had me committed?"

"At least you would have been safe!"

I laugh. "Drugged up in the hospital because my best friend didn't believe me."

"Because you didn't give me a chance, Eddie. Now we're going to be digested by a bunch of wolves! Can this night get any worse?"

Unable to find a fitting argument, I press my lips together. I want to be a smartass and tell him not to tempt fate with that last question, but the look on his face tells me it's not the time for dark humor. Despite the wolves barking at our trees, my adrenaline cools enough to remind me I'm not dressed for this weather.

Neither is Lex. "Why aren't you wearing a coat? How did they get you?"

"I was so worried about the best friend that has been keeping dangerous secrets from me that I didn't put one on when I rushed out to save her. They were waiting, Eddie. They swooped in the second it was safe to do so, then knocked me out. Who knows how long they've been watching? They probably followed you to the house and laughed the whole time you were breaking in!"

Lex needs to stop yelling things I've already questioned. I doubt he'd enjoy me pointing that out right now. "I didn't know they were watching."

"But you knew what they were! What was that thing about mates, Eddie? What did he mean? Are those three wolves too?"

When I stare in silence for a while, he actually snarls at me. "Fine! They aren't wolves, Lex. They're bears. Is that what you wanted to hear? He used the word mates because I've bound myself to Anders and Warrin. I'll also choose Draven too if he'll get his head out of his ass. Happy now?"

"Three guys?"

"You don't have any right to dictate what I do with my social life or who I decide to spend the rest of my life with."

Lex hits his branch with the side of his fist. "It is my business when you put my life in jeopardy. Did you even think about what this would do to me? Was my life anywhere on your list of things to think about?"

"Every single day. I'm riddled with guilt and afraid of losing you, but I love them, Lex. If I knew some way to keep you out of this and still have the men I love, I would have."

"You chose three practical strangers over me."

The grief in his voice curdles the blood in my veins. I swallow. I never wanted to hurt him. "I'm sorry. I was trying to have them and you at the same time."

Lex sighs and turns his head away. No more words come out of his mouth. I wait for a few minutes. "Please, Lex. I don't want to lose your friendship."

"Then you shouldn't have lied to me. Not that it matters right now. We're delicious chopped liver."

Tears freeze on my cheeks. I've lost my best friend in the end—at the end. I'm going to die with the only person who ever truly understood me hating me. Warrin is going to die. Anders is going to die. They'll pick Draven off when he's reeling from the loss of everyone. All because I couldn't listen to my intuition. I let everyone down.

A slow clap brings my attention to the darkness between the trees. Steven Hodge steps out from the shadows as snow begins to fall around us. The amusement in his eyes is too much. It may be childish, but I can't help flipping him off.

The leader of the enemy chuckles. "That was even more entertaining than I expected. Dinner and a show."

ANDERS

We watch as Draven circles the house, keeping strictly to the shadows. Eddie's car is abandoned a few blocks away. As expected, her scent leads to the lair of the alpha wolf. There's no sign of her. Either she came in and didn't come out, or they've abducted our mate.

Draven returns. "From my hiding place, I believe I can tell she went over the back wall. I don't smell her coming back out. When I got close to the front, I think I smelled blood, but I can't be sure, which means it's not enough for me to tell it's hers or for it to mean it's a fatal injury."

"What would the wolves do with her?"

Draven shrugs. "They may have cells in the basement like we do, or they might have transported her somewhere else. I could smell strong exhaust. We can try following that."

"I don't like leaving here in case she still remains and a chance presents itself," I say.

"I'll stay. You two go."

"Draven..."

"You two have the best chance of following her scent. I can pick it up, but we aren't mated yet, so it's harder for me. I'm smaller and better suited for stealth if I happen to see her."

My mind goes over everything. Splitting up is the last thing I want to do, but he's right. We need to cover all angles. This is the only way to do that.

"Could you tell which way the vehicle you smelled went?" I ask.

Draven points down the road. "I think that way. It was hard to tell. You'll know when you get closer."

"We'll make sure we're far enough down the road to avoid picking up attention, then we'll see what we can find. Be careful, brother."

Draven's only reply is a grunt as we hurry in the direction he indicated. They'll want to take her somewhere secluded. I have a few places in mind, but we'll see which is more likely as we go. I just hope the scent doesn't get too old before we have a solid idea. We have to find her. I can't let them murder another mate. Eddie is depending on us.

CHAPTER THIRTY TWO
COLD DANGER

"Go to hell."

Hodge chuckles. "I'm sorry I caused distress to such a strong relationship. Friendships are built on lies, after all. Oh, wait."

"Screw you."

"Unlike those despicable bears, I don't diddle with humans. Your people are inferior in everything except your breeding rate. Sometimes a little extra irritating, like you. You'll be out of my hair soon."

Scrambling makes me look down. The wolf below my tree continues to try to climb, dislodging pieces of bark. I'm not sure why they don't turn back and come for us. Unless this is nothing but a big game to them. Wouldn't surprise me if it is.

"Looks like your minions can't get to me," I say.

"They're merely waiting."

"For?"

"It's pretty cold tonight. Something else humans don't have going for them. You can't withstand the cold. I can already see your body shuddering and covered in goosebumps. How long until you freeze too much? You'll either die where you sit or fall. My bet is on fall when your limbs go numb. All we have to do is wait because no one is coming for you. No one knows where you are."

He's right. I know he is. Even now, I've lost all feeling to my fingers and toes. That doesn't mean I have to give in to despair. No matter how hopeless the situation seems, there has to be some form of escape. I look over at my angry friend to see him using his arms to hug the tree tighter. Anything to keep his seat. I follow his example. I'd rather freeze to death in a tree than be eaten by wolves.

Howls rend the air, and my gaze sweeps the dark forest. I have no idea where we are. When I find no other wolves, I look down on the CEO of the company intent on hurting my bears. The sneer of annoyance on his face tells me something is going on seconds before a white blur hits the wolf fighting to scare me.

"Warrin!" I cry out, excited to see my polar bear here.

That is, until more wolves come out of the trees as if they're answering some kind of call I can't hear. Fear makes me stand on my branch, my butt numb from the cold. Warrin fights like a crazed bear fighting for his life. I guess he is.

Blood darkens his red coat, making my heart stop. Anders joins the fight, knocking one from his white furred brother. Hodge stands back, watching the battle with pursed lips. He observes but doesn't interfere. It's as if he's waiting to see what happens before making a move.

The grizzly bear rears up, paws in the air. I could reach down and touch his furry hands if I wanted to, but it would only distract Anders. Both front paws land on a wolf, crushing it on impact. I yell my encouragement, adrenaline warming my body once more.

Movement from our enemies' leader draws my attention. I watch with growing tension as he pulls a gun from the back waistband of his pants. Frozen limbs protest as I force myself to stand. I hop from one branch to the next, channeling my inner cat burglar. Even a cat can take down a wolf if she's smart about it. He won't hurt my bears.

So focused on my men, Hodge doesn't even bother to look up. I drop from the branch above him as he takes aim. The gun goes off, but I have to trust that I disturbed his aim enough to save whichever one he was aiming for.

We roll in a tangle of limbs, him growling his frustration. I'm pretty sure my elbow hit a rock, but the pain is a distant flare. My mind is only on surviving this battle on the ground and making sure my bears are safe.

Our roll ends with the angry wolf man on top of me. His hands go around my throat. He doesn't need to be in fur to ruin me. Numb fingers fumble at his wrists as my lungs realize no more air is incoming. Failing to get a good grip, I try to bring my fists down on the inside of his elbows. Hodge is locked tight. This feels hopeless.

Unconsciousness threatens when I realize my attacker has lifted off me far enough to enable him to press all of his wait down on my throat. I bring my knee up. The resulting howl sounds nothing like a wolf, and my lungs pull in greedy bucketfuls of oxygen. My triumph only lasts for a moment.

Angrier now than I've seen him since pulled from the trunk, Hodge's muscles twitch and bunch. His eyes are heated as a snout grows from his face. He's about to go full wolf on me, and all his weight is still pinning me down.

While fur sprouts over his body, my mind turns. That's when I remember my lock picks. Fumbling with cold fingers is difficult, especially with the weight of a wolf on top of me, but I manage to pull one from my pocket. I plunge it into his eye.

This time, his howl of agony is half wolf and half human, an eerie sound that I'll never forget. I'm sure I'll have nightmares of it from years to come, and it's something I hope never to hear again. By my calculations, I have seconds. My eyes fall on the gun he dropped.

Rolling, I manage to grip the weapon. When I look back, Hodge is completely in wolf form. He lunges, and I roll toward his blind side. Unused to being half blind, he snarls and corrects, but it's already too late. I've never used a gun before, but no one can miss at this range. The bullet punctures his skull.

Hodge's limp weight lands on me, and the air is forced from my lungs. Stars flash before my eyes, dull ones unlike those that my bears show me. Blinking, I try to take a deep breath, but my lungs can't fully expand with the wolf on top of me. The weight is slowly pulled off, and I'm able to inhale a grateful breath.

Lex stares down at me. This close, I notice the cracks in the glass of his spectacles. I'm sure we can get him new ones. There are still enough savings, or the guys will probably offer.

The guys. Gasping, I sit up and look around. If Lex is able to be on the ground without certain death, the fight must be over. My searching eyes show me I'm right. Warrin stands naked to the cold air without a hint of a goosebump anywhere on his glorious form.

Anders is still a grizzly. His massive shoulders are sagging, making my heart stutter. When he transforms, he remains on all fours with his back moving up and down. He collapses.

"Anders!" I cry, rushing over to him.

Warrin already has him rolled onto his back to reveal the bullet hole in Anders's muscular chest. It seems the bastard didn't miss like I hoped. I fall to my knees.

"I need to get him back to the office," Warrin says.

I nod, standing to look at where Hodge changed into a wolf. Warrin lifts Anders and stumbles toward the vehicles that wait where we came in. The bright moon gives me enough light to look, leaving me frantic with the thought he had them on him.

"What are you looking for?" Lex asks.

"Keys."

"They're probably closer to the SUVs."

With a grunt, I stand, conceding the point before hurrying back. I can't think straight right now. As Lex assumed, Warrin is waiting with one of them running. I slip in back to keep Anders company while a reluctant Lex slides into the passenger seat.

Breathing shallow, Anders looks pale. My heart doesn't stutter this time. It stops.

"Tell me he'll be okay," I say to no one.

Warrin answers anyway. "It's difficult to tell, but Anders is a tough one. If anyone will pull through, it's him. Since it's not a shifter bite, I'm going to assume he'll heal in decent time. We just have to get him home, stop the bleeding, and stabilize him."

Swallowing is hard, but I manage with another nod. This is my fault. They came to save me because I didn't trust my instincts when they screamed danger. I should have pulled away when my intuition told me to. Now I might lose my big grizzly.

I don't care what Warrin says. This strong man looks so weak and sunken. How could I do this to someone so full of life and strength? He's survived so much, and I came along to put him in an impossible situation. They all would have been better off without me.

"We need to talk," Lex says, twisting in his seat to look back at me.

Not now. I can't do this now, so I keep my mouth shut and my eyes on Anders's still form. My hand cups his cheeks, alarming me with how chill his skin feels. Tears blur my vision.

"Eddie, we need to discuss everything that just happened and why you didn't trust me," Lex says.

Fury fills me. "Not now, Lex!"

"Then when? Are we going to avoid it forever?"

"I told you not now! I know you think this is nothing but a careless fling, but you're wrong. All three of these men are entrenched in my body and soul. One of the men I love is dying right now because of a mistake I made. This is not the time for your righteous anger. Leave. Me. Be."

"Fine. I'll get my stuff and go stay with Jared."

Annoyance fans the flames of rage. "You will not. It's safest for you there, and I won't let you get yourself killed because you're mad at me for not trusting that you'd believe me if I told you that men can shift into bears and wolves. Let it go. We can fight later."

"You can't stop me."

"Want to make a bet?" I ask with teeth clenched. "Even try it, and I'll have Warrin lock you in the cell in the basement."

"He won't."

I glare at my friend, still hoping he sees me the same through both of our anger. Warrin saves me from answering. "While I normally wouldn't do it, if she asked me, I would. I'd do anything for her."

Satisfied that Lex's shocked look shows a bit of understanding, I get back to gazing worriedly at the bear lying unconscious. I put his head in my lap and stroke his hair. It must be my imagination, but I swear I see a little color come back to his cheeks.

When we arrive, Lex sulks back to our suite while I follow Warrin to Anders's. His living area reminds me of the cabin, all rustic luxury. We bypass everything to lay him in the soft bed.

Warrin tears his shirt open to reveal the bullet hole. It doesn't bleed any longer, but it's not healed either. I sit down and take his large hand in mine while my gentle giant pulls his phone out of his pocket. He leaves the room.

"I'm sorry," I whisper.

Climbing under the covers, I snuggle in close. Warrin returns after a few minutes. "Draven is hot wiring your car, then he's going to dispose of the one we drove home."

"Okay."

Speaking that single word breaks the dam holding my emotions. Warrin slides in next to me, pulling me close and letting me sob. I bury my face in his chest.

"I'm so sorry. This is all my fault," I say when I can speak again.

"It's not. You have a big heart and only wanted to protect us. None of us blames you."

"But I got Anders shot."

"And he won't want to see you crying over him. Trust me when I say we'd do anything for you. None of us will ever blame you for loving us because we feel the same."

"Not even Draven?" I say with sarcasm.

Warrin chuckles. "Not even Draven."

I let him think his words dispel my guilt. They haven't, but I don't want him worrying about me. "I'm going to have to tell Lex all of it now."

"I know. We understand. He's seen too much. I told security not to let him leave if it makes you feel better. You can deal with that tomorrow. All of our problems will wait until tomorrow."

"I don't want to leave him."

"You don't have to."

"Will you stay?"

Warrin holds me tighter and kisses the top of my head. "Always."

CHAPTER THIRTY THREE
DISTRUST

The steady rise and fall of Anders's chest assures me that he still breathes. Sleep didn't come easily last night, so my eyes are burning like crazy. The bullet holes seem to be healing, but Anders has not regained consciousness. This keeps me from relaxing into complacency. My grizzly has to make it.

"Eddie."

Tired eyes find Warrin standing next to the bed. He had gone to check with Draven to make sure that the wolves' vehicle was disposed of and mine retrieved. I have yet to see the cranky black bear. I know it's coming soon, and I'm sure he will have something to say about me putting the three of them in danger. Draven is not known for keeping his mouth shut.

Warrin crouches beside my position on the bed. "You are still in last night's dirty clothes and need to clean up the cuts and bruises you gained."

"What if Anders doesn't make it?"

"He will. He's healing, and the color is returning to his skin. He's on the mend. Do you think he'd want you to stay in bed with him instead of taking care of yourself? I'll stay with him."

The question makes me flinch. No. Anders would not like that. All he ever wants to do is spoil me. If he wakes up with me a mess, he'll be unhappy. I won't be scolded, but his disappointment will hurt just as much. I can always come back when I wash last night from my skin.

With a nod to my concerned polar bear, I give Anders a soft kiss and climb from the bed engulfing me. Warrin brushes soft lips over my forehead. One last glance at Anders tells me there won't be any significant change if I take care of myself. Although, I'm not looking forward to coming face to face with Lex so soon. That thought alone makes me want to ask if I can shower here, but I'm smart enough to realize Warrin is also trying to give me a break from my vigil.

The elevator ride down to my floor goes too fast. Our apartment is quiet when I enter, so I sneak into my room to grab some clothes before making my way to the bathroom. My reflection causes a grimace to add to the chaos I see in the mirror. My blonde hair sticks out in all directions, and I take the time to pick twigs and leaves out of the rat's nest on top of my head. A nasty scab on my forehead is surrounded by blood that stiffens the skin. Various cuts and bruises can be seen through the holes in my black clothes. I'm a mess.

I strip and step into the hot stream of water in my large shower. The warm liquid stings the cut from the lump made from the man knocking me out at Hodge's home, right over top the broken fang wound. My washcloth comes away pink with flakes of dark red. That's going to take some time to heal, and I'm wondering how many times a supernatural shifter is going to leave me a headache upon our first meeting.

Done, I exit and search my bra. The drive is still there, flooding me with relief. At least it wasn't all for nothing. We can only hope that something useful is on this thing. The wolves need to be taken out.

Lex is turning on the television when I walk out, ignored by the dark-haired man standing next to the couch with his arms crossed over his chest. My friend—I hope he's still a friend—looks uncomfortable in his seat next to the annoyed black bear of a man. Draven directs him to turn to a news station. A reporter stands in front of a large building.

"Steven Hodge, CEO of Lunar Financial, passed away last night. It is said to be a peaceful passing, and his family asks for privacy in this time of grief. His son, Jackson Hodge, will take his place when their mourning period is done. He promises nothing will change."

Lex grunts while Draven mutters something I can't make out. Neither is happy with the news, and I can't blame them. "What else could we really expect?" I say.

My voice startles Lex badly enough to make him jump. He looks up at Draven, who I'm sure has a smirk on his face. "You knew she was there, didn't you?"

"I could hear and smell her, so yes."

"Of course. You could have warned me."

"And miss your reaction?"

With a scowl for Draven, Lex turns a glare on me. "And you! What the hell did you drag me into?"

Here we go. "I never expected it to happen like this, Lex. It was just another way to make the money we need to help others more."

"Don't give me that. Even if you didn't expect it, you should have told me when you knew."

"We told her not to," Draven cuts in, surprising me with his defensive stance.

"It doesn't matter what you told her," he says before turning back my way. "I thought we were friends."

"You wouldn't have believed me, Lex, and you know it. What would you have said if I told you I found out that all three of our bosses can shift into bears? You would have told me I needed to see a doctor."

"How would you know when you didn't give me a chance?! Friends don't keep these kinds of secrets. Even when I was put in danger, you didn't think to give me the whole truth."

I bite my lip. No matter how much I argue, I can't dispute that. I should have told him. I wanted to. It still wasn't my secret to tell.

Lex isn't done. "Besides that... three men, Eddie? Three? What are you thinking?"

"My sex life is none of your business. Even then, I never lied to you about that."

"But *you* have," Draven cuts in with a cold look directed at Lex.

When my friend's color drains, I clench my fists. "What do you mean?"

"It took me a while to figure out whether she knew or not, but it's clear to me how clueless she is."

I want to take issue with the clueless part of that, but I look at my friend instead. He glances between me and Draven, his mouth opening and closing like a fish. "I don't know what you're talking about."

"Even now, you deny it?" Draven asks. "I could smell it on you that day in your apartment. I could smell him on you. No judgment from me, but I don't think you deserve the right to judge her for keeping secrets."

My brows furrow in thought. What is he— "Jared?!"

Lex flinches, and it all comes crashing in on me. Their constant companionship. Their late nights in his room. The fact the man never left our damn apartment and felt the need to butt into everything.

"Why didn't you tell me?" I ask. "It all makes sense now, but I'm hurt that you felt you couldn't talk to me. I would've been a little more tolerant of the freeloader if I knew."

"Don't come at me like that. Not after what you have kept from me."

"I didn't tell you that men that can shift into animals are real because I was asked not to. It's not exactly an open club. You didn't tell me you were screwing Jared. Big difference. I would have been supportive of your secret."

My heart breaks knowing Lex wouldn't come out to me. I thought we told each other everything, except about the secret presence of the supernatural world.

"You don't know what it was like growing up in a home that wouldn't support me. I was nervous you'd look at me differently."

"Damn it, Lex. I grew up unsupported by everyone but you. You should have told me, but I guess we weren't the friends I thought we were."

His brown eyes flash. "You put me in danger. As we just learned, I'm probably still in danger because of your secrets. It's not the same."

My jaw clenches. "You're right. I kept a secret that wasn't my own from you. You didn't tell me you were dating your jock friend. Such a huge similarity there. You know what? Forget it. I'm not going to stand here. I need some space. If you really want freedom from me and all the trouble I cause, then figure out what's on this and how to use it to our advantage."

I stomp over and slam the drive down on his desk before leaving, with Draven following behind me. In the elevator, I feel lost. I stare at the numbers without seeing them.

"Where do you want to go?" Draven asks.

"I was originally going back to see Anders again, but I can't like this. He needs peace and calm, not my messy emotions. I don't know where to go."

Draven reaches over to press his floor, and I don't bother to argue. It's as good a place as any right now. His is the only suite I haven't seen. Although, I'm surprised he hasn't laid into me yet. Maybe I should say something first.

As the door opens, I decide to. "I'm sorry for last night. I didn't mean to cause problems and get Anders shot."

"As stupid as what you did was," Draven days, stepping off the elevator in front of me, "none of it was your fault. You putting your life in such danger makes me angry, but I know you were only trying to help. Doesn't mean I'm happy with it though."

That's it? No scathing words. No heated scolding. No smoking derision. All I get is told that I did something stupid, he's not happy about it, and he understands. "Did the wolves change you out for someone else?"

Draven chuckles, a dark sound that gives me goosebumps. "While I'm quick to anger, I'm actually pretty intelligent. All my raving and ranting was done alone last night. Now that I'm calm, I see where you're coming from. That doesn't mean I don't want to punish you for it."

His words halt my steps, and I find myself against the wall with his hands boxing me in. All thoughts of anger and concern drift away on the wind, along with any moisture in my throat. Lex has me at a distance. Anders is in another room and alive. The only people here are me and Draven. I lick my lips.

That signature smirk returns. "Thirsty?"

"What?" I croak.

"Sounds like you are."

When Draven suddenly walks away from me, it takes all my willpower not to groan in frustration. He needs to stop doing things like that. To occupy my thoughts, I turn around to take in my surroundings. Black leather furniture. Gray carpets. An electric fireplace. This place screams Draven.

My eyes fall on a pencil drawing surrounded by a black frame. I move closer to look. A small child dances in front of a group of trees. She looks happy and free.

"Merigold," Draven says behind me, making me jump.

"Did you draw this?"

He hands me a glass of water. "I did. It was shortly before I lost her forever. I wasn't the nicest to her that day."

"I'm sure she knew you love her."

"She was so full of life that no one couldn't love her."

My eyes follow the lines on the paper as I take a sip of water. "You draw really well."

"I used to."

"Used to?"

"This was the last picture I ever drew."

Pressing my lips together, I turn to gaze into his dark eyes. There's pain deep in those depths. This isn't the cocky, attitude-filled black bear I'm used to. This is a man, one deeply injured from a terrible loss. This is a brother who looks upon the sister he lost with regret.

I place my glass on the table by the door and surprise him with a kiss. The shock only lasts a moment before he changes my soft caress into a devouring of my mouth. I find myself pushed against the wall again, my hands running over the planes of his chest. The elevator dings, and Warrin walks through.

He stops with wide eyes. "I went to your apartment. Lex is at his computer and said you weren't there. I figured I'd check here."

Still pinned against the wall, I say, "Did something happen with Anders?"

"He's awake."

"You probably want to go see him," Draven says, pushing away.

I grab his wrist. "I do, but I want to do something first."

"What's that?"

"I want to ask you to be my third mate."

"I thought you'd never ask."

With a growl, he lifts me. My legs wrap around his waist of their own accord, and I use my fingers to motion for Warrin to follow. He grins and doesn't need to be offered twice.

Draven tosses me on his bed hard enough to make me bounce on the firm mattress. He removes my pants while Warrin works on my shirt. The heat rising in me keeps me warm, producing an ache that can only be calmed with one thing.

My polar bear goes straight for my breast, sucking one nipple into his mouth while the other enjoys the attention of his thumb. Draven pulls the sheets out from under me, twisting them as I writhe from the pleasure Warrin gives me.

My hands are pulled above my head and tied with the sheets. It only takes a moment for me to realize what's happening. Warrin pulls up and looks over with his eyes narrowed. "What are you doing?"

"Making sure she can't escape."

"I'm not going anywhere," I interject, "but I've always wanted to try this."

Warrin looks shocked. "I didn't know this is what you liked. I've always tried to be respectful. I'm sorry if it wasn't as fun."

His blue eyes fall, and I pull him into a kiss, which is hard with my hands tied above my head. "I like everything, my gentle giant. All three of you bring something different, and I love it all. Don't change. I like you just as you are."

"If you're sure."

"As sure as anyone can be. You're perfect."

Any further conversation is lost when Draven enters me. I gasp and arch my back, which gives Warrin greater access to his favorite part of me. Draven thrusts in and out while Warrin nibbles my throat and kneads my breasts. The pressure builds.

"Don't let go now, Mutt," Draven says with a moan.

"I'm trying, but you have no idea how good this feels."

"Trust me; I think I have an idea."

Draven thrusts harder, practically ramming into me with each move of his hips. There's no pain, only mind-numbing pleasure that leaves me breathless. When I can take no more, I release the built up pressure with a loud cry. Draven follows me over the edge, sinking his teeth into my neck.

All three of us lie on the bed. Panting fills the small space as Warrin frees my wrists. I need to check on Anders, but right now, my heart is too fast. I'll take a couple minutes with these two. All three bears are mine.

ANDERS

Everything hurts. Just moving into a sitting position in my bed fills the room with grunts and groans. Warrin told me he was going to let Eddie know that I'm awake, but it's been a while. They probably got distracted, which I can't blame them at all. She distracts me merely by being in the same room.

This is strange. I never really expected to take another mate. My need to take down those that murdered my mate years ago is what keeps me going. Even more, I never expected to love a human. There's something about Eddie that pulled me to her from the start, even while unconscious in our cell.

The door opens, followed by multiple sets of footsteps. Eddie rushes in and carefully slides onto the bed next to me, almost squeaking when the mattress tries to swallow her. I smile and wrap her in my arms, taking a deep inhale that leaves me pleased. "You mated Draven."

"I did. That's why it took me so long to get back to you. Warrin made me leave you."

"He told me, and I'm glad he did. You couldn't do anything to help while I was unconscious." I kiss the top of her head. "When I'm well enough, we'll complete the mating ritual."

Her shiver sends a delicious feeling through me. I am definitely looking forward to it. I'm sure we all are. Eddie may be unexpected, but she's absolutely perfect. I look forward to taking the time to explore this bond with her for the rest of our days.

"I'm so sorry I got you shot," she whispers.

Ignoring the sharp pinch of pain, I pull her tighter against me. "I get why you did it, and I'm not mad. The last thing I want is for you to put yourself in danger over us. We're here to protect you; not the other way around."

"I refuse to only take. You have to let me give too."

"We will, but let's not do this again. You are forgiven because you are not at fault. It was a high emotion time, and you did what you felt you needed to." I look at my newfound brothers. "Fallout?"

"I took care of the vehicle they brought you home in," Draven says. "My associates didn't get much from Jeff because they kept him mostly in the dark. News of the alpha's death is on all the news stations, but they're keeping it close. To the public, it's labeled as a peaceful passing. His son is gearing up to take his place."

"So, we're right back where we started?"

Eddie pulls away, taking her warmth with her. "Not completely. They destroyed the physical evidence I found, but I had a flash drive hidden in my bra. Lex hacked into his computer with it and downloaded everything. I'm hoping there's something on it that can help."

"We have a direction. I'm going to clean up, but the day is going to start soon. We need to make sure we're present."

"I have some locksmiths coming in today. Shouldn't you rest longer?"

"Fit as a bear," I reply, giving her a soft kiss. We'll figure this out. I won't let them get away with trying to kill my second mate.

CHAPTER THIRTY FOUR
HAVING WORDS

I stare at the door to the closet, sad that the lock will never get stuck with me trapped with a polar bear again. I'll have to ask for a set of keys. An inability to get stuck doesn't mean I can't lock my bears in the room. Construction on the new safety deposit room still goes on, but the lesser locks are being taken care of today. Electronic number pads are being replaced next week. Soon, even I won't be able to break in.

My mates are in their offices and making rounds on their business floors to assuage any worries. The excuse for the day off was a broken water main, so it's not like they know of the breach. Only the guard at the computer that day has any idea, and he's signed a non-disclosure. Turns out that my bears pay well enough to inspire loyalty.

Lex still types away in our suite, searching for anything to take the wolves down. I expected him to have it figured out faster, but I know he's determined enough not to give up without answers. Even if it's only to be able to walk away from me without putting Jared in danger.

That thought makes my heart sink. He didn't trust me. I don't care one bit who he sleeps with, dates, or falls in love with. I'd never judge him like that. He should know this. It hurts that he can't trust me enough to tell me these things.

Sure, I don't care much for Jared. That doesn't mean I will judge him for it.

The thought of losing him after this is all over doesn't make me feel any better. I have my three men, but I need my non-related brother in my life too. We have been best friends for so long. It seems like a terrible trade. I won't give up my mates for anything, but I don't want to lose my best friend over it all.

As if my thoughts summon him, Lex runs over to me. "I got it. Have the guys meet us in our suite."

He rushes away without any other words. I purse my lips in thought. For some reason, the glare I've been dealing with since he found out is gone. Maybe he's just happy about finding an answer so he can leave. Clenching my teeth, I send all three men a text. I'll deal with that when the time comes. Even if Lex has the holy grail of dirt on the enemy, it will take time to work. A few days of peace may make speaking with him easier.

By the time I reach our floor, Draven and Anders are already there. Warrin enters shortly after. Instead of angry and annoyed, Lex looks happy and excited. This is a good sign.

"Why did you run me down and not just text or call?" I say.

Lex blinks in confusion. "I was so excited I forgot about phones."

I shake my head but drop the subject. "Did my flash drive help?"

"Yes and no." The guys look at me in question, and I shrug. Lex continues without prompting. "His laptop was actually pretty boring for a murderous werewolf. What it did give me was access to their professional security system, which allowed me to slip in without detection. I may not have been able to take that security company head on, but I'm quite proud of sneaking in through another source."

"You got into Lunar Financial?"

His grin is all I need. "I did. As it turns out, these people are pretty nasty. We've seen a lot of underhanded dealings in our profession, but this is something else; connections with police, emergency personnel, even the justice system. Not to mention money laundering through their many subsidiaries. Bribes, threats, prostitution. You name it, and I found proof."

"If they have so many in their pockets, how are we going to take them down?" Warrin asks.

"Don't underestimate him," I mutter.

"Thank you for the much deserved confidence, Eddie." Lex is absolutely giddy, his normal crankiness nowhere to be seen. "What they don't have complete control over is the media. Watch this."

After a few taps, nothing happens. Draven narrows his eyes. "What are we watching?"

"I just sent all the incriminating evidence to all the major media outlets; news, black market sites, and any group that would be interested enough to throw this information all over social media. With this much exposure, the government agencies will have to step in. I'm talking feds, CIA, the works. Local judiciary won't be able to put a cap on it. All we have to do is sit and wait."

Squealing, I tackle Lex hard enough that his chair almost spills us both to the floor. I kiss his cheek with a hard smack. "I love you!"

"Of course you do. How could you not?"

I laugh and look at my bears. "They probably agree."

Warrin is emphatic in his agreement while Anders laughs his approval. I raise an eyebrow at Draven, who sighs and says, "Fine. I am thoroughly impressed."

"You should be," Lex replies without any regard for the resulting scowl.

Anders slaps Lex on the shoulders and thanks him. Only time will tell what the repercussions will be, but there's hope in all of us. I watch the men file out to get back to work. I need to as well, but I'm not ready yet. Instead, I turn back to the man I hope is still my friend. "Thank you for this. I'm sorry I dragged you into all of it."

Lex adjusts his cracked glasses before leaning back in his chair with his fingers laced behind his head. "I get it. Holding it over your head so strongly was an asshole move. It wasn't your secret to tell, and it was wrong of me to blame everything on you. Besides, this is what we do?"

"Get threatened by men who can change into wolves?"

"No. That's definitely new. I'm talking about working against corrupt corporations. As much as I hate to admit it, your bear boyfriends run a very straight and altruistic company. I can't complain about working for them. If we take down Lunar, it will just be another part of our job."

"So, you're not leaving?"

"Another thing I hate to admit, but this place is growing on me. All I ask is that you feed your damn cat. The only time he comes out of your room is to eat and use the litter box. If I'm not quick enough with the food, he goes after my wires."

I laugh. "I'm sure he doesn't leave my bed. Active is not a word I'd ever use to describe him."

"Someone needs to use the bed. Oh, unfurrow your brows. It's not judgment. You're right; I have no right to judge your relationship choices. Three hot men though. You have me beat."

"About Jared..."

Lex shakes his head. "No. I was wrong not to trust you. I really should have told you. Although, I think you lied by saying you'd tolerate him better if you knew. We both know you two aren't on a tolerable level. I appreciate you trying though."

"Thank you. I promise not to keep you in the dark about supernatural beings ever again. Still friends?"

"Always."

My best friend extends his hand for a peaceful shake. Instead of taking it, I lean down for a hug to hide the tears in my eyes. After an awkward second, Lex returns the embrace. When I stand, I have to wipe my eyes.

"Don't get all mushy on me," Lex grumbles.

I laugh. "I can't help it. I was worried I lost you."

"You have to try harder to pry me out of your life."

My phone dings. I look. "The guys are inviting us out to lunch to celebrate our hopeful victory. You in?"

"Is it expensive?"

I ask and wait for a reply. "Very."

"Then I'm in."

"You have no shame."

"Not when it comes to food."

That's how we find ourselves crammed into the backseat of the car. I'm thankful Warrin is driving, because I don't think the three of us would fit back here with his giantness. Even Draven's smaller frame makes it a bit tight. I'm squeezed between my best friend and my latest mate. I'm relieved when we finally reach the restaurant.

As usual, the food at this place is much too fancy for my tastes, but we're celebrating. Not that we will speak of that in public. The feeling of being watched nags at me again, so I know the enemy is still out there. It's best to act like everything is normal. They won't know what hit them until it's too late. At least, that's what I hope.

There is still a lot of uncertainty in the future, but as I look at the four people who have become the family I deserve, I realize we will get through it together. I'm loved. I'm cherished. There's nothing more I need in life. We may need to wait to see if our plan really worked. That doesn't mean we don't have things to celebrate. We are all truly blessed in our lives. No mangy wolves are going to take that from us.

CHAPTER THIRTY FIVE
THREE BEARS

"All of Lunar Financial's assets have been seized and all business transactions canceled in light of the ongoing investigation. The list of laws broken continues to grow as more evidence is found. It seems like no business was too shady for this crumbling company. The entire business will crumple shortly after the death of the CEO, Steven Hodge."

Anders mutes the TV as he plops onto the black leather couch beside me. Draven sits in his armchair beside the sofa while Clancy snuggles in Warrin's lap. I keep the orange cat where I am. All the men have made their floors a home for him. Anything to not hear Lex complaining about chewed wires. Although, he'll need to deal with it when we return to our weekend vacations.

It's been a month since the last excursion, but it doesn't feel safe... until now. Shortly after the funeral of Steve Hodge, we received a note tied to a brick thrown through the lobby window. The guys have sensed wolves prowling whenever we leave the building. They told me his son probably wanted revenge, even if he brought it on himself. That all stopped when the investigations started. They're a little preoccupied.

I can't wait until we return to the cabin tomorrow night. All three bears alone with me in the secluded forest. What more can I ask for? The wolves will be too busy licking their wounds to even consider it was us that leaked the information. The cabin will be safe.

"That was Bernard," Anders says. "The wolves are scattering, the pack fleeing in all different directions. Those that haven't been arrested are lying low. We've won."

"And we did it cleanly like you wanted," I say.

"All thanks to you." My grizzly leans in to plant a soft kiss on my lips. "How about a true celebration, Darlin?"

I feel a shiver run up my spine. "What do you have in mind?"

"I'm well enough to complete what the four of us started."

Draven lifts me, making me squeak in protest. He tosses me over his shoulder, giving me a complete view of the other two standing up to follow. Clancy gives Warrin an indignant glare that says repercussions for removing the warmth would be coming if he wasn't so lazy. We enter Draven's bedroom, and I find myself dropped on a bed that's a little too firm for my liking. Before that thought can fully register, all three men are on me.

Anders leans down to kiss me while Draven pulls my wrists above my head. Warrin moves between my legs, crawling over me until he's at my breasts. A warm tongue circles my nipple, making me gasp as the ache between my thighs builds. Anders moves to my neck, and his lips are replaced by Draven's. My senses are almost overwhelmed with the pleasure of having all three on me at once.

My polar bear moves from my breasts to my stomach, caressing every inch of me with a kiss. His tongue slides from my entrance to my clit, and my breath hitches. It circles over and over. My moan is the only sound that covers the panting that I'm not sure is mine or not.

"There's my good girl," Draven says into my ear.

He pulls my chin up to devour my mouth again when Anders moves to my breasts. Sparks flash in blinding brightness that obscures my vision. Before I can recover, Warrin thrusts his length into me. My heart races as the tension in my core builds to unbearable levels. Unable to reach Warrin, I fist Anders's hair. He doesn't stop sucking and circling my pebbled nipples. All the attention pulls me over the edge. I call out Warrin's name as he grunts his release.

Without a break, my grizzly and my polar bears switch places. Anders is inside of me before I even have the chance to come down from the pleasure-filled high. My breath comes in short gasps, unable to catch up to the sensations rolling over me. His hands snake up to caress my breasts in time with each thrust. My black bear slips a hand between us to massage my clit. Warrin nibbles my neck, chin, and ear.

The pressure builds once more, spreading heat through my veins. I gasp and moan, holding on for as long as I can. Draven's hand moves as Anders shutters and growls. I let myself go. The rush washes over me again with the threat of pulling me under into oblivion. I yell my mate's name so loud it echoes. Warrin moves to my mouth as the shudders ease. I lose his lips when Draven pulls me down and flips me over.

"I want you to scream for me, Mutt," he whispers hoarsely into my ear.

Before I can answer, he rams into me. Even through the growing soreness, pleasure sparks flashes in my eyes. His fingers move to my clit while Anders lifts my head to kiss me. I can't hold back at all this time, and I follow Draven's whispered orders. His name bursts from my mouth as if my life depends on the world hearing it.

I collapse onto the bed, unable to take any more. Warrin stretches out beside me, then pulls my back against his chest. Anders sandwiches me while Draven curls up beside my head. As my breathing returns to normal, exhaustion pulls me into slumber.

Waking brings a delicious soreness that reminds me of what happened before I passed out. I'm lying on Anders's chest with Warrin's arm draped over me. Draven is nowhere to be seen. Careful not to wake these two, I slip out from between them and throw on the gentle giant's shirt. I step into the bathroom before leaving in search of my black bear.

I find him on his balcony, sipping what is probably hot chocolate and looking out over the city. Snow falls around him, highlighting his dark features in the bright white flakes floating in the light of the balcony. For a few moments, I decide to stand back and admire his beauty. Even in the cold, his lithe frame is naked. I admire his strong back muscles as he leans on the railing, along with the curve of his ass. Long dark hair blows freely in the breeze.

How did I get so lucky to gain the attention of three hot, dedicated men? Sure, it was quite a battle to get here, but it was all totally worth it. I'd do it all again as long as these three are waiting on the other end. I'm theirs as much as they are mine. I don't care what I must do to ensure it remains that way.

After thoroughly committing his nudity to memory, I lean over the couch to pick up the fleece blanket and wrap it around me. The sliding door doesn't make a sound, but I know his incredible bear hearing doesn't miss the whisper my ears don't pick up.

I inhale, taking in the woodsy scent that is my black bear. I've determined this is a side effect of the mate bond they keep talking about because I couldn't smell them before. Draven smells like a forest right after the rain. Warrin has a musky, icy scent I can't get enough of. Anders reminds me of sweet honeycomb. Each delicious. Each leaves me wanting more.

I pull the blanket tighter and step out onto the balcony, instantly regretting my lack of shoes. To warm myself, I steal Draven's hot chocolate. Instead of getting angry, he chuckles with his signature smirk. I turn to lean my back against the metal railing.

My eyes find my mate. "Why out here in the cold?"

"Thinking over everything that happened recently took away my ability to sleep. I didn't want to wake the three of you."

"There's a perfectly good couch in the warmth," I say, taking a sip of his drink.

"Too cold?"

"Not at all."

"Your shivering tells me otherwise." In the blink of an eye, Draven is pressed hard against me. "Need warmed up?"

My breath falters as he leans in to plant a passionate kiss on my lips. He pulls away before I can get too into it. "You need to stop doing that."

"What do I need to stop?"

"Turning me on and stepping away."

He grins and looks back toward the bright lights of the city. "I think your body needs a little rest, Mutt."

"How do you know what I need?"

"I can feel your exhaustion and soreness in the bond. It's complete now, between all of us."

I frown. "I don't feel any different."

"Give it time. Being human, you won't feel it as strongly as we do, but you'll still be able to feel us. The group mating is complete, and we are now one. Is this what you expected when you broke in?"

"Not at all. Is this what you expected when you caught the would-be wolf that was stealing from you?"

He laughs. "Not at all. A human mate was never in the cards for me, but you have a way of turning the odds in your favor, Mutt. I have no regrets."

"Even if you did, it's a little late."

"Most certainly. You're cold."

"I am not," I say through chattering teeth.

"Again, I can feel you. Lying does not make you a good girl. If you weren't so exhausted, I'd feel the need to punish you. As it is..."

I'm lifted into the air and thrown over his shoulder, which seems to be becoming our thing. Afraid of waking my other two bears, I bite back my squeak of protest. Once inside, Draven drops me on the couch and tucks me in with the fleece blanket. My body starts violently trembling. My black bear shakes his head and slips in behind me. His body heat lessens the shudders.

"I'm not used to the calm and caring Draven," I say with a yawn.

"I can go back to being an asshole tomorrow if you want. Right now, sleep."

"At least you admit it."

His fingers running up and down my arms relaxes me, but I fight my eyelids. I don't want to commit this night to a mere memory yet. I want to live it a little longer, so I hold off sleep. It's not an easy feat.

"I never denied it," Draven says, his own voice sounding drowsy. "Who do you want me to be?"

"Yourself."

"Really?"

"Well, maybe a little less anti-human."

He sighs. "My views on humans will never change. You've softened the feeling a bit, but I'll never stop my dislike for your people. Don't worry though. I'm purely pro Edith Hart."

"Ewww. Don't call me by my real name."

"It's either that or mutt."

"I much prefer mutt. It's totally a Draven thing."

"I'm glad you think so. Now, sleep."

"Yes, master."

"Careful, or I'll find other ways to make you say that."

I shiver, but I'm no longer cold. He's right though; I'm too tired to act on the desire that sparks deep inside. Until he starts snoring, I continue to fight sleep. He needs to be here when I wake, so I can't fall asleep first and wake to find him gone again. As soon as I hear the loud rumble, I let slumber take me.

EPILOGUE

The darkness embraces me, keeping me hidden from unwanted eyes. Okay, that's a little dramatic. There are a few dim lights on, but it's more fun to act like I'm one with the shadows.

"Earth to Eddie. Are you going to move or what?" Lex says into my ear. "You have three minutes."

"Got it."

My trusty lock picks turn in the hole. It clicks. Alarms sound.

"Lex!" I groan as the alarm shuts back off.

"Sorry. That one was on me. I missed one of my own triggers."

"This is our fifth failure. I give up."

"You say that like it's a bad thing," Anders says from down the hall.

I pout. "You'd think we'd have this down since we're the security consultants. We should know this like the back of our hands."

"You're just that impressive," Warrin says before wrapping his arms around my waist and spinning me.

"Can you not do that when I'm in your ear?" Lex groans.

"Then hang up."

My best friend grunts before a click sounds in my ear. Draven appears at the end of the hall. "Now that you're done playing, can we get moving? The helicopter won't wait forever."

I agree to join them after I settle Clancy in with Lex. When I enter with the orange cat, he's on the couch, playing games with Jared, who is still blindly oblivious to what Lex was doing. Jared sends me an exaggerated wave without looking. I shake my head.

True to his word, Lex has stayed in our suite. We were able to salvage what we could from our apartment before breaking the lease. The wolves missed our safe and savings. I learned Betsy made it through her attack. She's a wryly old cat.

While Lex has made this home, I'm barely here anymore, choosing to stay with my men more than him, but he doesn't mind. He gets more time alone with Jared. Clancy immediately goes for some wires, so I quickly exit and make it to the elevator before I hear Lex yelling.

Despite Draven's dramatics, we make it long before the pilot needs to leave. We lift off, and I watch the city shrink below us. To think, the wolves couldn't share a city of this size. Ever since we took them down, other shifters are moving back in. They're not all bears. Anders spoke of a feud between the bears and the wolves, but it seems that they pushed all other shifters out. Everyone else is willing to share territory. No one is so greedy to want to push others away.

For now, our future is secured. Everyone swears not to let the wolves win again—if they ever find a way to bypass all the warrants and try to return. It's a peaceful existence. Of course, fights break out, mainly between predatory and prey shifters. Peace is still prominent. It's a good future, one I'm proud to be a part of.

At the cabin, I don't bother arguing as Warrin shoulders my bag with his. I stop to enjoy the sight of the snow-covered mountainside and glistening trees. The whole weekend with my three bears in seclusion. Hot tubs. Fires. Barbecues. Snow angels and snowball fights. We will make lots more memories, lots more noise.

"Are you coming, Darlin?" Anders yells from the porch.

"I wouldn't miss it for the world."

Follow the Author

For more information on Kiera A. Reynolds and upcoming titles, please visit:

Facebook: https://www.facebook.com/kieraareynolds
Instagram: https://instagram.com/kieraareynolds
TikTok: http://tiktok.com/@KieraAReynolds
Newsletter: https://subscribepage.io/IA2DJe

Kiera A. Reynolds can be contacted at kiera@kieraareynolds.com

Milton Keynes UK
Ingram Content Group UK Ltd.
UKHW011023050224
437294UK00005B/264

9 798224 081998